FORGED
IN
FIRE

AWAKENED BY TERROR BOOK 1

L.L. BROOKS

FORGED IN FIRE
Copyright © 2019 by L. L. Brooks

ISBN: 978-1-68046-776-5

Published by Satin Romance
An Imprint of Melange Books, LLC
White Bear Lake, MN 55110
www.satinromance.com

Published in the United States of America.

Cover Design by Ashley Redbird Designs

1

Phoenix, Arizona—1980

WITH SIX DEAD, ONE DYING, AND ONE GONE CRAZY, HE HAD LITTLE interest in his surrounding, not that he wasn't aware. All the beauty and craftsmanship of the wall mosaic of a flaming Phoenix bird rising in rebirth went unappreciated by Dwayne Pratters, F.B.I. The who and why of the reason he was there dominated his mind, his thoughts surging ahead, as his lanky, bony frame stalked through the terminal.

No one was there to meet him, not that Pratters gave a damn. To see the bodies, the survivors, write his report, and leave without any contact with the local law would suit him just fine. Any taxi could take him to the morgue and hospital, and if they didn't like it, too bad. They should have had someone there to meet him.

Even more annoying, his name was called over the loud speaker system directing him to a white paging phone. He answered in his usual way. Growling his name savagely made the unsuspecting person on the other end stammer.

"Th-th-is-this is Deputy Sheriff Hu–Hume. I was sent to–to meet you."

"I'm claiming my suitcase." The tone was curt, rude, and he hung up before Hume could say more.

Not knowing who he looked for put Deputy Hume at more of a disadvantage. Pratters had no trouble recognizing him. Young, neat, and tidy in a freshly pressed suntan uniform, and flushed with embarrassment, Hume stood out like a sore thumb.

Pratters saw no reason to put him at ease as he waved him over. "I'm Pratters."

He turned his back to wait for his luggage, not missing how Hume fingered the butt of his holstered gun, while he told Pratters, "Sorry, I'm late. Another report was coming in as I was leaving. I thought it might be important."

"Was it?" he asked without bothering to look around.

"Yes, sir. They found another body. That makes seven now, two women and five men. This one had his arm blown off. He bled to death. Had to be from the same gun John Doe had."

"Why?"

"He was the only one who had a gun with that large a caliber. The others only had thirty-eights."

Pratters gave a derisive snort, reaching for his bag. Hume jumped forward to carry it for him. Relinquished his hold, Pratters gazed coolly at Hume, long enough to make Hume color a deeper shade of red, duck his head, and turn quickly.

"The car is just out here."

Pratters fell into step beside him. "What's Doe's condition now?"

Hume shrugged. "The doctor won't say much more than he ought to be dead. Would have been if that woman hadn't covered his sucking chest wound with her hand."

The glass door opened, and the heat blast hit him like stepping into an oven.

"I left the refrigeration going in the car," Hume told him.

The shock of a Phoenix summer in full force passed, and Pratters went back to business. He slid into the car, appreciating the protective cold cocoon of metal and glass, not that he showed it. As soon as Hume deposited his bag in the back and crawled in behind the wheel, he said, "I understand he has injuries other than the bullet wound."

"They had them quite a war out there. Doe played hell with them before they stopped him, and they died doing it. The way the detectives read it, Doe killed the first man in a fight, broke his neck. The others retaliated."

He hesitated and swallowed distastefully. "He either got away or they were foolish enough to let him go. He retaliated in spades, burned their camp, including their bikes, and poisoned their water, the reason the women died. Exposure is a damned hard way to go. He's got to be sick to do a thing like that."

Shaking his head, he obviously still found it hard to believe. "I never saw anything like it before. If he hadn't overlooked the ice chest and it hadn't rained, they wouldn't have lasted as long as they did. Jane Doe wouldn't have made it. It's the worst kind of premeditated murder I've ever seen."

"You haven't seen it all then," Pratters said in a flat, indifferent tone.

Hume's head swung around. "You haven't seen anyone die of exposure."

"Compared to some of the things I've seen those animals were responsible for, exposure was a kindness. They died."

Hume swallowed hard, remembering the other survivor. "He still killed them," he said tightly, looking back at the road.

"You can take my word for it. They intended to kill him."

"Sure, after what he did."

"Before—they never let him go."

Hume glanced around at him again. "You're the expert on the motorcycle gangs. So why didn't they kill him then?"

"Maybe Jane was more interesting."

Hume blanched. "She was beaten and raped repeatedly."

"But not killed."

"The doctors say she won't ever be the same."

"That's what I said. Sometimes dying is easier."

Hume's fist pounded the steering wheel. "They're animals, filthy, rotten animals."

Pratters stared ahead, unaffected by the rush of emotion from Hume or the subject.

"How do you stand it?" Hume asked.

"I keep my temper under control and use everything I can get to use against them. This isn't the first time I've taken a spur-of-the-moment flight. I'll seize any opportunity to get even one piece of evidence on any of them."

"Ought to castrate the bastards."

"You get the law passed, and I'll do the cutting."

"She's just a kid, just a tiny little kid."

Pratters knew Hume didn't necessarily refer to Jane Doe's actual size or age. Seeing someone mentally shattered made them seem smaller. Her state of mind, however, didn't soften Patters' voice.

"Any ID on her yet?"

"No and there's not much chance of it. She either can't or won't tell her name. With so many run-aways, dozens fit her description."

Hume went from fury to drowning in compassion. The latter appealed to Pratters less than the former. He changed the subject. "I understand you were the first at the scene. Mind giving me a first-hand account of what you found?"

"Sure," he said willingly.

Pratters suspected Hume's eagerness to comply came from this case being the most important thing to happen in his career and probably always would be.

"I picked up a distress call on a citizen's band. At first, I thought it was because of all the flooding. The woman was hysterical, repeating her message without letting up on the button long enough for me to answer. When I finally got through, she calmed down. She gave me an accurate location and was telling me she needed an ambulance when she broke off. I couldn't raise her again. I could see why when I got there. They shot the hell out of her RV."

"What kind of RV?"

"Motorhome. Nice job, twenty-four-footer with everything. She even had—"

Pratters was getting more detail than he wanted. "What did you find when you got there?"

"The way she was parked, I thought maybe she'd had a heart attack or something. I pulled up behind it. I saw the bodies and motorcycles down the embankment when I walked around the end. Even from there, there was no doubt they were dead, heads were gone. The side of the RV was shot up, windows shattered, and Doe's legs were sticking out the door."

His air of importance diminished with the seriousness of what he described. He paused and swallowed. "You don't expect to find something like that. I don't mind telling you, I didn't like the idea of walking up to that door. I felt like an idiot when I jumped out, pointing my gun at them. She didn't even look up, and he couldn't."

He shook his head. "I thought he was dead. You'll see why when you see him, and they were both covered with blood. She was crying, and she kept stroking his head, like you'd see someone do to a hurt child. Man, it was weird. Her hand was cut, and she kept rubbing blood in his hair."

"I take it she was in the door with him," Pratters said drily.

"Yeah, sitting on the top step, holding him with her legs and arms. When I tried to move him, she screamed at me. She said she had to hold him, or he'd die. Hell, I didn't know what to do. I could see why she was holding him like that with her hand pressed on his chest. Anything more was past any first aid I knew, and I couldn't have gotten him away without fighting her. I left them alone and called in."

"What did she do then?"

"Nothing," he said glumly. "Other than when I tried to move him, she didn't seem to know I was there. I checked on the other two. He shot one of them twice, the other one three times. He pumped bullets into their heads after they were dead. He just did it to mutilate them."

Pratters' voice was as dry and indifferent as ever. "Or to make double sure they were dead."

"Well, they damn sure were. He blew their heads off. It seems to be a favorite thing. He did it to three of them."

A head shot was the surest way to be positive the men wouldn't get up again, but Pratters let the thought pass unspoken. "What about the woman?" he asked.

"She didn't come out of it until the medic talked to her. When they started finding out the extent of damage done to him, they called for a chopper. I could see a little of it, but I didn't have any idea how bad he was until they started looking him over."

"Did the woman?"

"She just knew he was hurt. She found him on the side of the road, helped him inside, and then called for help. She was talking to me when the other two showed up. That was why she cut off like she did."

"If she wouldn't let you move him, why did she let the medics?"

Hume shrugged. "They talked to her while they took his vitals and didn't try to move him away from her until she seemed to understand who they were. They said she was the only reason he was still alive. She held him up so he could breathe with that lung filling with blood, and she kept her hand over the wound, keeping the chest cavity from filling with air. It's kind of spooky the way a person can be that far gone in shock and still be able to do the right thing. She could just as easily have gone screaming and running into the desert to end up like the other two women."

"What did she do when she came out of it?"

"Not much at first. The medic took her hand, telling her he wanted to clean it. She jerked away from him and looked down at herself, kind of funny like, then jumped up, saying something about being dirty. He followed her back into the RV and waited until she came out. Then she let him—"

"Came out of where?" Patters asked, showing the first sign of interest.

"The shower."

"Shower!" he roared. "You let her take a shower?"

Hume stared at him long enough to drift over the center line. A blast from an oncoming car snapped him out of it. "Why not? She was all bloody, and the medic said—"

"What shape were her clothes in?"

"Bloody."

"Torn?"

"No, just bloody."

"What does she look like, how old?" Patters questioned rapidly.

"What has what she looks like got to do with anything?"

"Pretty, plain, what?"

"Plain as a mud fence."

"How old?"

"Thirty or so."

"She said she found him on the side of the road?" Hume nodded numbly. "What else?"

"Not much. She didn't know much. It all happened too fast. When he heard the bikes, he pushed her. She hit her head, and it stunned her. The medic said that's probably why she didn't remember much."

"Neat," Patters said with a snarl of contempt.

"I don't know what you're getting at."

"I'm not getting at anything," he told him flatly.

"You act like she did something wrong. If you're making something out of her wanting her name withheld, I don't blame her.

Other people would do the same thing you're doing, and she doesn't deserve it. She got the hell scared out of her, and she'll probably never stop for anyone again."

"She probably wishes she never had."

"Which would be natural. A person like that has never been any closer to real violence than news on T.V. She stopped. That's more than most would have done."

"A person like what?" Patters asked, dropping back to detached indifference.

Hume rolled his eyes in exasperation. "She takes pictures of nature. Pick up a copy of Arizona Highways. Some of her work is in this month's edition."

"What did the doctor's examination come up with?"

Hume got lost in what seemed like a change of subject to him. "Which one?"

"On her."

"The medic found a lump on the back of her head and cuts on her hands and knees from crawling in the glass. There wasn't any sign of concussion, but he still thought she should have gone to the hospital."

"Did she?"

"No, she wanted to go home. He advised her to see her own doctor." He asked again, "Why?"

Pratters dropped it with a slight shrug and changed the subject. "Any chance Jane Doe is faking?"

Hume shook his head, his face flushing with anger. "This wasn't the first time she'd been beaten. They suspect brain damage, but she's so hysterical it's hard to tell how severe it might be."

"There's not much chance of getting any information from her?"

"No," he answered tightly.

"John Doe's the only chance then," he stated, exhibiting as much indifferent to Hume's anger as to the condition of Jane Doe's mind.

"He wouldn't give you the time of day."

"He might if it makes things easier for him."

Hume twisted to stare at him. "You can't offer him any deals."

"Watch where you're driving," Patters told him, watching a parked car coming up fast on his side.

Hume turned back to the front, speaking through a partially locked jaw. "You can't, not after what he did to those women. It's not in your jurisdiction. County and state have priorities. You're just here as an advisor. He isn't going to get away with murdering those women."

"I'll tell *you* something about those women you're wasting your compassion on. They were just as vicious as the men. Some of them are like your little Jane Doe, but most of them want to be there. If you could get Jane to tell it, you'd find out they did as much to her as the men."

Hume showed how naïve he was. "They couldn't!" he exclaimed.

"She has rope burns on her ankles, doesn't she? It's the women's job to tie them. They strip them naked, hitting them as many times as it takes to get them to submit. They tie their hands behind their backs and their legs apart with a stick between their ankles. If it's a mock or initiation, the stick ends aren't sharpened to a point. If it is, it's a blow-out, a slow agonizing death while every perverted sex act thought of is done, and it isn't always a man or his penis that—"

"God," Hume groaned.

"Make you sick? Good. Keep it in mind when I tell you I'll use any means available to stop them, including letting one bastard go to get two or three. That bastard is always left, and it won't be long before I'll get him on something else if his friends don't kill him first for dealing with me."

"You're as bad as they are."

"Would you like me to tell you how they do it to a man or how much easier it is for them to do it to a child?"

"You don't even know if they have done those things!" Hume cried.

"Yes, I do. That's why they send for me. I know this gang, and I know their methods. The stick thing is their favorite. For variation, they put the stick between the—"

"God damn you, shut up!"

"If John Doe is someone I can use, I'll take him," he told him coldly. "I don't care whose toes I step on."

———

Hume led Patters to the intensive care unit, but wouldn't go in. A doctor stood at the nurses' station reading a chart. Pratters went to him. The hiss thump of respirators and beeping of electronic equipment were the only sounds in the quiet, hushed cubicles, until Patters spoke.

The introductions were short, accompanied by a show of Patters' credentials. The doctor barely looked up, gave his name as Doctor Daniel Thristen and answered Pratters' question absently. "Critical."

"You can be more specific," Pratters told him tartly.

Calm, grey eyes rose to study Pratters' face. Without a word, he handed Pratters the chart.

Pratters worked his way through the bad handwriting. One item struck his interest and explained Hume's uneasiness at one point. "Sodomy?"

"That's an uncomplicated way of putting it."

"Interesting but hardly the cause of his impending death."

The doctor's voice was droll in his answer. "Interesting is hardly the word I would use, but you are right, a torn rectum and bruised genitals are not the cause of his critical condition. It's internal hemorrhaging." He paused, no doubt waiting for a response from Pratters and got none. "We can't stop it without surgery, and we can't operate until it stops. So far the whole blood and coagulants haven't overtaken the bleeding enough to stabilize him."

"There is some hope?"

"Remote at this point, but as long as the machines keep his heart and remaining undamaged lung functioning, there is some."

"I'd like to see him."

The doctor didn't like him. Pratters knew it and didn't care. John Doe was one of them. If he'd done something to turn the gang against him, he'd only received what he had done to others. Fitting punishment and one the law would not dispense.

They crossed to a cubical with the front curtain drawn to shut the sight away. The doctor pulled the curtain before he folded the covers back from the still form on the bed. Pratters could easily see why. Nothing could be more destructive to the morale of visitors to a seriously ill person than seeing a sight like that.

"We shaved his head, face, and pubic area. Easier to get rid of lice that way. We also cut his throat. The tube through it is for the respirator. It's the only reason he's still breathing."

Pratters' gaze went to where he pointed. "Rope burns on the neck, wrists, knees, and these bruises on the ankles would be if he hadn't had boots on. Lots of pressure, broken blood vessels. Feet are undamaged. Knees, rope burns already mentioned, and lacerations on the inside of each. Right is more severe. Object was sharp, irregular, and wood to judge by the bits we dug out. Contusions and abrasions on the front, indicating he crawled or was dragged. Thighs, more contusions from blows by blunt objects."

He skipped the torso going to the head. "No serious injury to the skull or brain. Rather amazing when you consider what was done to the face. Two more teeth were knocked out."

"More teeth?" Pratters asked, staring hard at the mutilated face.

"The first and second incisors were lost at an earlier date. No denture. He either lost it when that happened or never had one. The laceration through the cheek is minor. The one through the lip will require plastic surgery if he's ever to be pretty again."

Pratters looked at the misshapen lump of a nose the doctor pointed at and doubted if he ever had been.

"Old break," the doctor informed him. "Nasty one and healed without attention. The other abrasions and bruises are minor. Shoulders and arms are covered with abrasions, bruises, and shallow lacerations. Left shoulder seems to be sprained, some swelling. His kidneys are not functioning, a common occurrence in trauma." He pointed to a needle embedded in the right arm, "That we did."

Pratters gazed as indifferently at the tubes inserted in a muscular forearm with as much disinterest and lack of compassion as he did everything else. He didn't care if the man had to have a machine draw out his blood, filter it, and send it back into a body no longer capable of doing it. No more than he cared that a machine filled and emptied one remaining whole lung with life sustaining oxygen for the same reason.

The doctor pointed to the groin area. Pratters' eyes followed to stare at something he'd noticed the second it came into view.

"Nasty scars," the doctor stated, "but they have nothing to do with his present condition, so I'm sure you aren't interested in them."

"Wrong," Pratters told him curtly. "I'd like to know how he got them."

"They weren't made with a knife. The edges are too irregular. My guess would be shrapnel."

That did interest Patters. He looked up to ask, "Nam?"

He found the doctor watching him closely. "Probably. He's too young for Korea. That was where I saw the same type of wounds. He's fortunate surgery techniques have improved since then. They did a good job on him."

"Are you talking about plastic surgery?"

The doctor nodded and pointed. "Corrective work. I'd guess the cuts were deep enough to have affected the genital nerves."

"Enough for him to be impotent?"

"That would depend on how deep or how well they sewed him back together. I haven't tested for it. Would you like me to?"

His sarcasm wasn't missed. Patters glared at him. "Just go on with your story."

"Where did I leave off? Oh, yes, chest, abdomen, and groin. All have various bruising from blunt objects, except for that, which appears to be a bite mark." He pointed to one mark before pointing to a small bandage on the upper left chest. "This is where we begin to get serious. Bullet wound, the bullet is still in there. The lung is punctured by a fractured rib as well and hemorrhaging. The tube through his nose is sucking out the blood to keep him from drowning."

His finger dropped to point to a swollen black and blue area the size of a cantaloupe, still on the left side, but to the lower end of the ribcage. "This is the critical. Underneath the fractured ribs is the lung and below it is the spleen. We don't know yet how extensive the damage is to either. We do know there is hemorrhaging, and there is nothing we can do about it."

"Yet."

"Yet," he agreed. "Anything else you would like to know?"

Pratters ignored the sarcasm. "How long could he have moved around like that?"

"Not long enough to walk out of this room, and he couldn't have walked."

"According to the report, he did."

"According to what I understand, he rode a motorcycle." He pulled the covers back over the man, taking the time and care to place the arms with the various tubes connected to them, on the outside.

"He had to walk to it."

"Or crawl." He straightened to stare at Pratters in distaste. "Or it wasn't far. Or he hadn't punctured the lung yet or been shot and started to hemorrhage."

"Those ribs could have been fractured without causing the hemorrhaging immediately?"

"Fractured ribs don't always puncture or tear at the tissue beneath. Binding prevents it and if binding isn't possible, care in movement can. He would not have been able to lift or twist, and he would have had to have carried his arm to his side. If he had lifted it above his shoulder, it would have caused a puncture."

"This couldn't have happened before he fired the camp?"

"If he did."

Pratters gave him a cutting look as he turned and walked out. He'd done it, all right. That kind of violence was just his style. Pratters stepped into the hall with reaction setting in. Bell! It had to be Bell. Pratters always feared this was going to happen, had ever since the man started blackmailing him. If Bell died, there would be no problem, but men like Bell didn't die. They held on to extort and blackmail. How could he make the payment Bell would demand now? How could he possibly protect him?

———

Pratters couldn't totally hide his reaction. He didn't, however, want anyone seeing it, including Hume. He refused to answer when Hume asked if he recognized John Doe and walked off, demanding to be taken to Jane's room.

His reaction to being told he could not see her was nearly explosive. Hume moved to prevent what he seemed to think was a threat of violence to the nurse who barred Pratters' way. Pratters spun off, demanding to be taken to the morgue.

At the morgue, Hume's attitude changed to disgust he didn't hide over Pratters' and the coroner's callousness as they walked down the row of drawers, pulling them out to view the bodies. Neither batted an eye or suffered from difficulty with breathing at the sight of mutilated heads, blistered faces, or the early stages of decomposition.

Pratters read through the autopsy reports with as much concern —less than most people read the daily paper. From the tone of voice both used when Pratters finished, they could have just as easily been discussing the weather.

"Six days?" Pratters asked.

"Seven as a maximum. I'd say four as a minimum. The weather element out there alters the normal decomposing times. First, we had the dry heat, then wet from rain, then damp heat. Broken neck was first. He laid on his back during rigor mortis. Then he was moved and buried face down. Four to six days from the time he was brought in. Two to four days later the other two were killed. The one missing an arm was not moved from the time he fell and died. The last one brought in was killed about the same time. He laid on his back during rigor mortis, and moved, either to be thrown in the wash or by the flood water. The first two brought in were easy. The women were still hot, but they had been dead several hours. The heat and rain make it tricky."

"How much time do you estimate between the first two gunshots and the last?"

"One to two full days."

"Same gun killed them all?"

The coroner shrugged. "I just measure the holes. Same caliber gun, but there were no bullets for ballistics."

Pratters mused aloud. "Four to seven days from start to finish."

"Sorry I can't be more accurate."

"You do what you can."

———

Pratters recoiled from the heat build-up in the closed car, and Hume wasn't so disgusted as to not feel sorry for him. "Let me get the air conditioner started before you get in."

Pratters waited, his head already pounding from the heat. When

Hume signaled, he crawled inside and leaning into the cool air pouring out of the dash ports. "How do you people stand it?"

"July is a bad month."

"What's a good month?"

"January." He eased into traffic. "Where to now?"

"The lab."

Hume sighed. Pratters had no sympathy for the hours more Hume waited while he went over everything the lab boys had gathered from the charred remains of the camp to the clothes taken off John Doe.

He also spent time, to Hume's ire, searching through the shattered RV. "Did she remove anything?"

"Not personally. She asked for her camera. The department had someone take it to her."

"Was it in a case of some kind?"

"Yes, and it was searched and dusted before it was released."

"I'd like to see her statement."

"I've got a copy of it in the car."

He started out, and Pratters followed. "I'll read it on the way to the scenes."

Hume stopped short. "I don't think you better go out there."

"Trying to keep me away?"

Hume retorted. "If you're smart, you'd stay away. You can't take the heat."

"I wouldn't be stranded."

"No." He turned away in disgust and started for the car again. "There'd be someone there to rush you to the hospital."

"Don't think—"

He whipped back to face Pratters. "I'm not being smart. Look at yourself. You're sweating like a horse and not cooling off. If you don't watch it, you'll have a heat stroke or go into heat exhaustion. They aren't fun, either one."

He shoved the door open and marched to the car. Head throbbing, Pratters waited as the car's cooling system cranked out cool air before getting in.

Hume tossed a bottle to him when he slid in. "Salt tablets."

"I'd rather have some aspirin."

"Those will do more for the cause." He jerked the gear lever and moved out on the street.

Pratters looked at the bottle, looked at Hume, and held his head. "What's the difference between a stroke and exhaustion?"

"Convulsions with one, cramps and vomiting with the other, and both will knock you out or kill you."

"What is it now?"

"Sick," Hume said, sounding like he had something bad tasting in his mouth. "A cold shower, a cool room, and a nap will take care of it."

"I guess living out here you'd have to know all about strokes and such to survive. I suppose Miss, ah…" He waved his hand trying to recall a name he hadn't heard.

Hume didn't fall for the ploy and give Pratters an answer he wanted. "I suppose so. She goes out in that desert all the time. She'd be an idiot if she didn't."

"Did she seem like one to you?"

"No, just shook. Why don't you lay back and rest?"

"Sounds like a good idea, but I can rest later. Where's that statement?"

Hume pointed to a folder of papers. "Where do you want to go now?"

"Back to the hospital."

———

Hume seethed again, and as usual, Pratters didn't give a damn. He had a plan, and a uniform or witness didn't fit in. He made Hume stay in the hall.

As he suspected, Jane Doe was not tiny, though she was young.

She jumped to her knees and drew herself into a huddled ball in the middle of the bed when he walked in. Her pupils were huge with fright, and her face was scarlet with sunburn.

Pratters glanced behind him to make sure the door was closed and pressed his finger to his lips. "Your old man sent me," he whispered to her.

"Al?" she cried, rising out of her huddle.

"Shh." He looked over his shoulder at the door, moving closer to the bed. "Yeah, Al sent me to look out for you."

She whispered, loud enough to be heard twenty feet away. "When's he coming after me? I don't like it here. They keep asking me questions."

Pratters hoped the door was thick enough to keep the conversation private. "You haven't told them anything?" he asked sharply, though still in a whisper.

"Noooo." She shook her head from side to side, assuring him she hadn't. "Al told me never to tell anyone anything."

"Good." He sat down on the edge of the bed. "Al can't come for you right now. The pigs have him." Her eyes filled with tears and fear came back into her eyes. Pratters kept talking. "That's why he sent me to take care of you. You're supposed to do what I tell you."

"He isn't ever coming," she whined.

"Sure, he is, just as soon as he gets out. That's why I've got to talk to you. You can help."

"I want to, really I do. Al takes good care of me. He's my old man."

"Good. You know how it is in the slammer. It's hard to talk. Al couldn't tell me very much, and I have to know what happened."

"Are you a lawyer?"

"Right and more importantly, I'm on the outside. I grease the wheels to make things go easier."

"Are you Davidson?"

"You got it," he agreed, tucking that name away for future use. "Tell me what happened."

"When?"

Pratters bit his tongue. "In the desert."

"I got lost looking for Al."

"Before that. Why did Bell kill Joey?"

With a shrug, she said, "Made him mad."

"What did Joey do to make him mad?"

"He was just mad, and Joey was closest."

"Why was he mad?" Pratters forced his voice to a gentle level, and it wasn't easy. He knew he had to go easy if he was to get any answers out of her.

"They tried to get Prissy."

Pratters quickened in interest. "Prissy?"

She nodded. "Bell's old lady. He never shares, and Al says he should."

"Okay," he said with satisfaction, beginning to understand. "Al and the others wanted Prissy, and Bell wouldn't let them have her. They got into a fight, and Bell killed Joey. What happened then?"

"Al and Dago went to look for Prissy."

"Did they find her?"

"No." Her eyes filled with tears. "They used me."

Pratters backtracked quickly. "What did Bell do when Al and Dago left?"

"He just laid there."

Pratters took a deep breath to quiet his impatience. "He was unconscious?"

"Al hit him with a rock."

"Then someone *hurt* Bell." He used the word with a twist.

"Ready's mean. I knew she was going to hurt him. I went in the tent so I wouldn't have to see. That's what made him mad, and what Fingers did. That hurts more than what Ready did. I know. It hurts."

Her eyes filled with tears again. Pratters hoped they'd go away on their own. He asked, "But they didn't kill him?" She shook her head. "Why not?" She shrugged. "They were going to kill him." She nodded again. "Why didn't they?"

"Al hit Ready. He said it was all her fault. She was supposed to tell him when he woke up, but she didn't. She hurt him more, and he got loose while they hurt me."

Tears spilled out of her eyes, and Pratters' voice grew hard and cold. "What's the big deal? That's what you're for, isn't it?"

She choked back the tears, nodding at him. "Don't tell Al, please."

"I got better things to do. What happened after Bell got away?"

"I went to sleep."

Pratters groaned. *God, what a simple creature.* "What happened the next day?"

"We looked for Prissy."

"Not Bell?" he asked in surprise.

"Oh, no," she told him emphatically. "Bell told Ready they better not cross the wash, or he'd think they were coming for him. He said he'd be back in two days, and Fingers better be there, or the deal was off. Al said he must have met Prissy, and she must have seen what really happened and told Bell, and that was why he came back and burnt everything."

"You're sure it was Bell?"

She nodded. "He made Al awful mad. When Fingers got back, they went after him, Al figured out he wasn't across the wash at all, 'cause it was always the hill he took Prissy to, and he figured out that's where he had Prissy hid, and he must have been right, 'cause we heard shooting, and no one came back but Bell. He took the Jeep."

Pratters stopped her quickly. "What Jeep?"

"Prissy's Jeep. Bell wouldn't share her, and Al says he should share, that she should be initiated if she was going to stay, but he said she wouldn't be there that long. He never kept one more than three days."

Pratters stopped her again. Once he'd got her started, it was a flood of rattle that barely made sense. "How long did he keep her?"

She shrugged. "He told her he was going to take her home, but Ready and Jolene told her he lied, and it made him mad when she wouldn't mind, and he suffocated her."

"He killed her?"

"Not then, but Al figured he was going to when he said it'd be two days before he'd come back, and he sent Fingers for the stuff and guns, 'cause Bell had a gun, and he used it to stop a claim fight."

"Who'd he shoot?"

"No one, but I was afraid he shot Al when Al didn't come back. I went looking for him, and I got lost when it started to rain, and I couldn't find him or the camp, and—and–I got so scared."

She started crying, making what she said difficult to understand. "I didn't want Bell to find me. He wanted to take me home, and he comes back covered with blood. Al said he must use a knife for so much blood. Dago says he must stick them with a knife 'cause he can't get it up."

"Calm down and back up," Pratters told her curtly.

Pratters couldn't quiet her as she went into hysterics. In a rage over losing control, he stormed out of her room, heading for the intensive care unit, too much in a rage to care that Hume followed. While Hume stopped in the hall, Pratters marched straight to the foot of Bell's bed.

The doctor came up quickly behind him. "He's the same."

"If I didn't need the bastard," Pratters told him with the hatred drawing his mouth into a snarl, "I'd pull the plugs myself."

He spun around. The curtain thrashed as he threw it out of his way. When he came out of the door, Hume stood there.

"Get off my tail. I don't need a babysitter, and you can tell your bosses that."

2

ONLY ONE WOMAN'S NAME SHOWED AS A PHOTOGRAPHER IN THE table of contents of the magazine Hume mentioned. She was listed in the phone book, and Pratters only got lost once finding his way to the upper middle-class home. The rented car's cooling system wasn't as good as the one in the county car, and the heat was unbearable. Pratters' head pounded furiously when he knocked on the door. When it finally opened, he found himself looking into a pair of the deepest blue eyes he had ever seen. Maybe the heat was playing tricks on him, slowing down his thinking, or he had the wrong one. Hume had described her as plain. The woman in front of him was attractive in a classical way, style and grace over actual beauty of features.

In her early or middle thirties, she wore light makeup. Her brown hair was pinned atop her head without a strand out of place, At least five-foot-ten with every inch slim, well-proportioned, the only thing that detracted from her appearance was a look of weariness, and despite the temperature, she wore a long-sleeved blouse.

"Annalisa Summers?"

"What do you want?" she asked tonelessly.

"I'm Inspector Pratters, Federal Bureau of Investigation."

She didn't look at the identification he held out, and she interrupted him before he could say more. "I've already told you people all I can."

He did have the right woman. "Just a few questions."

"I've already answered all the questions."

"Not mine. Do you mind if I come in?"

"Yes," she told him flatly, not moving.

"Easy or hard, lady," he told her curtly. "You choose."

Choosing hard, her features set, and her arms crossed in front of her. "I may have to answer your questions, but I do not have to ask you in." Even that was delivered in a monotone.

"You sure don't, but it'd be a damned sight easier."

"For who?"

Pratters wanted to hit her. He was sick with the heat, and she could see it. He shifted tactics quickly. As much as it chafed his pride, he softened, the only thing to do against her quietly delivered, yet strong resistance.

"Miss Summers, I apologize."

"Mrs."

"Mrs. Summers, it's the heat. I'm not used to it."

"I can see that. Loosen your tie. It might help." Her tone was still flat, but she stepped back without shutting the door in his face.

He stepped inside gratefully. The air was cooler, and the room dark after the stark glare of the desert sun. He closed his eyes to speed up the adjustment to the light change, and when he opened them, she was nowhere in sight.

"Mrs. Summers?"

Her voice drifted in to him from further back in the house. "Sit down. I'll be there in a moment."

Taking the nearest chair and holding his head, he closed his eyes against the pain. He intended it to only be a brief respite, one she wouldn't see, not knowing she was back until she spoke.

Standing in front of him, she held a glass in one bandaged hand

and a wet cloth in the other. She handed them to him, saying, "Drink one, put the other on your forehead, and loosen your tie."

"Thanks," he told her in an ungracious snarl. He did loosen the tie but held the cloth in his hand as he took a mouthful of the water. He choked and broke into a fit of coughing. "That's salted."

"Yes, it is." She moved across the room and settled in a high-backed chair in front of the window.

Pratters couldn't see her clearly for the bright light coming in the window behind her and wondered if it was a deliberate move. As a photographer, she would know all about the effects of back-light. "Why does everyone keep feeding me salt?" he asked and dabbed at his watering eyes with the cloth.

"It isn't because you aren't salty enough," she told him without the slightest trace of humor.

"I apologize. It's this heat."

"It does tend to make tempers short."

"Does it yours?"

"Not usually."

"Does anything?"

"Small talk or are you still being rude?" she countered.

Her tone never wavered, and that puzzled Pratters. Her voice wasn't just toneless and flat, it was listless. So was she. She sat without moving so much as a fingertip.

He tried a weak smile. "Seems like we got off on the wrong foot."

"It seems we still are."

"Shall I go out and start over?"

"I doubt if it would help."

"Tell me, is it the situation or me?"

"Both."

He backed off again. "Is this really the best thing for what ails me?" He held the glass up, and he would drink every drop of it, if it would get her to loosen up.

"It would help the pending sun stroke," she said as he sipped sparingly.

He drew in a deep breath and let it out slowly. "Mrs. Summers, I was mad about something else when I got here. I took it out on you. Every time I have to work on one of these cases, I get mad. I have to repress it, and it bubbles up at the worst possible times."

"Bullying didn't work so now sincerity?"

"No more tactics. This is just me, and I need your help."

"I doubt it."

"I do, more than I can explain to you now. I may never be able to explain it to you, but I do need your help. A young girl's life may depend on it."

"Whose?"

"They called her Prissy. Did Bell mention anything like that?"

"Bell?"

"The man you saved. Did he mention the name Prissy?"

"No."

Pratters chewed his lip. "Did he ask you to give anyone, *anyone*, a message?"

"No."

It was like talking to a pre-recorded machine, frustrating Pratters. "Did he mention a place?"

"No."

"Can you say anything besides no?" he snapped.

"He didn't talk to me. I said that in my statement."

"I don't believe it." He stood up, furious with her, digging a card out of his pocket. "If you should happen to think of something more." He tossed the cloth on the nearest table. "If it doesn't inconvenience you too much." He flipped the card after the cloth. "That's the number I can be reached through."

————

He drove back to the hospital, but before going in, he made a call from the phone booth, making sure no obstacles were near enough to hide a listener. He dialed the operator and gave the number he wanted to call collect, cradling his throbbing head in his hand. He still held his head when the party accepted the call.

"This is Dealer. We've got a mess," Pratters told them without preamble.

"It's someone we know."

"Yeah, and I want a three on him."

"That's pretty drastic."

"There's too damned many loose ends. He got sloppy, and the deals have always had the stipulation, *within reason*."

"I just hate to lose a client."

"I really don't give a damn," Pratters hissed.

"We have our reputation to consider."

"Screw the damned reputation. I'm here, and I'm telling you, it can't be washed. I want a three."

The man gave in without further argument. "Very well, Dealer. I'll get it started."

Pratters slammed the phone down, took two steps away from the booth, and passed out cold. Hume was right, a sun stroke was no fun, and he was there to say 'I told you so' when Pratters opened his eyes in the emergency room.

"Guess I do need a sitter," he told him weakly.

Hume pushed away from the wall. "I wouldn't have let you pass out in the parking lot."

"At least I was trying to get back to my sitter."

"You were coming here and not to find me or help."

"All right, Hume, I'm sorry. I had no right jumping you like that. I had no right jumping you at all. I was letting off steam, and you got caught in it."

Hume told him stiffly, "My superiors would like to know if your trip here was worth anything."

Pratters gave up mollifying him. "John Doe is Simon Bell, and you won't find any prints on him. He's a runner for the gangs, carrying merchandise and money for drug buys. The women were called Ready, the redhead, Jolene, the brunette, and Jane was called Prissy, I think. She isn't too clear on who she is. Ready and Jolene ran with men called Al, Dago, and Joey. Joey would be your man with a broken neck."

"She told you all that?" He obviously didn't believe she had.

"No," Pratters admitted. "She babbled a lot of names. I put them with what I know about the gangs. Jolene's fairly new, but I've heard of her. Ready's well known and has been for years."

"If she's so well known, why didn't her record show up?"

"I said she was well known. I didn't say she had a record."

Hume leaned back against the wall with his arms crossed. "All right, what's your idea of what happened out there?"

"Probably started over Prissy. Bell has a reputation of claiming a girl, then refusing to share her. He's been known to take one after they got started with her, which made a lot of enemies. He's done it to this gang before, and it was one time too many. My guess is they got him down, did a little, and then went to the woman. Knowing their twisted minds, they probably had it in mind to make him watch since he wouldn't share to begin. Or the main gang took her away from him and forgot about him. They may have just tied him to keep him out of the way while they worked on her. Fingers, the fat man with his head blown off, wasn't part of that gang, even though he did do a lot of business with them. What was done to Bell was his specialty. Fingers and his lover, Blake, the one missing an arm are the only two homosexuals in the bunch."

Hume eyed him suspiciously. Pratters ignored it.

"Fingers treaded on dangerous ground. Bell has a unique position in the gangs. No one blows up a runner and gets away with it. It's one of those unwritten rules. If it's broken, it cuts them cold with the other gangs. They figure they can't trust them, and they lose the protection of the mass. Al and his group must have stopped Fingers and a fight broke out. That would explain how Bell managed to get away in the shape he's in."

"If Fingers was the one that did it, why would the other ones go after Bell?"

"Another of those unwritten laws is the host gang protects the runners. They failed, and they wouldn't have wanted Bell getting back to the gang that sent him to tell it."

"Then why stop Fingers at all?"

"Killing a runner is one thing. What Fingers had in mind was all together something else. They can kill a runner in a claim fight. He takes his chances the same as any other member there. I know of several who have been killed, and it's one of those things they all accept, but like I said, what Fingers had in mind, wasn't."

"How do you know what he had in mind?" Hume asked hatefully. "Are you a mind reader?"

"I don't have to be. Remember what I told you about the stick business. For a man, it's placed between the knees, and if it's sharpened, he's staked for a kill."

Hume looked like he was choking, but he got out, "Dead is dead. From what you've said, how shouldn't matter to them."

"Hume," Pratters said, sounding as patronizing as he felt. "Bell is like a diplomat. If they took his body back in one piece and said he made a claim and couldn't back it up, nothing much would have been said. If they took it back the way Fingers would have left it, the gang that sent him would have felt their honor had been offended. They would have defended that honor, and it's a bigger gang."

"I don't believe you."

"That's a strange way to phrase a different view point. You make it sound like you think I'm deliberately making it up."

"I think you are."

Pratters laughed, but he felt anything but amused. "Why would I?"

"You want to white wash John Doe so there's no hassle over jurisdiction."

"There won't be a hassle," he told him smugly. "My gang's bigger."

———

As soon as Pratters was released, his first visit of the morning was to Bell's bedside. As soon as the nurse saw him, she picked up the phone. The doctor appeared as quickly as before, not missed by Pratters.

"Don't worry, Doc. I won't try to pull any plugs. I told you, I want him alive."

"Why?" he asked.

"For the information in that ugly head of his." The nurse opened her mouth in protest but caught herself. Pratters saw it though. "Don't you think he's ugly?"

She flushed a bright red, but she answered truthfully. "No."

Pratters looked at the swollen, disfigured side of the face visible from where he stood. He walked around to the side, much less damaged. "Does that kind of man attract women?"

"Well, no, not that kind of man," she answered with embarrassment.

"His looks, I mean."

"He isn't bad looking. He's, ah, he's…"

"Sexy," the doctor supplied, making her flush brighter.

"Masculine," she corrected quickly.

Pratters walked to the foot of the bed, looking Bell over from shaved head to blanket covered feet. "He is built," he admitted.

"Excellent shape, it's the only reason he's still alive." The doctor waved a hand at Pratters, pointing to the exit. "I'd like to talk to you."

He took him to a small lounge and treated him to a cup of coffee before he hit him with his displeasure. "I won't be dragged into any kind of game you're playing."

"Meaning what?" Pratters asked in honest surprise.

"I never said he couldn't have done the things he's been accused of. I said he couldn't have done them after he began to hemorrhage."

"Isn't that all the same thing?"

"I don't believe so. The coloration in bruises change, torn flesh heals at the same rate. He received some of the injuries much earlier than others."

"For instance."

"Several of the bruises and the sodomy happened at an earlier date than the fractured ribs."

Pratters stared at him while he absorbed that. "Are you trying to tell me, they had him twice?"

"I wouldn't know. I'm simply saying not all the injuries occurred at the same time."

"Just how much time are you talking about?"

"Several days."

Pratters considered it for a moment, before shaking his head. "Not even Bell could have gotten away from them twice."

"As I said, I wouldn't know. What I am saying is I will not be drawn into any games you're playing."

"This is not a game. It's life and death stuff I'm dealing with."

"I always deal with life and death, on an altogether different level than you. Right now, I'm the one responsible for saving the life of a man you're using as some kind of political pawn. I'm letting you know I won't support you or them in it."

"Now I understand. The local law boys have been after you."

"I told them the same thing."

"Good for you." The doctor looked at him in surprise. "Doc, I don't care what they think. He's mine, and I'll get him. How is he anyway?"

"Anyway? Wouldn't it be a shame if he died and you had nothing to fight over?" Pratters answered his question with a glare. "I'm taking him to surgery in a few hours. Ten minutes after we start, he may no longer be a worry to any of you."

————

Pratters went back to Mrs. Summers. With a lot of time during the night to think, too many things about her bothered him. When he first heard of her, he had a hunch there was more to the story than she told. The more he saw of her and the more he learned, the more certain he was.

She still wore long sleeves, and as soon as she saw who it was, she tried to slam the door in his face. He blocked it with his hand, talking fast.

"I have to talk to you, and I swear my temper is under control. I won't forget my manners."

"I can't tell you anything more."

"Mrs. Summers, I have to know everything he said. It may have seemed unimportant to you and still have been a message."

She still held the door, but asked, "Why would a man like that give a message to a policeman?"

Pratters hadn't said it was for him, but he would take advantage of her conclusion. "Because—can I come in?"

She hesitated, then stepped back, releasing her hold of the door. "Was he undercover?"

"Not by a long shot." He shut the door and motioned her to a chair.

She shied away from the one he indicated, going again to the chair in front of the window. He knew then it was deliberate. Shadowed was where she wanted to be.

He sat down, deciding what he would tell her. He had to give her an explanation she would believe and not say enough to incriminate himself. Clasping his hands together, he leaned forward, elbows on his knees.

"I'm sure you realize that in my profession I have to make concessions at times that seem contradictory to the job. My dealings with Bell have been like that. He's the most despicable man I've ever encountered. I've never met him face to face until now, but he's been in contact with me for months."

She made no comment, waiting silently for him to continue.

"He has no loyalties. He cares for nothing other than himself, and he trades in anything that will insure his safety. What I have to tell you, if you repeat it, I'll deny. There's no way you could prove it."

She still made no comment as she gazed at him or, at least, in his direction, as he couldn't see her eyes clearly enough to be certain.

"Giving a criminal immunity in exchange for information is not unusual in my business. Bell carried it a step further. He's insured his safety beforehand. He's given me information for months. Now it's my turn to pay. That's why I believe, if he were capable, he would have asked for me."

"To protect him?"

"Yes."

"To keep giving you information?"

"He's through with that. There'll be too much suspicion and too many friends of those he killed for him to go back. I'll provide him with a new identity and the promise if he steps out of line again, his old friends will know where he is."

"You hope he does," she stated.

"I'd rather he didn't. He's a dangerous man. A threat like that will be the only way to keep him straight."

"I doubt if it would be enough."

Pratters leaned forward anxiously. "What really happened out there?"

"I already told you."

His mouth dropped open in surprise. Then he jerked up straight in anger. "You're lying! You wear long sleeves to hide bruises. Your obsession to be clean, your refusal to be examined, and your hostility towards me are all for the same reason. You got raped, and you don't want anyone to know."

She stood up, all grace and dignity. "Good day."

He shot to his feet and stormed to the door. "I'll be back," he promised hatefully.

3

The First Day of Hell

THE MOTORHOME TOWING THE LAND CRUISER BOUNCED AND JOLTED down the dirt road. The tires threw up a thick cloud of powder-fine dust nearly hiding the roofless, doorless cruiser from view in the mirrors as it bucked wildly behind.

Annalisa wore a look of grim determination. Her jaw set, her hands gripped the steering wheel hard as she fought the bumps and jolts. She was not yet where she wanted to be.

This valley had become her favorite place. Not too far ahead a level, solid spot lay hidden in a circle of trees where she could pull the motorhome off without worry of it sinking in sand. The spot was out of sight from the road and possible vandals. She had been taught that lesson once, returning to find the RV in a shambles. What they couldn't rip out to steal, they'd torn up. A disgusting waste and the incident had caused her many hours of listening to lectures. The general opinion her family held of her activities was she was a fool.

They'd only began to accept her fascination with the desert when she turned it into something that brought in money, and she'd only begun taking pictures to show them the beauty she saw when she tried to explain why she went. Money they could understand. Maybe the fault lay in her ability to explain. They certainly never looked at her as if she were making any sense when she used words like peace, but they understood profit.

Maybe they were right, and something was wrong with her. Why else would she deliberately go out in that hot and dusty desert, where there was no one to talk to? Why else would she leave the comforts of walls, glass, and refrigeration, or grass surrounding the pool, or a quietly humming car with the windows rolled up tight and the air conditioning running at high speed? Why would anyone want to leave the city life with its technology and conveniences? For what? A barren wasteland?

The plant or animal life wasn't what drew her time and time again, nor did any of the beauty she found and recorded with her camera for others to see. What drew her was a feeling she experienced when out there, one she had never felt in the city, in buildings, or in her own home, least of all in her own home. Solitude and quiet had totally different meanings in the desert.

She shrugged, a visible, physical effort to push away thoughts and feelings she didn't want. She parked the motorhome safely away within a thorny thicket of mesquite trees and hurried to free the cruiser. Though late afternoon, enough time remained to reach the spot she wanted and try for the pictures she planned to take this trip. With slight cloud cover, she hoped it would form the backdrop for a point of rock when the sun set. From the first time she saw it, she visualized it in silhouette with a red and gold sky behind it.

Since she would be going only for a few hours and just a few miles she hurried. She didn't load anything in the cruiser. All she needed for a short time was her camera and one canteen. Emergency supplies were already under the tilt back driver's seat, just in case anything happened.

Leaving the cruiser on the side of the dirt track road, Annalisa walked to a small rocky knoll a few hundred feet away. Roadrunners had a nest below it, and she could further record the growth of the chicks as she waited for the sunset.

The khaki colored jeans and long-sleeved shirt she wore blended in well with the sand color of the rocks. The camera sat down among the rocks to conceal it from the sharp eyes of the birds.

Atop the knoll with her face held into the hot, dry breeze, she breathed deep of the clean air, and peace began to settle within her. With the camera case at her feet, a slight smile graced her lips.

Pulling a narrow-brimmed hat from her pocket, she shook out the wrinkles and folds. The inexpensive, unattractive headgear was crumpled, but out there, she didn't care how it looked as long as it covered the lightness of her hair. Out there, it didn't matter if her hair was mussed or if she didn't put makeup on in the mornings. Out there, no one cared if her face showed her thirty years with wrinkles around her eyes. Out there, it didn't matter if she was alone.

Twisting, she looked back at the road to identify a sound. When she could see the motorcycles, long and low slung, she was glad she was out of sight. They weren't kids out looking for a good time jumping washes. Those bikes wouldn't jump anything. The people riding them didn't look as if jumping washes was anything they would be interested in, either. They were more interested in stealing anything not bolted down in her cruiser. She took up her camera and locked on the telephoto lens.

Of the four bikes, each with a man driving, three had a woman behind, holding a sack of groceries. The solitary man caught her attention first. He seemed separated from the main group not only in the sense he was the only man without a woman, but he held himself back from the others. He stayed on his bike and watched with his arms crossed over his chest while the three men swarmed over her vehicle.

Despite the heat, black gloves covered his hands. He wore Levis, a denim jacket hanging open in the front, the sleeves cut off, and no shirt underneath. His black boots had a metal plate up the front with buckles down the outside, and a rolled bandana encircled his forehead.

Annalisa took a picture of him, then another, extending the reach of the lens for a close-up of his face, what could be seen of it. Older than the others, he was at least as old as she. A full beard was long enough to reach the first button of his jacket, were it buttoned. His dark, almost black hair hung well past his shoulders, the filthy band keeping it out of his eyes. His nose, large and misshapen, bore a large lump on the bridge. Heavy brows met in the center while he watched the others.

She recorded him on film before turning the camera on the others. One of them, busy hot wiring her cruiser, lay in the seat with his head dropped under the steering wheel. She took a picture of that. She took a close-up of his face when he sat up, happy and satisfied with his work.

With no shirt, a black leather vest hung open from his shoulders. Levis, much too tight, covered his lower half, and the same type of metal adorned boots covered his feet. No beard, but he needed a shave. His hair was even longer than the first man's. Looking the 'all bones, little flesh' type, he was skinny compared to the heavy muscular build of the first, though he was probably taller and much younger.

The third man was much smaller in build and height. He looked to be Mexican or Italian, black hair, swarthy colored skin. He wore a blue, un-pressed shirt, hanging loose and open. His hair was collar length, and a mustache drooped down around the corners of his mouth.

The last man had a beard of sorts, skimpy and thin compared to the first man's. Of medium height and weight, he looked to be the youngest of the men, late teens or early twenties.

The women were shockingly dressed, both by moral standards and common sense. They had no protection for their skin against the sun. Cutoff Levis were what they all wore for pants, cut as short as possible. With the telephoto lens, it was disgustingly apparent they wore no underpants. The side seams were split nearly to the waistband on all of them.

Their upper apparel was just as skimpy. A redhead wore a halter top. A brunette, about the same age and build as the other, wore a sleeveless blouse tied in front and unbuttoned above the tie with no bra.

The last female was no more than a girl of sixteen or seventeen to the other two's early twenties. Timid, she hung back while the others scrambled over the cruiser. She didn't seem to belong with them, even though she stayed close to the man in the black vest. She dressed in the same mode, a bathing suit top, no more than a few patches of cloth held together with strings.

Their heads all turned to the lone man. Annalisa turned the camera as well, twisting down the lens to be able to watch all of them at the same time.

They seemed to be having an argument, the main group anyway. Their attention was given to the man on the bike, who didn't look the least disturbed. He wasn't even scowling any longer.

He hadn't moved, even so much as to uncross his arms, but he held their attention. She decided he had to be the leader. He obviously was the eldest by ten to fifteen years, and he had two teeth missing in the front. She took another shot of him. She took another when he stood to restart his bike. Another when he started rolling away. When he stopped to say something else to them, Annalisa turned the lens down to take a shot of him, another when he rode away.

The women tossed the sacks they carried into the back of the cruiser. The redhead got behind the wheel. The brunette got in beside her. The young blonde got on the bike behind the man in the leather vest. When they drove off, they laughed and shouted at each other. Words drifted up to her to make her blush.

A dust cloud rolled down the road as they drove away. The loss would cause her some inconvenience, but like everything else in her life, there was no overflow of emotion connected with the theft. The insurance would replace the vehicle, and there was nothing to be disturbed over. She certainly wasn't as she wound the film, the practical thing to do, even if the roll was not fully exposed. The police would not be interested in pictures of mountains she would take on the fresh roll she put in.

She lost interest in the dust and turned her attention to her camera, took off the telephoto lens, and returned it to the case. The wide-angle lens went on, ready for the shots of the point she came for. The sun had dropped too low and cast too many shadows for good shots of the roadrunners.

When she heard a falling rock rattle, she was surprised that the animals were moving so soon, she looked and saw nothing. The sound shouldn't have made her nervous, but it did. She listened intently for sounds of movement. It was too quiet, much too quiet. She jerked, looking behind her.

He was five feet below on the back side of the knoll, bigger, uglier, and more menacing that close. All her well-practiced composure deserted her. She dropped the camera, jumped, and ran.

He caught her before she reached the bottom. One jerk of her wrist and she fell into his arms and against his chest. The odor of his unwashed body overwhelmed her sense of smell, and Annalisa turned her head away, pushing at his chest.

"You smell," she exclaimed, in shock that anyone would allow themselves to be so offensive.

The force of her pushing against him sent her to the ground when he let go. The jolt of landing sent out a cry of surprise and pain. Indignant, she brushed dirt from her hands, telling him, "Your manners are just as bad."

He dropped to one knee in front of her, and she shrank away from the smell. Her face distorted in disgust, and her attention centered on the small scrape on the palm of her hand.

His voice was a deep, rolling rumble. "What are you doing out here?"

She looked for and reached for her hat, telling him, "None of your business."

He made her look at him by grabbing her wrist and twisting until she did. Annalisa knew again the fear and feeling of panic that swept over her when she first saw him close.

"What are you doing out here?"

"You're hurting me," she whined, prying at his fingers to loosen them.

"Answer me or I'll hurt you a lot more." He proved it by increasing the pressure on her wrist. "Now, what the hell are you doing out here?"

She answered as fast as she could get the words out. "Taking pictures."

He let go and settled back on his heel to stare at her. "You damned fool."

"I don't know where you have the right to—"

He cut off her indignant reply. "What do you think they'd do to you if they knew you took pictures of them?"

"They should think of things like that before they take something that doesn't belong to them."

He shot to his feet with an explosive exclamation.

She lunged to her feet, too, backing away. "There is no need to be profane."

"Stay where you are," he warned quietly, staring hard at her. She took another step back. "If I have to catch you again, I might hurt you."

"You already have." Her posterior smarted, but she certainly would not rub it in front of him.

"Don't you have any idea what kind of trouble you're in?"

"I'm not. I didn't steal a vehicle."

He looked straight at her. "You're in trouble, lady. I can't let you go."

"You can't possibly intend to keep me against my will."

"Yes, I do."

She took one step back, and her hand went to her throat, clutching her shirt tighter to her neck.

He laughed at her. "Don't worry. I don't go in for that."

She didn't believe him. She ran again. At her heels, his arms swung out to encircle her waist. She dropped to escape them. He caught her by her wrists, jerked her up, and turned her to face him by forcing her arms to fold behind her.

"Let go of me."

"Quit fighting me."

He captured both of her wrists in one of his hands, freeing one of his to grab a handful of her hair. Pulling her head back, arched her back, pressing her hips against him.

"Don't fight me," he ordered again.

She froze, staring up at his face. "I won't. I swear I won't. Just let me go."

"I'm not going to rape you, and I won't hurt you if you quit fighting."

She didn't believe him. The terrible scar across the lump on his nose and the gap where teeth were missing told her how violent he was. She wanted away from him, and she couldn't even pull her hips back from contact. "Take the cruiser," she told him frantically. "Take the camera. Just let me go."

"Straight to the police—if you made it out of here."

"No, I won't tell anyone."

"What will dear hubby say when you come home without the Jeep?"

"It's not a Jeep."

"Jeep is close enough and don't correct anyone else. Now answer my question."

"I'm a widow."

"The kids then?"

She arched violently to push him away. "I don't have any children!" she screamed.

The sudden violence caught him off guard. She jerked one hand free before he recovered, but he quickly recaptured it. Within seconds, he held both wrists again in one of his hands and had her bent backward with a hold of her hair. All her efforts to free herself caused their pelvic bones to grind together. She gave up with a groan and a plea to be let loose.

They both jerked and stiffened at the sound of another voice. "Might as well, Bell. We'll take care of her for you."

Bell's voice changed from rumble to growl. "Get the hell out of here, Al."

He released her hair, freeing her enough to see who spoke. Two of them, the man in the leather vest, and the smaller, dark one watched them. They both rubbed their crotches.

Annalisa looked at Bell in wonder. For all the contact of their bodies, pressed together the way they were, he was not aroused. The other two were, showing it beneath the cloth of their jeans.

She shifted her weight, leaning toward him, taking the drag off the arm he had around her. He rewarded her by easing his grip on her wrists.

The other two saw it. "How the hell does he do it?" the smaller one demanded, though he used much more descriptive words than her mind cared to recall. She could not, even in memory, deplete all that embarrassed her, no matter how hard she tried.

"Just makes them think he's safer than us," the other one answered, with a nasty grin. "No flagging prick to scare you, baby?"

"Get out of here," Bell warned quietly. The man chuckled, moving closer. So did the other. "You, too, Dago."

They separated as they moved closer. "Hey, Al, how do you figure him to be the one to smell out a cunt?"

"Maybe that's how he does it, smells them to death."

Confused by the things they said, Annalisa still knew what they meant to do. She could tell in the way Bell held himself and watched them. There was going to be a fight.

He released his hold of her wrists and shifted her to his side with an arm around her waist. With one hand, she held to his waistband in the back. With the other, she clutched his jacket in the front. She wouldn't look at the other two. She stared up into Bell's face, waiting for whatever he was going to do.

Al reached out to touch her. She gasped as his fingers brushed her hip and gasped again when Bell swung her around. Her head snapped, he bent her over backwards, only to jerk her straight again.

In seconds it was over. She clung to him, sagging on his arm. Al was on the ground, holding his mouth. Dago held his stomach gasping for air. Bell wasn't even winded.

"Want to try again?" Bell asked calmly.

"Nope," Al said, wiping blood from his mouth. "Ain't no bitch worth losing teeth over."

Dago regained his breath. "He tried to ball me!"

"Bell wouldn't ball you," Al said, getting back to his feet. "He might break your neck or back, but he wouldn't ball you. Would you, Bell?"

"I would if I needed to."

Annalisa dropped her head to his chest with reaction setting in. Shaking, she felt like she couldn't breathe. With each breath she did take, she nearly gagged from the smell of old sweat. Nothing seemed real. Men didn't jump out of rocks and fight over a woman they had never seen before for the chance to rape her. Things like that happened in movies where everything was exaggerated for sensationalism.

She knew they were talking. She didn't hear what they said or see the other two leave. Bell sat her on the ground, squatting in front of her, holding her by the arms. He shook her until she looked up at him.

"That's only a sample of what you're in for. I can't let you go now."

"I won't tell anyone."

"They've seen you."

If that was supposed to explain something to her, it didn't. "I just want to go home. Keep the cruiser. Keep the camera. I just want to go home," she whined.

He shook her again, harder, making her bite her tongue. He stopped shaking with her head thrown back, forcing her to look at him.

"You're staying with me. Understand?"

"If you let me go—" She cried out in pain as he increased the vise grip on her arms.

"We're going to the camp. You stay close to me and do what I tell you. As long as you do, nothing will happen to you."

"Because you can't?" she asked dumbly.

He jerked back as if she'd slapped him, shoving her away. Her head bounced hard on the ground. "That's right," he told her hatefully. "I just smell."

"How can you smell anything over yourself?" she retorted, rubbing the back of her head.

His hand moved, making her flinch from an expected blow, but he jerked her up by one arm instead. None of her struggles to pull away succeeded. In a matter of seconds, he had her in front of him, arms locked around her chest. She walked where he wanted to go.

4

PRATTERS STOPPED ON HIS WAY BACK TO THE HOSPITAL LONG enough to make a call to the local FBI office. He wanted a search for Nam veterans who suffered wounds in the groin.

As soon as he appeared in the ICU ward, the nurse snatched up the phone. Other than the nurse, no one noticed him, something Pratters planned to change immediately.

"We're taking him up in a few minutes," the doctor told him, appearing at Pratters' shoulder.

"When you bring him back, I want him taken to a private room."

Thristen cocked a grey eyebrow in a manner conveying extreme patience with a fool. "He isn't going to run away."

"How would you like it if someone walked in here and blew his head off?"

"You for instance?"

"His friends in particular. They won't like the idea of him making a deal."

Thristen studied him for a moment before saying, "He can't be moved to a private room. They aren't set up for the intensive care he will need. That's why he's in the Intensive Care Unit."

"A guard then."

"Outside is fine. You arrange it. Now move aside."

Pratters moved and moved again to make room for the interns and nurses. He stood outside watching them hook and unhook equipment and tubes from permanent to temporary to keep an un-responding mass of flesh and bones in a living state. Brakes were released from the wheels, and the bed moved.

He followed until a hand planted in his chest to stop him. A finger pointed to a "No Admittance" sign. He paced the hall while he waited and nearly pounced on the doctor when he appeared hours later.

"Well?" he demanded.

"The machines are still working," Thristen said wearily.

"He isn't?"

The doctor had little compassion for Pratters' concern. "His brain is still functioning, if that's what's worrying you. It still says, 'beat heart, breathe lungs.' They still listen, but they can't do it on their own."

"You don't think he'll make it."

The doctor sighed. "I realized when I first saw him that making book on his chances could be a losing game."

"You think he will."

"I wouldn't give him a snowball's chance in hell."

Pratters' temper snapped. "Damn you. Give me a straight answer!"

"You won't like it." Pratters glared at him. "It is now in the hands of God."

"He doesn't stand a chance then."

"Maybe *God* does not agree with you."

Thristen turned to walk away, and Pratters grabbed him by the arm, spinning him back around. "You think I'm playing God?'"

"You do seem to have decided who should live and die."

"Did you see any of the bodies?"

"Not my department."

He tried to turn away again. Pratters still held him. "You heard their names. Ever wonder why a man would be called Fingers?"

"I'm not interested."

"Get interested. It's people like you who hide their heads in the sand and make my job harder. You give us all those right and wrong laws we have to follow, and men like Fingers use them to keep right on doing their filthy work."

"I don't need any lectures."

"You're getting it. Fingers wore a necklace. Bones, each one the top joint of the little finger of the right hand of his victims. One was a nine-year-old boy who received the same treatment Bell did."

The doctor's face paled, but Pratters didn't stop anymore with him than he had with Hume. "One of those nice right and wrong laws is the accused had the right to face his accuser. What do you think it would have done to that boy to face the man who raped and mutilated him, and how long do you think he would have stood up to cross examination?"

He released his hold and stepped back. "I'm a cold-blooded bastard, but if I can use scum like Bell to stop scum like Fingers, I damn well will."

To judge from the expressions flashing across the doctor's face, Pratters was sure thoughts of human rights, civil rights, wrong, good, and bad went through his mind, but he couldn't catch a hold of any of them. The picture of a nine-year-old child in Bell's condition was in was too strongly implanted. His mouth opened, but no sound came out.

Pratters turned on his heel and walked out.

———

"Told you I'd be back," Pratters told her as soon as the door opened.

Annalisa Summers' voice was as flat and toneless as always. "Since I know it does no good to shut the door in your face, you may as well come in." She left the door and crossed immediately to the same chair.

"Why do you always wear long sleeves?" he asked, closing the door and watching her closely.

"For the heat."

How prim and proper she sat in the chair, and the question seemed not to upset her at all. He still dug. "A little backwards, isn't it?" He moved to the seat nearest her, the end of the couch, perpendicular to her chair.

"Ask any Arab."

"They always stay covered, but that's their religion."

"They shroud and veil their women for religious reasons, but they cover themselves against the sun."

"Seems to me, the less you have on, the cooler you'd be."

"The quicker you'd dehydrate. Are you really interested?"

"Yes," he told her with a grin. "I had a heatstroke after I left here yesterday. I spent the night in the hospital."

"You should have taken the water." A spot on the floor held her attention while she spoke.

"Why?"

"Probably because you don't take the time to drink enough liquids." Pratters was beginning to feel like he was talking to Jane Doe again. Annalisa paused, but she did continue without prompting. "There has to be a balance. Too much salt and you don't perspire enough. Too little and you perspire too much. One will cause a stroke. The other will cause heat exhaustion."

"Which is which?"

"Exhaustion is caused from depletion of salt, from perspiring too freely, or not enough salt. With a stroke, your body temperature builds from not perspiring enough. Too much salt or not enough moisture."

"What do you suppose those women died of?"

47

"Idiocy." She straightened slightly and turned her head to look at him. "Clothing—long sleeves and high necks, loose so the air can flow freely to evaporate the moisture of perspiration slowly to cool the skin. Without clothing, the sun hits directly, burns the skin and dries the moisture off too rapidly to cool. Dehydration kills."

"I didn't realize they published pictures of them."

"None did that I'm aware of, but there were very vivid descriptions on the news." She looked away, back to the spot on the floor.

"Did they rape you?" he asked bluntly, hoping to catch her off guard.

She answered without hesitation and without showing the slightest shock over his question. "No."

"They tried?"

She looked up at him, not answering.

"I'd like to see your arms."

"I'd like to see your identification," she countered.

"Why?" he asked, being the one to be surprised

"Don't I have the right?"

"Of course, but I already showed it to you." He knew she hadn't looked. He dug it out and held it out in front of her. As she stared at it, he added, "It's authentic."

"I wouldn't know if it is." Her eyes went back to the spot on the floor. "It's the name I wanted to see."

"Why? Did he give you a message?" he asked eagerly.

"He tried to say something once. It could have been your name."

"Probably. Did he say anything else?"

"No."

"Mrs. Summers, what really happened out there?"

"What do you think happened out there?" she countered.

"I think they found you out there, kidnapped you, he claimed you, and they fought."

"Why would he claim me?"

"Christ, woman, what happened?" he shouted in exasperation.

"I made my statement."

Pratters stood up, glaring at her. "You left out him trying to say my name. What else?"

She did the first graceless thing he was to see her do. She shrugged.

Mad enough to shake her, he ground out, "More than that happened, enough that you held him in your arms, crying your head off."

"I was in shock."

Pratters sank back down on the couch. "You were grateful enough to help him."

"I found him on the side of the road. He was hurt. I couldn't just leave him there."

Pratters tried a new angle of attack. "They operated on him."

"It was on the news."

No question of Bell's resulting condition came from her. Pratters gave up, for then. "If you do think of anything else, you have my number."

5

The Camp

THE CAMP WAS ARRANGED IN A SQUARE OF SORTS, IN A LARGE cleared area. Bell pulled up to the other bikes and her cruiser, serving as one border. Directly opposite, a space of forty-five feet, three two-man pup tents in a row formed another side. To the right was a canopy of sorts, strung between two mesquite trees. The sagging canvas sheltered two tables with a narrow space between, loaded down with cooking equipment, food, and debris. Across from that, another tent stood alone.

In the center of the crude square was a dead campfire, and the others stood around it. The little blonde standing behind Al was the only one who didn't wear a grin. Al stood slightly to the front with the other two men flanking him. The redhead leaned against the third man, and the brunette had Dago's arms around her waist.

Bell held Annalisa on the seat in front of him. At the sight of them, she ceased her struggles. Any fear or anger she felt toward him and riding on the motorcycle whipped away with the terror of seeing them and increased when Bell stated, "You're going to try again."

"We got one more," Al answered smugly.

Bell leaned forward to turn the bike off and lower the stand. It caused him to press against her and placed his mouth at her ear.

"Stay here or the women will get you down," he told her softly.

Her hand went out to him as he moved away. Only terror of what he moved toward kept her from following. The same terror made her too weak in the limbs to run, hands gripped together in her lap as her eyes followed his movements.

He walked up to the three, separated then by several feet. He pointed at Al with his right hand. "You're first," he told him, and at the same instant, his left shot out as he moved forward, doubling the third man over.

Something touched her. She brushed at it without looking. It touched again, harder. That it was a hand shocked her. She jumped off the bike away from the woman only to bump into the other, the redhead. Unable to believe a woman would touch her on the breast, Annalisa pushed the hand away when the woman reached for her again.

The redhead laughed. "Ain't you never done it with a woman?"

"Bet she hasn't, Ready. Look at her face," the brunette said with a deep chuckle. She reached out, over the seat of the bike for between Annalisa's legs.

Annalisa dropped her hands to block, only to jerk them up when Ready pinched her hard on her breast. Crying out as much in horror, as in pain, she slapped at Ready's hand.

"Tender, baby?" Ready cooed. "I'll kiss it and make it better."

She moved forward, and Annalisa backed until the bike's handle bar held her. Fingers closed on each breast, squeezing hard. Annalisa screamed, shoving with all her strength, giving herself room to twist free of the bar. She backed away from her tormentors still unable to believe women would be doing that.

"It'll be like doing it to my old lady." Ready advanced slowly. "I hated that old bitch."

They went at her the same way the men had Bell, one from each side. Annalisa threw an arm out in reflex when one started at her and turned her head away from the other.

Ready gasped as Annalisa's stiff arm caught her in the chest, but she still found Annalisa's hair with both hands. She shook Annalisa, tossing her around while the brunette tore at the buttons on Annalisa's shirt.

The women forced her to the ground, the brunette on her legs, holding them down. Ready leaned on the hold she had of her hair, keeping her head on the ground, laughing as Annalisa cried out.

Each effort to hold her blouse together, ended with it being torn from her grasp. She pulled on one hand only to have another take its place. All the time, hands rubbed and pressed on her breasts causing pain. She sobbed, begging them to stop until she felt the snap on her jeans jerk open.

Annalisa screamed with something more than fear, and she no longer felt pain. She jerked herself up, freeing her head by pulling out hair. Twisting against the weight on her legs, she swung an arm at Ready

Ready dodged the blow, laughing, and then dove in for Annalisa's hair again. "Get those pants down," she ordered, bearing all her weight on Annalisa's head.

Annalisa still hit, but the open-handed blows had no effect. The brunette laughed, jerked on the pants. The waist folded down to Annalisa's hips. In desperation, Annalisa arched and twisted, throwing her off her legs.

Someone other than Annalisa screamed. No one held her down any longer, leaving her free to huddle in a ball and frantically pull at her clothes.

The brunette stood in front of her, rubbing her head, Ready behind her. Another figure stood beside Annalisa.

Ready taunted. "What's the matter? Don't you want your pretty prissy soiled?"

"Not by you," Bell answered, pulling Annalisa to her feet by one arm.

She jerked away, frantically pulling her blouse together. She jerked again and shied away when he jerked her pants back to her waist from the back. Both women laughed.

"She needs breaking in," Ready told him.

"Not by a slut."

Ready screamed vile, filthy names, and Annalisa huddled with her head swinging from side to side looking for a place to run that wouldn't take her toward one of them. When Bell put his hand on her neck and turned her, she walked blindly, holding her clothes to her, too ashamed to raise her head.

Ready screamed, "If I ever catch Prissy Pants out by herself, I'll show her how it feels."

Bell didn't look back or raise his voice. "You do, and I'll beat the shit out of you."

Ready snorted, but she made no further comment. No one did as Bell walked Annalisa to the solitary tent. She didn't lift her head, but from the corner of her eye she saw the three men he left before stopping the women. The only one still standing was Al, and he held his stomach. Dago sat on the ground, holding his head with both hands. The last man was unconscious, lying flat on his back.

Bell pushed her down and into the tent, told her to stay there until he called her, and folded down the flap. The air in the small tent was stifling. The flap left open would have given her fresh air, but she was grateful for the sense of being hidden the closed tent gave her.

An hour passed before she could stop crying. A half hour more before her hands stopped shaking enough for her to attempt to re-button her blouse. The thinner fabric had not fared as well as the heavier material of the pants. She re-pinned her hair with the few pins that remained and buttoned the shirt for the fourth time in holes too ripped to hold when Bell came back.

He threw the flap up and squatted in the entrance. She cowered to the back, hunched over beneath the sloping tent sides. Clutching at the blouse, she held it tight at the waist and neck while he stared at her in the fading light of day.

He moved again, and she shrunk back further, but he only sat down, leaning in on one elbow. "You'll have to help fix dinner," he told her in a soft rumble.

She shook her head. She wasn't ever going out there again.

"You have to or don't eat."

She found her voice, a weak whisper. "I'm not hungry."

"Don't make it any harder for yourself. Just go along with it."

"For how long?" she wailed.

"Until we leave here."

In her anxiousness, she leaned toward him. "How long is that?"

"A day, maybe two."

"Then what?" she asked, afraid of the answer.

He made her wait a moment, studying her before saying, "I'll take you home."

Biting at a trembling lip, she wanted to believe him, but he was the one who took her there to suffer the degradation. "I won't tell the police, I swear."

"I don't care if you do. I won't be here then but keep your mouth shut about it to the others."

"Why?"

"Because I told you to. Give me your things."

"Things?" she asked dumbly, not following the shift in subjects.

"Your rings and anything you have in your pockets."

He held out his hand, and she stared at it. When he snapped his fingers impatiently, she jerked and pulled off her wedding rings, dropped them in his hand, and quickly emptied her pockets of her keys and a packet of salt tablets. He handed the last back and dropped the rest in his jacket pocket.

Straightening, he told her, "Come on."

She didn't move fast soon enough to suit him. He leaned back inside and dragged her out on her knees. Inside, his voice had been low and toneless. Outside, it turned hard and cruel. He shoved her toward the canopy, telling her loud and clear, "Help fix the grub."

Freezing, she stared at the two women who waited for her. Bell shoved her again, nearly knocking her down. She moved stiffly, walking a wide circle around the two women outside the tables.

The little blonde stood under the canopy between the two tables. She looked almost as terrorized as Annalisa felt.

"You help Bunny," Ready ordered.

Looking at the one between the tables, she said, "I thought everyone had to help."

"Not if you're strong enough to make someone else."

"It's all right," Bunny said quickly.

"They've no right to make you do their work."

Ready laughed and asked, "Are you going to change it?" She jabbed the brunette in the ribs. "She thinks she's going to change it."

She was jabbed back in warning. Bell moved up behind them.

"You can't stop us from—" Ready began.

He cut her off. "Unless you're strong enough." Then he looked at Annalisa. "Come here."

She was afraid to move. He was so big, and he seemed angry. Bunny bumped her from behind. Annalisa knew what she was trying to tell her but still couldn't move. Bell went after her, grabbed her by the neck and walked her away from them.

Ten feet away, he jerked her around to face him, but he didn't release his hold on her neck to allow her to raise her head. She cringed from the tone of his voice, low but mean.

"Keep your mouth shut. If they jump you for any reason other than sex, I won't interfere. Got that?"

She nodded awkwardly. The answer didn't satisfy him.

"Say it—loud."

"Yes."

"Louder."

"Yes—ow!"

"Now go back there." He shoved her away and walked off.

Rubbing the back of her neck where he pinched her, she fought the instinct to run after him. The women laughed. Humiliated, she had to walk back by them and listen to them snicker while she opened cans of chili. She listened until she couldn't stand it anymore.

"Shut up."

Ready laughed harder. "Come make me, *Pretty Prissy*."

The way she said it sounded vile, and she wiggled her fingers, inviting Annalisa to go after her. Annalisa looked past Ready to Bell. He looked the other way, ignoring what went on but had told her he wouldn't interfere.

"I don't suppose you ever considered anything fair like one-to-one?" Annalisa asked.

Ready shook her head and nudged her companion. The brunette immediately circled the tables to come in from behind. Bunny quickly got out of the way.

Annalisa had never been in a fight in her life, unless she considered what happened earlier, and she hadn't done well then. Her panic built, and she wished she had done what Bell told her—kept her mouth shut.

"Backing down, Prissy?" Ready asked, closing off one end of the narrow aisle between the tables.

The brunette closed off the other, and Annalisa grabbed for a weapon. The nearest thing handy was the pan, filled with chili. Throwing the contents in the brunette's face, she twisted and hit Ready alongside the head with the pan. They both screamed, and Annalisa ducked under the table to get from between them. She nearly went back, when she saw the men running toward her, all but Bell.

Pride kept her from running, but she didn't breathe until the men went by her, running to their mates. For a few moments, a complete bedlam of screaming, whining, and shouting of obscenities by both men and women reigned. When the noise quieted, all of the women pointed at Annalisa.

When Al started toward her, pride deserted her. She backed away. Panic nearly took her again when she backed into something that didn't move. She looked over her shoulder, saw Bell, and ducked behind him.

Al's advance stopped short. "She ruined the food!" he yelled.

"Ready and Jolene started it." Bell paused, looking at Ready. "She finished it."

Annalisa felt a surge of satisfaction. She *had* finished it. She had been in a fight, and she won. Her triumph, however, died quickly.

"She ruined the food!" Al shouted again.

"There's more." Bell reached for Annalisa and jerked her to the front. "Get it fixed and quit fucking around."

———

The women's position in the camp was servant and slave to the men. The men lounged around the fire while the meal was prepared. Their meals and drinks were carried to them before the women were allowed to get their own, taking two trips each before they were allowed to sit on the ground to eat.

The ground, without cushion or backrest, was uncomfortable. Bell, however, was comfortable, sitting with a big rock as a backrest and a folded blanket beneath him. Eating like a hog, he shoveled the food in, drained the bottle of beer in noisy gulps, and belched. He tossed the empty bottle into the fire and settled back.

Annalisa stared at her paper plate of food unable to eat. By the time the men were served, it was dark, and from where she sat, with her back to the others, all she saw was the solitary tent.

Four men and, counting her, four women meant one for each man and a tent for each couple. The thought of being forced to be in the same confining space with Bell appalled her. The smell would be overpowering in the airless space.

The thought of what he might expect of her, made her insides threaten to expel what little food she'd managed to swallow. If she understood the things the others said, Bell was incapable of normal sex. She shuddered at the thought of what he might demand instead.

Clenching her hands in her lap, Annalisa didn't see his hand coming and gasped when it closed around her arm. He jerked her to him, making her fall on his chest. She pushed away, but his arms were steel bands forcing her down to his chest and trapping her arms between them.

"Cold, Bell?" Al asked.

"What happens when you get warmed up?" Ready asked maliciously.

Annalisa shuddered, wondering the same thing. What kind of satisfaction did he seek?

Bell didn't answer, but Ready shrieked. Annalisa looked, only to snap her head back. The rank smell of his body filled her nostrils, but it was much preferred to not seeing what was happening on the other side of the fire.

Ready shrieked again. "Oh, Joey, do it. You know how much I love that."

"You love anything, you horny bitch," Joey told her huskily. "You've got the best love handles in the world."

"I think I'm going to be sick," Annalisa whispered, swallowing compulsively.

Bell stood up, dragging her with him.

"Is she ready, Bell?" Ready asked sweetly.

"To piss."

"Excuses? Can't you stand to watch?"

Bell looked straight at Ready to answer. "Nothing here worth watching."

"You..." Ready growled.

Something grazed Annalisa's head. Bell caught it easily before the bit of material hit him in the face and deliberately tossed Ready's halter into the fire. Ready screamed the usual obscenities at him while Bell walked Annalisa away from them, and Bell didn't have to hold onto her. Annalisa trailed after him like a trained dog. He walked past the row of tents to an area not hard to identify.

She stopped ten feet short of the canvas stall hung haphazardly from a large Palo Verde tree. She could smell the enclosure, and the breeze blew the other way.

"Either that or squat," Bell told her.

"Do you have to be vulgar?" she asked miserably. "I don't have to go anyway."

"I'm not bringing you out here again tonight. If it offends you, use the ground." He added, as nastily as Ready used it, "Prissy."

"That isn't my name."

"It is here and don't give them any other. Now, are you going or not?" he asked.

She did, approaching the stall with her breath held. Inside was a metal stand with a plastic ring. A bag was suspended from the ring, filled to overflowing.

While she shuddered in disgust, he relieved himself on the ground outside. She told herself the degradation was necessary, and she could stand the embarrassment as long as it kept him close to protect her from the others.

Annalisa trained so well and so quickly, she never questioned his order not to tell the others her name. She simply accepted, following him back to camp, keeping her eyes on his back to avoid any chance of seeing what the others did by the fire. She couldn't close her ears. Neither could he have, yet he stretched out on the tent floor as if he heard nothing. He made no move toward her, much to her relief, and he obviously had every intention of going to sleep.

Annalisa sat as close to the edge of the tent and the door as she could get, as far as possible from his feet and legs. "It…it must be hard to take their taunting all the time."

He rose up, cruel and brutal. "Don't feel sorry for me. If I could, I'd have fucked you ten minutes after I found you."

Cringing at his language and what he said, she retorted, "You're as bad as they are."

"Don't you forget it."

"What do you want from me? Why did you bring me here?"

"I brought you here to keep you from going to the police. As long as you're here, you can take care of me. Do it right and I won't have to teach you any *hard* lessons."

"You mean you'd beat me?"

"To a black and blue pulp. Now shut up and go to sleep."

"What makes you so cruel?"

He sounded even more menacing in the hoarse whisper he used. "Don't ask stupid questions. Don't ask *any* questions. Keep your mouth shut and go to sleep."

"I won't ask you anything. I won't even talk to you."

"Good." He stretched out again. "Now lie down and be quiet."

"I won't lie beside you."

"Sleep sitting up then."

She sat, but not to sleep. He was hateful, filthy, vicious, and a criminal. He'd kidnapped and dragged her there, placed her in the danger he protected her from while telling her he would rape her if he were capable. She was going to get away from him, all of them.

Gradually the sounds outside faded into the other tents. Annalisa waited awhile longer to be sure they were all asleep, but as soon as she eased to her hands and knees, Bell's head went up.

"What are you doing?"

"Lying down," she said quickly, prompted more by fear than intelligent thinking.

"Do it then and quit waking me up."

She dropped flat, and she didn't believe he had been asleep. He couldn't have heard her, and she knew she hadn't touched him. She made sure she didn't by staying as close as possible to the side of the tent. Flat beside him, she stayed as close to the side as she could get, with her nose pressed against it to keep from smelling him. As determined as she was to out wait him, every time she moved, he did. In the end, she woke to find herself alone.

———

At first, Annalisa couldn't remember where she was. When she did, and knew she hadn't suffered a hideous nightmare, she feared he had left. She scampered out on her hands and knees, jerked to an ungraceful stop, sitting back on her feet when she saw him.

Bell stood by the dead fire with a paper cup in his gloved hand. One foot rested on the rock he had used for a backrest the night before, and he leaned with an elbow on the raised knee. He stared at her and did so without moving or speaking for so long a time, she began to fidget.

His stare made her conscious of her terrible appearance. Raising a hand self-consciously to her hair, her movement seemed to draw him away from his thoughts. He walked over to her and held out the cup, towering over her, making her even more uncomfortable.

Dropping her head in embarrassment, she saw that her blouse hung open. In her haste to cover herself, she spilled the coffee, knowing it was silly of her. He certainly saw more than a tiny strip of belly every day, but it was more than she had ever showed.

When he knelt on one knee in front of her, she stiffened and drew away when his hand moved to her waist.

"I thought we had that settled," he told her.

She stared at him in amazement. Of all the voices she heard from him, never before was the tone the soft gentle one he used then. She didn't move while he tied the shirt tails in a knot at her waist.

61

"That will keep it closed." He sat back on one heel, looking at her face.

"Thank you." The words sounded faint to her. She cleared her throat to repeat them, tugging at the shirt, terribly conscious of being stared at, and it made her throat dry.

"It looks fine."

Even though certain she saw amusement in those green eyes of his, she didn't feel he was laughing at her. That puzzled her, and he saw it.

"Come on," he told her with the gentleness disappearing from his voice.

"Where?" she asked, eagerly jumping to her feet to follow him.

"Keep your voice down."

His voice was curt, but still low. How he could change his tone without changing the volume amazed her. She couldn't. She whispered, half-running to keep up with his long stride. "Where are we going?"

He stopped, looking straight into her eyes again. "Right here for now. Fix some breakfast."

"Then where?"

"To see if anyone is looking for you."

The words were a rude reminder, dashing her hopes cruelly. "Do I have to go?"

"No, you can stay here with them."

Not a choice and he knew it. Shooting a glare at him, she flounced to the tables. He reached by her for the pot of coffee. She deliberately stepped away, her silent act of defiance ignored. He poured himself a cup and sipped coffee, waiting for her to serve him breakfast and continued to ignore her while he wolfed down the scrambled eggs. Finished, the paper plate and plastic fork went into the fire pit as he walked by her to his bike without a word. He knew she'd follow and get on behind him, just as he knew she wouldn't try to run away. Damn him, he knew everything.

Sitting behind him instead of in front, Annalisa began the ride determined not to hold on to him. In a very short time, she clung to him like a limpet. The wind made her eyes water and made it hard to catch her breath. His long hair flipped into her face with such force it stung like tiny whips, though none of that was the reason she held on to him so tightly. The narrow seat beneath her offered little in the way of security, especially each time they hit a bump. If there was any place for her to put her feet, he hadn't shown her, and they constantly banged and dragged the ground.

They left the road and started up the incline to the very point she had come to photograph. After one particularly bad bump, she got off, deliberately, but her landing wasn't graceful. Standing up seemed the thing to do. Her feet were already on the ground, so she kept them there, only the bike had been moving faster than it seemed. The ground did not stay under her feet, and she ended up in a sprawl, again on her butt.

Bell stopped the bike and looked at her. "What did you do that for?"

"I'd rather walk," she retorted. Amusement was what she saw in his eyes then, to goad her anger. "If you want to kill yourself, go ahead."

"I'm not the one who fell."

"I wanted off."

"You made it." He swung his leg over the seat and moved the bike into a position that would keep it up on the stand on the uneven ground.

During that very brief time, Annalisa got up and brushed herself off, ready to follow him when he walked the last of the distance up to the point.

The view was beautiful. The early morning breeze blew cool and fresh. That was her desert out there. She felt the peace returning to her, and she forgot he was there until a wren flew by, carrying a bit of something in its bill. Her eyes followed and found Bell in her line of sight.

"You like it!" she exclaimed in surprise.

Her exclamation surprised him. "Why wouldn't I?"

"I wouldn't think a man like you would appreciate anything of beauty."

He raised an eyebrow at her. "Maybe I like it because it's ugly."

"It is not!"

Her obvious anger amused him, reminding her she'd sworn not to talk to him. She certainly wasn't going to be baited into saying silly things to entertain him. "The only thing ugly in it is you and your friends, contaminating it with your filth."

The humor vanished from his eyes. "Don't ever say anything like that in front of the others."

"Or what?"

"I'll have to do something about it." He shoved her, pushing at one arm to turn her.

Seeing him angry, part of her was glad, another sad. Annalisa concentrated on the glad. She had to be with him but did not have to like him. Nor would she pander to him while obeying his orders or be upset by his anger. She did believe he was going to take her home. He had no reason to keep her, once he left the area. She believed him, until Ready told her different.

———

When they returned, he was ready for lunch. The others were just having breakfast. He sent her back into the lion's den with no more than a short warning. "Don't get between them."

Ready wore a shirt, tied in front like Jolene's, as filthy as the halter Bell had burned the night before. Ready, as usual, started trouble.

"My, my, look at Pretty Prissy trying to be sexy." She gave Annalisa's shirt a tug as she said it with a nasty smirk.

Annalisa stepped back to get away from her. Remembering Bell's warning in time to avoid Jolene, she side-stepped.

Ready saw the movement and laughed. "Getting nervous?" she

asked Jolene, "How nervous do you think she'd be if she knew what Bell really had in mind for her?"

"She'd shit her pants," Jolene answered maliciously.

"Be careful about going on long trips with him. They're always one way."

A trip home would be, but Annalisa was sure that was not what Ready meant. Ready made sure she understood.

"He's kinky. Haven't you figured that out yet?"

Jolene helped explain, happily. "You ought to ask him what he did with his other old ladies."

"Ask him. You'll just love hearing that lie."

"What do you suppose he's told her? The same thing?"

"I wouldn't know. He's never had reason to lie to me."

Annalisa retorted without thinking. "He wouldn't bother, either."

Ready went after her with both hands, aiming for her hair again. Annalisa ducked, and Ready's weight carried them into the table holding the stove. The table went down with a crash as they thrashed around. Annalisa held Ready's wrists to keep her away from her hair as they spun around in the narrow space. Annalisa remembered Jolene too late. A blow in the back knocked the wind out of her, and her knees buckled. Ready got her hair then, using it in an effort to slam Annalisa's face into her raised knee.

Annalisa shoved with both her legs in an instinctive effort to throw Ready off balance and suddenly felt like she was flying, no longer on the ground, not any part of her. Bell had her around the waist, but Ready still had a hold of her hair. At the same time, Al had Ready around the waist, pulling her back. Annalisa felt like her scalp was being pulled loose until Bell put a stop to all of it.

He closed one hand around Ready's nearest wrist. "Let go or I break it."

Ready let go. Bell flipped Annalisa up and set her on her feet in time to face Al.

"You better keep that bitch of yours under control!" Al screamed.

Bell answered without raising his voice in the slightest. "Joey's bitch started it."

"Who saw it?" Al demanded.

"Ready jumped her," Dago supplied.

Al spun around and slapped Ready in the face. "No more. I don't want to have to go to town for more food before the meet. You leave her alone."

He turned to Annalisa. She dodged behind Bell. Still gasping to catch her breath, each breath hurt. If she could help it, she wasn't going to get slapped as well.

If the look on his face was any judge, Al wanted to hit her, but he didn't want to pass Bell to do it. "Get rid of her," he shouted in frustration. "She's nothing but a troublemaker."

Bell's answer was indifferent. "Get rid of Ready."

"She's one of us." He pointed at Annalisa. "She isn't."

"I told you to leave that Jeep alone."

"You could have killed her."

"I didn't want to."

"Not yet," Dago murmured, breaking the tension with laughter from all with his remark.

"All right, but keep her away from the others," Al ordered.

Bell turned toward Annalisa, and she bolted in terror. Now she knew why he wanted her and that he lied. If Ready thought he was kinky, as perverted as she was, Annalisa couldn't imagine what Bell had in mind. She just knew it would be horrible. Terrified of him, she fought when he caught her.

"Didn't mean to make it hard for you," Ready called after them as Bell carried Annalisa to the tent.

———

Bell tossed her inside and only came back once to throw in a canteen, leaving her to the misery of suffocating heat and fear filled afternoon. If she hadn't been acclimated to the heat and not had the salt tablets, she could easily have died for all he knew or cared.

As the heat built to an unbearable level, her anger grew, more at herself than at him. Her protector! That was a sick joke. He was no knight, not even in black armor, and it was no castle he carried maidens off to, but a grave.

At five, he came for her. "Come on," he ordered with only his head in the tent.

"Where?"

"Get out here before I come in after you."

Al called out, "Too bad you can't train her right, Bell. Sure you don't want us to initiate her for you?"

Bell dropped his voice so only she would hear. "Is that what you want?"

Annalisa crawled out. He would keep her from them, no matter what his twisted reasons. He used deceit to keep her from fighting him. She wouldn't fight, but she could use deceit too. While he kept her docile with his lies, she would wait and watch for her chance to escape.

At that moment, she had to run to catch up with him. The others laughed, and Annalisa didn't care. She'd run after him. She'd play his slave, until the first opportunity came to escape.

"How long you gonna be?" Al shouted.

"Couple of hours."

"We'll see you again then, Prissy," Ready yelled. "It's only when he stays gone all night that he comes back alone."

Annalisa knew when it would be. When he told her he was taking her home, she'd be on her way to death instead. Without Ready's warning, she would hop on that motorcycle even more willingly. Amazingly, it was possible to feel gratitude to one of them.

Still frightened, but in a different way than before, Annalisa's thoughts weren't dominated by panic, hopelessness, or a defeated acceptance. She didn't know what she would do, but she would do something. Bell was going to pay for the lies he told her.

Bell took her back to the point. When he reached the base of the incline, he stopped long enough to hatefully show her where to put her feet. "See if you can stay on this time."

His remark made her determined to stay on at any cost. She felt like he purposely rode further up than he normally would have just to frighten her. He didn't stop until the bike refused to climb any higher and slipped in the loose rock. Finally stopped, he set the bike on its stand and left her to follow.

Below, the tiny orange dots of the tents were visible. Her eyes followed the course of the road. Five miles down that track was where he'd found her, where her camera lay exposed to the elements.

Seven or eight miles further down her RV was parked. Twelve or thirteen miles, but if she crossed straight from the camp, avoiding the westward swinging road, it would only be six, maybe eight. It was hard to tell from that height.

She could use the highest peak to the southeast for direction and walk until she came to the road that ran to the east to the highway. On a straight course, there was little danger of missing it. The road and a large wash made a crude cross on the valley floor. Where they intersected would be about half of the distance she needed to travel.

Settling down on the ground, Annalisa concentrated on memorizing the valley floor. She would have to watch that peak on the way back to camp. The formation would be different from another angle.

"What are you looking for?" he asked, making her start violently and answer much too fast.

"Nothing." She knew it sounded like the lie it was, but he didn't push. He wasn't ready, just yet, to let her see what he really was.

"Hungry?"

"No."

"Thirsty?"

His false solicitude irked her. "You wouldn't care if I was," she snapped at him.

"I do care, Prissy."

"Don't call me that!"

"Do you want them to know who you are so they can go after you?"

"Why would they?"

"You can give the police a description of them. They wouldn't like that."

"Or you!" She gasped at her own stupidity once the words were out.

"For me, it doesn't matter."

"Why not?"

"No questions, Annalisa Summers."

"How…"

He turned from his observation post on the end of the point and moved to her. "That cruiser's registration. You'll have to get a copy. I burned the other." He knelt down in front of her, reaching for her left hand. She instantly jerked it away. He didn't insist on touching. "Still wore the rings. Why?"

"No reason to take them off."

"Are you saying you are married?"

"Yes." It might be better if he did think there was someone missing her.

He shook his head. "Registration was in your name only."

"So what?"

"You aren't married. You've never had children."

"Did the registration tell you that, too?"

"Your smooth belly told me that. No scars."

"You wouldn't know!"

"I saw it when they had your pants down."

Her face flamed as she retorted. "You might at least have the decency not to mention it."

"I need to know if you're lying to me."

69

"I'm sure bringing that up will tell you."

Immune to any of her sarcasm, he sat back on the ground in front of her, watching her without speaking until she fidgeted again.

"You've got to have family, friends. A woman like you must have, and they'll miss you. You came out here with only a camera and one canteen. You've been gone for two days, but no one's come looking for you."

"They will."

"When?"

"Tomorrow." She gave the answer too fast again. "They're probably looking right now. They just haven't gotten here yet."

"When were you expected back?"

"Last night."

"I don't think so. That cruiser has a tow bar. I think you've got another rig near here. I think you left it in your camp with the rest of your gear."

"My things are at home," she said quickly.

"Where's home?"

"Phoenix."

"Long way to come on a full tank."

"It only takes half," she retorted, satisfied that he was wrong at last.

"Tank's full."

He'd trapped her into admitting she was lying, but she still tried. "I filled it in Cave Creek."

"Still too far."

"I had a can."

"Where's the can?"

"I–I...oh." To her fury, she couldn't run away from him, and she couldn't even lie successfully.

He didn't stop the questions, either. "When were you expected back?"

She could still try. "Tonight."

"You're going to be late."

The very brief satisfaction in him believing a lie was shattered. "You said two days. That's in the morning."

"There's been a delay."

"Oh, quit lying to me," she wailed. "You're not going to take me home."

"No, but I'll take you to your camp. You can get home by yourself from there."

She wanted to believe him. "You don't even have to do that. Just let me go."

"I can't, not yet."

"Why? If you're really going to, why not now?"

Bell leaned toward her. She screamed and scrambled to her feet, barely making two feet before he caught her around the waist. "I'm not going to hurt you. I swear that to you."

"You're going to kill me."

"No, I'm not. I know what they told you, but it's not true. I tell them that, and I make them believe it. They'd turn against me if they knew the truth, and I can't afford that."

She listened to him, stopped fighting to do so. He held her, but only to keep her from running. Without hurting her, he set her on her feet, turning her in his arms, making her feel safe and secure, until his hand moved to the back of her head. A caress? She stiffened like a rod.

Bell released her and stepped back. His voice had an edge to it when he spoke. "One thing you can be sure of, I won't do that to you. That's one thing they tell you that you can believe."

"Or another thing you make them believe?"

"Why would I?"

She could think of no answer that made any kind of sense.

Bell told her, "If you weren't so modest, I'd show you the scars. That would convince you."

"What happened?" The question was out before she knew it was coming, astonished that she asked such an intimate question.

"Standing in the wrong place at the wrong time." He quickly

dismissed the subject. "Come on, there's something I want to show you."

He held his hand out to her. She looked at it, then raised her eyes to look into his. Staring into those emerald green pools, she took his hand and walked beside him.

They went down the backside of the point. He helped her over the steeper places and lifted her down the last drop of seven feet into a narrow wash where a stream bubbling out of the rocks at the end. When he set her back on her feet, his hands stayed on her sides. She stiffened again.

He turned abruptly, walking away. "Over here. Come get a drink."

"Bell, I'm sorry."

"Never mind." His voice was gruff. "Come over here. I won't touch you again."

"I didn't mean it that way," she said helplessly, because she had.

"Yes, you did."

"Oh, all right, I did. You're filthy, and you smell."

"Taken a whiff of yourself lately?"

She turned crimson. "I haven't had a bath," she told him furiously, and it was his fault.

"Neither have I."

"You could. There's even water here to do it."

"That would spoil my image."

"My God, how can you stand it?"

"You get used to it. You get used to anything if you have to."

"You don't have to," she insisted.

"Yes, I do."

"Why? What possible reason could you have for living like this?"

He turned away. "Get a drink."

"I'd rather have a bath."

"No, I don't want them to know it's here."

That she couldn't understand at all. "Why?"

He didn't answer, squatting and cupping water to his mouth from a small pool.

She moved closer. "Why don't you want them to know?"

He pivoted on his feet to lean back against the rock wall. With his arms draped over his knees, he looked at her.

She couldn't stand it when he stared at her like that. She couldn't tell what he was thinking. What it might be made her uneasy, always reminding her of her horrible appearance. The last fight with Ready had knocked the last of the pins from her hair, and the afternoon in the tent had made it stiff with perspiration. She turned away before he finally spoke, turning her back in a whirl.

"If anything happens, I want you to come here. You'll have water and be safe until your people look for you."

"What could happen?"

"I might lose a fight. If I tell you to run, you run like hell. Come up here. You can find the way. I saw you picking out landmarks."

He saw everything. She couldn't hide anything from him or lie to him. Most frightening of all, he spoke of more fighting, fights he could lose, leaving her without his protection.

As soon as they got back to the camp, the need for his protection was again impressed upon her. Dark had fallen and the others were already gathered around the fire. The bike light shot across bare skin, showing they were indulging in the sex play of the night before. She noticed something that had been added or she missed the previous night, though it wasn't hard to guess the misshapen cigarettes were not tobacco or that Al was intoxicated when he struggled to his feet.

Al staggered, shouting out, "Hey, Bell. You were gone so long we figured you'd be coming back alone."

Dago got up beside him, staggering slightly more. "Yeah," he slurred gleefully. "We thought you'd taken her home for sure."

They all giggled and laughed. Ready added something Annalisa couldn't hear, and she didn't want to, no more than she wanted to see. Bell walked by them immune to all of it, and she followed, her eyes riveted on his back.

Bell spoke without looking at them. "If he isn't here tonight, I split."

"Tomorrow's the night," Al called out.

Bell stopped and turned. "You been fucking with me?" he asked coldly.

The sudden quiet rubbed at the nerves. Annalisa stared at the button on Bell's jacket, terrified at what might happen next.

"Just careful," Al answered.

"Meaning what?"

"He didn't mean nothing 'bout you," Dago answered quickly. "We was just being careful. There's been a lot of meets busted lately. We didn't want word to get out."

"Not exchange meets. You've had me sitting on my ass for four days," Bell countered.

"You've been occupied," Al snapped. "More than we can say."

The tone changed, and the tension grew. Bell turned nonchalantly, Annalisa on his heels. When he leaned down, she inched closer, urging him to hurry inside.

When Joey got up to join the other two in their unsteady progress toward them, she pushed at Bell's back. He didn't go in. He straightened and pushed her behind him. Al, Dago, and Joey froze.

"What do you need that for?" Al demanded.

"I'm through fucking with you," Bell told him.

"You ain't to have no gun. That's part of the meet rules. No guns."

"I carry the money. I carry a gun, especially when things aren't happening on schedule."

"You don't need it for this. Fingers is just a day longer than we thought. No big deal."

"I told you, I'm through fucking around. I've held off twice for the deal. I won't again."

"You ain't fucking," Dago complained, rubbing at himself again.

"Come on, Bell. We ain't had a break-in for weeks," Al pleaded, aping Dago's movements.

"She isn't a member," Bell told him dispassionately.

"All right, damn you, but if she's here more than a week, we get her. You keep hanging on the rules, you'll stick to that one."

"Shit," Dago complained, "he ain't never kept one more than a few days."

"Business before pleasure," Bell told them and then he added coldly, "It better be tomorrow."

"It will." Al looked at Annalisa. "There'll be some fun too."

"Not," Bell shoved the gun into his waist band, "with my old lady."

Annalisa stared at the gun when he turned to face her. It had been right there in the tent with her all that day. If she had thought to look in the bag he used for a pillow, she'd have found it, and she would have a weapon to use against them and him.

Bell pushed her inside, and Annalisa knew he'd seen the way she looked at that gun. He knew what she was thinking and wouldn't talk to her. He told her to go to sleep and stretched out, ignoring her.

Her mind in turmoil, Annalisa couldn't believe he was really going to take her home, not when she saw him with them. He couldn't be two men. He couldn't convince them he was like them if he wasn't. Yet he did convince her he wasn't when they were alone. A vicious, confusing circle of thought chased inside her head while she waited for him to sleep.

Every time she moved, he stirred. Every time they made a noise outside, she could feel the difference in him as he lay still waiting to identify the sound. She thought he slept over and over, only to have him tense at the slightest sound.

The others went to their tents, and the noises of their drunken lust stilled. Everything was quiet. She moved, he rolled his head, but Annalisa was determined to wait him out. She wasn't as exhausted as the night before, and she was more confused.

When Bell moaned, she didn't think it meant anything more than he was finally asleep. People moaned in their sleep. She eased to her hands and knees.

When he jerked, drawing a leg up, she fell to the side of the tent, certain he knew she tried to sneak out, but he turned to his side, away from her. He drew both legs up, moaned again, and rocked slightly.

Certain he was having a dream, or maybe a nightmare from the way he rolled his head back and forth, she, at least, knew he was asleep and inched forward.

He threw himself to his back, moaning louder. Both legs drew up. In the faint light of a full moon cast through the tiny back window she could make out his contorted features, and his hands were low, holding his abdomen or groin.

She forgot what she was attempting to do. She touched him on the shoulder, saying his name.

Bell sprang up and had her by the throat and forcing her backward but realized who she was. "God damn it, don't wake me up like that!"

"I won't," she promised fervently as he pulled away.

He sat back on his legs with his hands gripping his knees. His voice was calmer, as he added, "Don't touch me when I'm asleep."

"I won't," she swore, "but what's wrong?"

"Nothing."

She leaned forward, laying her hand on his arm. "Are you sick?"

He threw his arm up, flipping her hand off. "No."

He sounded sick, his voice strained and his body tense. "Is there anything I can do?"

"You can go to sleep," he told her hatefully.

"I was only trying to help. Maybe you should see a doctor."

"They can't do anything."

"Can't they give you anything for it?"

"Sure. It'll put me to sleep, and you can have visitors." He shoved himself around and crawled out.

She let him go without another word. If he was going to be that hateful, let him hurt. How could she feel sorry for someone like that, anyway? Yet, every time she looked out and could see he still suffered, she felt less indignant and more compassion, unable to sleep until she could see by the way he leaned up against his rock that the pain had subsided. She didn't know if he came back in that night or not. He wasn't there when she awoke.

———

The second morning started the same as the first. He waited for her, standing with one foot on that rock and holding a cup in his hand.

From there it was different. She went out to him, careful not to look straight at his face, even when he handed her the cup. She just as carefully avoided looking at the gun in his waistband.

"How do you feel?" she asked hesitantly.

"Fine," he answered sharply and then in a softer tone added, "Don't say anything to the others about it."

"All right."

"Better get something to eat."

"All right."

She walked to the canopy. He followed.

When she took four eggs out of the ice chest from under the table, he said, "I already ate."

She put two back. If he had, it hadn't been eggs. The pan was cold. He didn't look as if he felt like eating, either.

"Still hurting?" she asked.

"No."

If his words hadn't made it clear it wasn't to be discussed, his tone did. "Sure you wouldn't like something to eat?"

"Just eat, so we can get out of here."

Annalisa looked at the skillet, the scummy grease, and sand in the bottom. Her stomach rolled. She hadn't eaten since breakfast the day before, but the sight of the pan made her queasy, not hungry. "I don't think I want any."

"Then come on." He spun around, nearly knocking over the table behind him and snatched something off as he stormed away.

Annalisa had to run to catch up with him. The bike was running, and he glared at her until she settled behind him. They went back to the same point, and he got off, shoving something at her.

"That ought to be clean enough for you."

"I wasn't hungry," she retorted, then stared down at the can of peaches. That would be clean, but why should she have to defend herself for not wanting to eat out of a filthy pan?

"Then starve," he retorted, walking away from her.

"I would if it was left up to you."

He spun around to face her. "I gave you the damned peaches."

"How am I supposed to open them?"

"You helpless baby." He stomped back, making her flinch when he snatched the can out of her hands. "How the hell do you survive?"

"Just fine until someone drags me off to live like an animal."

"What the hell did you want me to do, leave you in the desert?"

"Rather that than you!"

She thought he was going to hit her, and she'd seen him hit, knew what he could do, but she had never seen him lose his temper. He did then.

"You'd have died!" he shouted at her.

"I would not. I know how to live in the desert."

"It was a fifteen mile walk to the highway."

They yelled at each other. He shook the can in her face, and her hands braced on her hips.

"I've walked that and more in a day. I wouldn't be out here if I didn't know how to take care of myself." They say anger blinds. It did her. "I'd have gotten back in plenty of time to see your little party rounded up. I still can."

She started off, forgetting he wouldn't let her go. She remembered when he lifted her off the ground again. She struggled with as little results as before.

"One more day, Prissy, I promised."

She went limp in his arms. "Why not now?"

"Is it really so bad you can't stand one more day?"

"Yes." She straightened up, and he released her so she could turn to face him.

"I guess it would be for a woman like you."

"What does that mean?"

"Pretty Prissy."

She stiffened like her spine turned to metal. "If that means being clean, not exhibiting myself, not treating sex like it was a parlor game, and not using every filthy word ever thought of, then I am."

"You are."

She stared into his eyes, not understanding how he meant it. No mockery sounded in his voice, and no amusement showed in his eyes. Her uneasiness built again, and she broke eye contact.

"Come on," he said softly. "I'll open your peaches for you."

He pulled a heavy folding knife out of his pocket to pry open the can.

"Where's your switch blade?" she asked.

He looked up, straight into her eyes again. "What switch blade?"

She looked away. "I thought all gangsters carried one."

"This one doesn't." He handed her the can. "Other than sticking someone, they're useless as hell. You couldn't open a can with them without the blade or spring breaking."

"I'll keep that in mind."

"This will kill just as well." He handed her the knife. "Use it for a fork."

He turned his back on her. He put a weapon in her hand and knew she wouldn't try to use it. He knew he had nothing to worry about if she did. In any kind of combat, she was sure to lose.

Annalisa ate the peaches while he surveyed the area below, watching for searchers. When he was satisfied, he took her to the spring. She used its cool clean water to wash the sticky peach juice from the knife before handing it back to him.

"Can I at least wash my face?"

"Go ahead, but if they should ask, you did it at camp." He stretched out and folded his arms under his head for a pillow. "I'm going to take a nap."

She could well imagine he needed one. "Before you do, I don't suppose you'd have anything as useless as a comb." He rolled to his side and pulled one out of his back pocket. She caught it when he tossed it to her, amazed to see it. The comb wasn't unusual—just a common one. She had one like it in the RV, but she never expected him to have one. He didn't look as if he ever combed his hair or that a comb would go through the matted mess.

That set her to imagining what he would look like with his hair combed or better, cut off. How would he look without the heavy beard and dressed differently or in clean clothes? She tried to visualize what he would look like in a suit and decided it was impossible. He was an outdoor man. She doubted if he would be comfortable in anything other than Levis, but if they were clean and he wore a normal shirt, he might even be handsome.

She studied his face. He wasn't really ugly. It was just that terrible scar, smashed nose, and missing teeth that made you think so when you first looked at him.

While she considered, she dragged and pulled the comb through her own matted and dirty hair. Its length, middle of her back, made it difficult and gave her plenty of time to fantasize about what Bell could be if he weren't the man he was. She could think of nothing his particular talents would prove useful for with the exception of possibly being a professional fighter. He could certainly fight.

When the comb passed freely through her tresses of naturally wavy hair, she shifted positions, leaning back against the narrow canyon wall.

Bell rolled his head and looked at her.

"I thought you were asleep," she said.

"I was."

Puzzled, she asked, "What woke you?"

"You moved."

"I didn't make any noise."

"I sleep light. How long has it been?"

"You've had your eyes closed for about an hour, but I don't think you were asleep."

"What difference does it make?" He sat up, rubbing the back of his neck.

It mattered. How could she ever slip away from him if he slept so lightly even the slight scraping noise she made shifting positions woke him? "None," she said, but it worried her.

"We better get back."

She forgot a worry for a real dread. "Do we have to?"

"Yes." He stood up, offering her his hand. "You can stay in the tent." She slipped her hand into his, and he pulled her to her feet. "You can stand it one more day."

He climbed the bank and reached down for her. "I'm not sure," she told him.

"I am. You're tough."

He pulled her up, and she laughed shakily. "No, I'm not, Bell. I'm scared."

He put his arm around her shoulders, walking her with him. "Shows you've got brains too."

She didn't feel smart. Why, knowing what he was, did she feel warmed by his compliments and comfort from his arm around her?

Bell spent some of that day in the tent with her. He slept, if that's what it could be called. Every time there was a noise, he tensed and laid still, listening until sure the noise meant nothing to him. That was eerie. The way his hand closed tighter on the gun in his waist band was frightening.

The noise was continual. The others spread blankets under the trees and drank beer, laughing and talking all afternoon. Ready was the loudest. Annalisa heard Prissy said several times. She wasn't too surprised that by dinner time it had been decided she had lazed around enough and would help Bunny fix dinner.

Annalisa didn't mind. Al saw to it that Ready and Jolene stayed away, and Bunny was too timid to be frightening. She didn't even get brave enough to speak for several minutes.

"Ready's mean," she whispered.

"That's an understatement. Is she always so quick to pick fights?"

Bunny nodded. "Jolene says she does it more to Bell's old ladies 'cause she's jealous." Once Bunny began talking, it was like a dam busting. "She wants him. I heard her say so, and she doesn't believe he can't fuck. She says he lies 'cause he thinks he's too good. I wouldn't want to be his old lady. He's nice, but Ready seen him one time. Al said he had to use a knife for that much blood, and I don't like knives. Al says he bets a woman gave him those scars, and he gets even with all them."

Simple-minded Bunny had no idea of the terror she created. She opened cans of stew, chattering innocently while Annalisa froze, staring at her in horror.

"Ready says she knows he's giving it to you, or you wouldn't mind so well. Jolene says it's 'cause he lies to you, that you really think he's going to take you home and likes you're special. Does he give it to you?"

Bell's voice came at them like a whip, making them both jump and cower. "Give her what, Bunny?"

"Your prick," she mumbled.

Ready saw something going on and followed Bell in time to hear the question. "His prick don't work," she put in, her eyes bright in anticipation.

Bell ignored Ready. "What else did you tell her, Bunny?"

His voice cut with cruelty. Bunny shrank away, looking from him to Ready as much afraid of one as the other.

"Leave her alone," Annalisa said, finding she still had a voice, and she could still stand up straight.

"Oh, oh, oh," Ready canted.

"Come here," Bell ordered.

Annalisa didn't move. She disobeyed, and Ready laughed at Bell for it. "Maybe your tongue isn't long enough, Bell."

The others moved up behind them. Al joined in, adding his opinion. "She needs the real thing to train her right."

Ready spoke to Annalisa. "That's what you want, isn't it, Prissy? You want a nice hard—"

"Shut your filthy mouth," Annalisa snapped.

Ready closed her hand tight, asking, "Maybe a fist. How'd you like my fist stuck up your ass?"

"Shut up!" Annalisa clamped her hands over her ears to shut the words out and stared at Bell as he moved toward her.

"Hey, Bell, I got a good-sized dildo. You can strap it on over that useless mess between your legs and stick her good, if it really is useless."

Bell rounded the corner of the table. Annalisa broke in a run. Futile, she knew, but she had to try. He caught her differently. He didn't overrun her, wrapping his arms around her. He grabbed her by the hair and jerked her back off her feet.

Annalisa screamed and twisted, going back to her feet, fighting in a way she never fought before in her life and not to get free. She fought to hurt and went after Bell's face with her nails, screaming at him.

He let go of her hair to catch her wrists. In seconds, her arms were twisted behind her back. She knew he'd catch both wrists in one of his hands, and she fought that, using her feet and heavy soled boots. He still trapped her wrists in one hand and grabbed her hair, but he didn't jerk her head back. He crushed it forward against his chest.

Unable to pull back or turn away, Annalisa opened her mouth and closed it again, taking all the flesh she could find between her teeth. Bell only pressed her face tighter.

The others stood around them, howling and cheering him on. The last distinct thing Annalisa heard through the roaring building in her ears was a male voice. "Hey, you're suffocating her."

———

When Annalisa came to, her head roared, but she could see. She rolled away from him.

Bell put a hand out on her shoulder to keep her down. "Lay still a minute."

She wouldn't. For whatever purpose he hadn't killed her and had dragged her away from the camp, she was not going to lay still and wait for him to finish the job. She grabbed at a rock. He leaned over her, holding her arm down before she could swing at him.

"Stop it. I don't want to hurt you again."

She screamed at him, rolling to her back. "You enjoyed it!"

"No, I didn't." He sat back, not touching her. "I warned you that I'd have to do something if you mouthed off in front of them. I don't enjoy hurting you. I wouldn't have if it hadn't been necessary."

"Necessary!" She jerked up to sit facing him. "Necessary to half-kill me?"

"If I hadn't done something, they would have taken it as a sign of weakness."

She stopped screaming and turned hateful, dropping her voice. "It takes a lot of strength to beat up on a woman."

"A different kind of strength. If I showed you any consideration, they'd take it as weakness."

Why was she listening to him? Why in God's name did she even consider what he said might be the truth? "You killed them!"

"I've never killed a woman."

"Bunny said you did."

"Bunny's been beat so many times her brain's rattled. She'd believe you if you told her you're the tooth fairy." He said it with as much compassion needed to say she'd been born with freckles.

"You don't even care."

"There's nothing I can do about it."

"You could take her home, if that's really what you do with them."

"She won't leave Al."

She tipped her head back to look at the sky in despair. He had an answer for everything, and no answers to her confusion appeared in the sky. She dropped her head back and flinched in pain.

"Are you all right?"

"I hurt!"

"I'm sorry."

He looked like he meant it, staring back at her with those soft green eyes. Could he really be that good an actor? She didn't know. She couldn't think, and she did hurt. Even her back from Jolene's blow the day before throbbed. Tears stung her eyes, and she didn't want to cry. She didn't want to be so weak all she could do was cry.

She might not have if he hadn't taken her in his arms. The gentleness, the concern, and the comfort broke the dam. She turned her cheek to his shoulder and wept freely.

"It'll be all right. Just walk softly until I can get you out of here."

"Let me go," she sobbed. "Just let me go."

"I will, tomorrow."

"You're going to kill me."

He slid his hand under her chin and tipped her head back. She didn't see anything but his eyes while he told her, "I am not going to kill you."

Staring into his eyes, hypnotized her. One finger rubbed gently along her jaw. When he leaned closer, she caught and held her breath. When he came close enough to kiss, she turned her head breaking the spell.

"I could take you to the spring," he murmured.

She turned back eagerly, to find his face still inches from hers. The finger returned to rub along her jaw.

"I'd have to know I could trust you," he whispered.

He leaned forward again, and Annalisa forced herself not to turn away. She held her breath and pressed her lips tightly together when his lips touched hers and let the breath out, only to take another when the side of his face pressed to her cheek.

"Is that why you never had any babies?" he asked in the same soft whisper.

She jerked back in puzzlement. Then the insinuation she was frigid penetrated. She swung at his face and within seconds, her arms were trapped behind her again.

He pushed her to her back, keeping her arms under her. "What's the matter? Didn't Pretty Prissy want any scars on her pretty belly?"

"No," she growled, straining to shove him off and free her hands. "He was a lying son-of-a-bitch, just like you."

Bell stiffened in surprise. "You mean he couldn't?"

She stopped fighting to tell him hatefully, "Sex isn't everything. He could, but he didn't want kids. Wait until we get a house, until the cars are paid for, until we get a new car, a pool, a savings account. Wait, wait, wait, until you're too old, then I'll tell you the truth."

"You aren't too old."

"I'm too old to start."

"I don't think so."

"That really makes me feel better," she told him with sarcasm more biting than her anger. "Let go of me."

"Just lay still and listen to me," he told her patiently.

"So you can lie some more?"

"I had to find something out. I didn't mean to hit such a sore spot."

"Like what?"

"How afraid you are of me and how much you trust me. Neither are enough."

She stopped struggling then. "Enough for what?"

"Me to trust you."

She half-laughed and half-cried. "What could I do to you?"

"I can't trust you to stay there."

"I would, I swear."

"I don't think so. You know the desert too well, and you don't trust me enough."

"Yes, I do."

"If they saw you after I told them you're dead, they'd turn on me."

"I wouldn't, Bell. I swear. What can I do to convince you? I'll do what you tell me. I swear."

She asked a question, and he meant for her to answer it. He kissed her again, starting gently, but knowing what she had to do, she parted her lips instead of giving him an unresponsive surface.

He drew back to gaze at her for a moment, then he kissed her again, the pressure grew in insistence, demanding more from her. Annalisa gave it. When she twisted her hands to free them, he released them. Her arms went around him. When his hand slid down her hip, she gave no resistance as he rolled her to face him. When he pressed against her, she pressed back.

Bell jerked away, pulled her arms from around him, and went to his feet in one rapid movement. Before he could speak or move away, whatever he intended when he left her so abruptly, never happened.

"Hey, man, don't stop now," Al yelled excitedly. "You got her hot."

Hands clenched in fists at his sides, Bell spun to face Al. Dago stood beside him. Both showed the discomfort of their arousals, massaging themselves, Dago with his hand down his open pants.

Dago spoke, breathless in his excitement. "He can't finish. He ain't flagging. That's why he pulled off."

"He can't flag, Dago. He got himself gelded."

"Get out of here," Bell ordered.

"How were you going to finish her? Stick her with a knife instead of a cock?"

"If you ever follow me again, I'll kill you."

If he had shouted it in rage, it wouldn't have sounded as much a threat as it did in the cold tone he used. He turned his back on them, reaching for Annalisa.

Annalisa shrank away when he touched her.

"Made her mad. Always makes them mad if you heat them up then don't take care of them," Al told him.

"She wasn't just heated. She was boiling," Dago put in.

Bell turned back to face them, and Al threw up his hands protectively. They were nearly ten feet apart, but Al wasn't taking any chances. Bell was furious, and it wouldn't take him long to cover the distance in an attack. "We just come to remind you," Al said quickly.

"Of what?"

"Fingers will be here soon."

Dago joined in. "We figured you might of forgot, being busy and all."

Bell didn't answer. He turned and jerked Annalisa to her feet by the arm. She struggled away from him, making him as angry with her as he was them. He jerked her around, her back to his chest and wrapped his arm around her throat.

"She'll give you hell now," Al called out as Bell walked her off. "Nothing worse than a frustrated broad."

In Annalisa's ear, Bell whispered, "Don't answer, just nod. Can you find your way to the spring in the dark?" She nodded. "Tonight, I'll send you to the tent early. You can slip off while we settle business."

She nodded again, but it was not the spring she would go to. She had made him trust her. Maybe it was worth the shame.

———

Once back in camp, their positions went back to slave and master. Bell sent her to the canopy to fix the meal she deprived him of earlier. He went to his rock by the fire. How he sat indifferent to the taunting he was being subjected to, she couldn't understand.

A new cruel note was added, and one she didn't understand at first. They had always taunted him, but with the understanding it was something he felt no loss or remorse over. Therefore, it was not a weakness. After what Al and Dago saw, they were sure he did care, and it delighted their wicked hearts to inflict what they thought was pain.

They grouped together on their side of the fire, throwing insults at him. Bell drank his beer like a deaf man. He belched after the last gulp and tossed the bottle into the fire, crossed his arms, and dropped his head with his eyes closed.

Ready grew tired of the game. Baiting someone who ignored you was no fun. She crossed over to the edge of the canopy and spoke in a voice that could be heard half a mile away.

"You don't know how, Prissy. If you were a real woman, you'd have made him come up and got what you wanted."

Annalisa furiously stirred the can of stew she heated. In some way it seemed if she hurried, it would make the time Ready had to talk less.

"That is what you really want. Your prissy manners don't fool any of us. You want a big, hard cock slipping in and out of your pussy, tickling your twat, making you hotter—Ow!"

Ready spun, rubbing her back. Why wasn't it hard to see why or who had thrown the rock that hit her. Bell picked up another one, large enough to fill the palm of his hand.

"You dirty son-of-a-bitch, cock—" She broke off quickly and dodged when he threw the next rock. "Joey, you gonna let—"

Joey cut her off. "Get the hell away from there and leave her alone."

"He ain't got no right throwing rocks at me."

Al shut her up. "Shut your damned mouth, cunt. I told you to stay away from her."

Ready stared at each man in turn. When no one backed her, she flounced off to her tent in a rage. Jolene left Dago to follow her.

Annalisa leaned against the table sick with relief. She straightened quickly when Bunny came up for a beer from the ice chest.

"Are you sick?" Bunny asked.

"No."

"Ready's nasty. It used to make me sick, but you get used to it."

Watching Bunny walk away, Annalisa remembered what Bell said about getting used to anything if you had to. She would not get used to it. She would die first, but she wouldn't have to. Just a few more hours.

Annalisa filled one plate and dug one beer out to carry to Bell. If he noticed she had nothing for herself, he gave no indication when she sat down beside him. He wolfed down the food, emptied the beer bottle, and tossed the bottle in the fire with his usual belch.

Joey bellowed for Ready to bring him another beer.

Bell settled back against his rock to observe the activities around him with disinterest. He didn't look up or turn his head, resembling a manikin or a sleeping lion or perhaps a sleeping jackal, something that would wake to be vicious and brutal, something magnificent to look at and to fear when roused.

Ready disturbed him, and she paid for it. She walked up to him, wiggling her hips suggestively. "A peace offering," she said, holding out a bottle of beer.

The others snickered over the innuendo. Bell only looked up, at her face, not the beer.

"Come on, baby, no hard feelings," Ready said, wiggling again.

Another round of malicious snickers followed, but Bell's gaze never wavered. He didn't smile, but then he didn't frown. Ready took that as encouragement. Dropping to her knees, she put the bottle between his legs, twisting it to work it down between his thick thigh muscles. When her hand slipped away, her fingers dragged up his leg to his crotch and stroked.

"You still have the thoughts, even if you don't have the hard. I can show you how to satisfy the thoughts."

Bell still didn't move or speak. She placed his hand on her breast, rubbed it back and forth, kneading him at the same time and took a deep breath of satisfaction when his fingers closed. Her expression rapidly went from pleasure to surprise, then fear.

"You're hurting me," she cried, both hands gripping his wrist to pull him away. Only when she screamed did he let go.

She swung at him, and he caught her arm, twisting until she screamed again. Joey dragged her away. "Keep the hell away from him," he ordered.

Bell saluted him with the fresh beer and tipped it to his mouth.

"How can you stand it?" Annalisa asked in a whisper.

"I told you not to ask any questions."

"You hate them."

"It's mutual." He tipped the bottle to his lips. "Just sit there and keep your mouth shut."

The hatred was mutual. She wanted to never have to repeat the earlier scene or go through what she had since with the jeering and cruel, vulgar jokes. At least those stopped. Once Ready stopped wailing over her injuries, the others got strangely quiet, speaking to each other in muted tones.

Bell, however, was restless. He shifted positions often. Each time he moved, she looked up, hoping that the time for him to send her away had arrived. Each time, he didn't so much as look her way. When he lunged up without warning, he twisted her arm dragging her to her feet.

"Where're you going?" Al asked.

"For a walk."

"Not now, Bell. Fingers will be here soon."

He stood there for a moment, looking at her. "The tent will do," he said with a shrug. Turning her, he drew her up against him with his arm around her throat. The move surprised and frightened her.

"Don't fight me. I don't have much time," he whispered in her ear.

He pushed her inside the tent, falling on top of her. While she struggled to get from under him, he floundered to roll off. When she tried to sit up, he grabbed her arm.

"What are you doing?"

Bell didn't answer. He jerked and pulled on her, taking her deeper into the tent. She hadn't realized he drank that much, but he had to be drunk. His movements were awkward, and he gasped and grunted. Yet, even uncoordinated, he had his strength.

He jerked her up to her knees with the painful hold of her arms, lifted her as if to throw her over his legs to the back of the tent. He fell instead, dragging her down with him.

"Bell, please," she cried in fright.

"Get out."

She tried, but when she sat up, he jerked her back. "Get out," he repeated in a strained voice. On his side, he pulled her up, still to the back of the tent, not the door, and pushed her.

Her hand hit the back wall of the tent and went through. At some time, Bell had slashed open the canvas.

In a tangle of arms and legs, Bell complicated their efforts by drawing into a ball, holding himself low as he had the night before. He was sick, she thought, not drunk.

She pulled herself up to a sitting position and reached a hand out to him. "Are you in pain?"

He threw her hand off. "You know I am. You think it's funny," he growled at her.

"No, I don't."

"You do this to me and think it's funny."

"I didn't do anything."

"You enjoy it?" One hand reached out to her. "You want it all?"

She edged away when he rose up on an elbow and tried to dodge, but there was no room. His hand closed down on her arm like a vise. "No, Bell, don't."

"You think it's funny. You do this. Then you laugh."

She didn't laugh. She screamed as his fingers dug into her arm and dragged her down. "Don't, Bell, please, don't."

He forced her to her back and levered himself up on top of her. "You damned bitch, you think it's funny."

What had been missing earlier that night was there, pressing down on her belly, through the double thickness of their clothes. Annalisa pleaded with him, pushing with all her might on his shoulders. He held her pinned to the ground with one hand on each of her shoulders.

"You think I can't. You think you're safe because I can't."

One hand grabbed at her waistband. She hit at his face, twisting from under the single hand that shifted to hold her down in the center of her chest.

He hit her. A single blow stunned her into an immobile state of knowing and feeling without being able to do anything to prevent it.

His breath was foul in her face, coming in great draughts as he gasped and panted in struggling to tear off her pants. He jerked the band, the snap opened, but the zipper held. The band felt like it was coming through her back when he jerked again, and again, drawing her out of the daze to see him on his knees above her, jerking her pants down to her thighs.

Rising up, she struck with both hands in fists. He stopped her by falling back on her, knocking the breath out of her lungs. She gasped to regain air while he forced her arms over her head to the ground, holding them again in one of his.

She kicked, screamed, twisted, cried, and cried out. Nothing helped. She begged and pleaded with him. That didn't stop him.

His foot between her legs pushed her pants further down. Barely able to breathe for the pressure on her stomach from the hand he held himself up with, she couldn't protect the tender inside of her legs from the hard, scraping edges of the boot toe

Not until the pants were packed tight against her boots did he quit kicking at them. A knee pressed between her legs, and when she didn't open them, he rammed it down hard, making her scream. Between her legs, deaf to her cry of pain, he forced himself into a dry channel, tearing at delicate flesh. A flame of pain shot through her, only to be repeated when he pulled out and rammed in again.

Falling on her, his fingers clawed into her shoulder, he moaned with each throb of ejaculation. She sobbed and gasped when he withdrew from the raw tunnel and cried out when he jerked her up.

"Go on, get out," he rasped in her face. He fell to his side and drew again into a ball.

She wanted to, desperately, but none of her limbs worked properly. He helped her on her way with a shove, sprawling her head first and face down out of the back of the tent.

Annalisa dragged herself the remainder of the way. He was through with her. She paid the price for her freedom and sat outside the tent, pulling her pants back to her thighs. She turned to her hands and knees, too weak to walk, to pull the cloth to her waist, and then she crawled.

6

THE LIST OF NAM VETS WHO HAD SUFFERED WOUNDS IN THE GROIN area was discouragingly long. Pratters put the multi-page list in his briefcase, giving a brief nod of thanks. Such things as shop talk with fellow agents held no interest for him.

His interest all centered at the hospital. His identification got him past the guard he'd ordered. Not satisfied with the arrangement, he accepted what he considered inadequate protection, for the time being.

In the cubical, the doctor leaned over Bell, and Bell looked dead with his eyes lax and opened a slit. "Is he…" Pratters began.

The doctor shook his head and pressed Bell's eyelids closed. "Deep coma, the muscles relax totally, but no, he isn't dead."

"He's worse."

It wasn't a question, and the doctor made no comment until Pratters looked at him questioningly.

"He isn't worse, but he isn't any better."

Pratters didn't see how Bell could be any worse and still be considered living. The tubes were still in his nose and throat. More were still attached to both arms. The covers were folded back, and another tube hung out of the incision on his side, draining some rank looking stuff out. Patches held wires taped to his chest.

"What do you think?"

"We're playing catch up. We've stopped the blood loss. We have to catch up before anything else comes along to finish him off."

"Such as?"

"At this point, just about anything, but infection is the most prominent danger." He shrugged in helplessness.

"I know how you feel," Pratters said.

"I think I understand that now."

Pratters looked at him in surprise. The doctor grinned self-consciously, making his seamed face look boyish. "Don't faint. I may be wrapped up in my tiny little world, not noticing much of what takes place on the outside, but when it's pointed out to me, I recognize it for what it is."

"A snake pit."

"Not all of it. You need to look at the other parts as much as I do."

He wouldn't just then. He went to Jane's room, still wanted a clue to Prissy. Only three ways were available to get information on her. First was through Jane, but her information was difficult to decipher. Second was Mrs. Summers. He was more than sure she was withholding something to avoid further involvement. Third, and the least likely, was Bell. Then he realized there was a forth, Prissy herself. From all he had learned it looked like she had gotten away in that Jeep of hers, but would she stay away?

Jane looked up in terror when he pushed open the door. She would probably never lose that look when a door opened, until she saw if it was someone to hurt her.

"Hi," he said cheerfully. He pulled up a chair and set it close to the bed. "Remember me?" She nodded. "How do you feel?"

"Fine," she murmured.

"Are you afraid of me?" She shook her head, but her expression gave a different answer. "I think you are, and I want you to know you don't have to be."

She stared at him with suspicion mingled with fear. That, too, was something he doubted she would ever lose when she looked at any man.

"I want to help you."

"Al takes care of me."

"When he can. He asked me to until then. What's your name?"

"Bunny."

"Al named you that?" She nodded. "What was your name before?"

"Caroline."

"Ah, now I like that better. Caroline is much prettier, like you are."

"I'm not pretty anymore."

"You're very pretty."

She dropped her head, and her hand went to her face. "Not anymore." Tears filled her eyes. "I used to be."

"I bet your friends thought so, the ones before Al, kids you went to school with. Where did you go to school?"

"Franklin."

"Back in L.A.?" He guessed Al and his gang's home area. They'd only moved to the Phoenix area three months ago. She nodded. "Good school. Were you able to graduate?" She shook her head. "Too bad. How long were you with Al?"

She shrugged, and he could well believe she didn't know. "Caroline. That's pretty. Caroline what?"

"Nothing," she said glumly. "It's just Bunny now."

Pratters didn't push. He had enough information for what he needed. He wasn't going to jeopardize his source by making her suspicious of his motives. He did carefully make a suggestion.

"You know, Al is going to be there a while. Maybe you should go back to your family to wait for him."

"Nooo, I can't," she wailed.

97

"Okay. It was just a thought. I'll find a nice place for you to wait," he told her quickly.

"I can't go home, not ever again."

"Hey," he said with a wide smile, "I'm not going to make you. I just thought you might like it."

"No, not ever."

"Fine. Now, I need to ask you a few more questions about what happened. Where did Al find Prissy?"

"Bell did."

Pratters jerked up straighter in his chair. "Bell kidnapped her?" She nodded, shrinking away from him. He forced himself to calm down. "Did you say Bell was the one who took Prissy?" he asked to be sure. She nodded again. "Where?"

She shrugged slightly. "Where they took the Jeep, I guess. He went back after we left, and Al and Dago found him with her. Al said he meant to cheat us out of something he'd seen, but it was only her. She hated him. She tried to kill him."

As before, once she started talking, she rattled with little more pause than it took for breaths. Pratters listened intently.

"He hurt her and lied to her. He told her he was going to take her home, but he didn't take them home. Ready saw him one time when he came back, all covered with blood. Al said he must use a knife for that much blood. He heard me tell her what Al said, and he got awfully mad. He told her to come here, and she wouldn't."

"Caroline," he interrupted, "how long was she with you?"

"Couple of days, but she wouldn't mind, and he punished her for it. He suffocated her till she went limp, then he carried her off."

He interrupted again. "Was that before or after he killed Joey?"

"Before. Al and Dago went after them, and they saw him holding her on the ground, but he couldn't, and she got mad and ran away. Al said he should have shared her, 'specially since he couldn't. Al said he gets mad when he can't and hurts them. He hurt her, and she ran away, and she was gone when Al and Dago looked for her."

She leaned forward as if she was telling a secret. "I think she hurt him too, 'cause he was moaning something terrible. That's funny, isn't it?"

"Yes, it is."

She straightened with a deep breath. "I wish she hadn't run away. I don't like it when they all——"

"Caroline?"

"Huh?"

He didn't get to ask. The door opened, and a nurse walked in. "You'll have to leave now."

"Not just yet." He put as much authority in his voice as she used in hers, but he lost.

"Unless you have official business here, you will leave now."

He couldn't very well flash a badge in front of Caroline without spoiling the trust he worked to develop. He left in defeat, but not the floor until he made sure all the nurses on duty knew who he was. He wouldn't be interrupted again.

He wandered down to the ICU ward and into the doctor making his rounds.

"Really, Inspector, you don't need to live here," Thristen told him.

"No change, huh?"

"Hardly."

"I was wondering, you said the injury happened at least a full day before the hemorrhaging started. Could shooting that gun be what started it?"

"I know very little about guns or shooting them."

"A forty-four magnum kicks like a horse."

"Possibly. I would be more inclined to think it was getting shot or possibly falling when he was shot. It could also have been a combination of all three. Why?"

"Just curious. Is there any sense in me hanging around here?"

"None at all. If he goes sour, a phone call will tell you. If he improves, it will be days before you can talk to him and a phone call will take care of that, too."

———

Pratters called the local branch to give his location and was immediately transferred to the supervisor's office.

"You're stepping on toes. We've already got complaints."

"From who?" Pratters asked sharply.

"The state and county boys. They don't want you to take this Bell person away from them."

"They don't have any solid evidence to hold him on."

"Motive and opportunity are pretty good starts."

"They'll never make it stick after what was done to him."

"I don't think you've got enough to make anything stick on a federal charge, either. I've read the file. All you've got is hearsay evidence."

"I'll get him on kidnapping."

"That's the one thing he hadn't been accused of directly."

"Name's Caroline. She attended Franklin High School in L.A., didn't graduate. She would have been taken in the last eight months."

"Jane Doe?"

"Yes."

"It won't hold. She would be the only witness, and she is mentally incompetent."

"It'll hold long enough to move him. Put the L.A. office on tracing her down for me."

"Will do, but I don't think you'll ever pull it off."

Neither did Pratters and unless he found what he wanted in that multi-page list of vets, he wasn't really going to try. Bell's past had always eluded his searches. Finding where he came from might possibly provide some hold to turn against Bell. After an hour of searching the lists, he was sure he had what he was looking for. He picked up the phone again. This time it was a special number, and he didn't need to worry about operators or phone records.

"Research."

Pratters gave a code number for identification and read the name and serial number off the list he held. "Got it?"

"Right."

"I want a full workup. You can start at the V.A. hospital. How long before you'll have something for me?"

"That depends. Medical records can be tricky sometimes. I may have to doctor up some papers to get anything."

"That's your specialty."

"Do tell."

"I'll call back tonight." He hung up with as much a goodbye as the hello he gave, none.

Pratters worried. He traded in too many camps, and it was close to coming down around his ears and had been ever since his deal with Bell. Now, Bell threatened, to tumble the whole house of cards, exposing all three, deliberately or not.

Nothing would give Pratters more pleasure than turning the tables on Bell, making him the one who hung on a hook. If he found the right name, if that was the man Bell left behind to join the gangs, Pratters just might do it and shore up his house, if Bell lived, and if he could wash the mess Bell had made of things. Way too many ifs.

Pratters picked the phone up again. "Hold off on the three," he said as the man answered.

"I'm glad to hear that. I hate to lose a source."

"The only source I'm concerned with is ours. There's no need to expose ourselves if he's going to die."

"He's that bad off?"

"That bad. If he does make it, I'll be calling back for that three. Keep it ready."

"They're on their way. I can have them there within an hour of your call, but are you sure there's no other way?"

"There is a very slim chance. I'm working on it, but he left a lot of loose ends."

"I only know of one."

"Triple it," he retorted before hanging up.

Or double it. Caroline wasn't any problem. She would be shuffled away into an institution without anyone knowing what disjointed information her rattled mind held. The problem was Prissy. Or the problems were Prissy and Mrs. Summers.

7

The Escape

ANNALISA HEARD MOVEMENT BEHIND HER AND TRIED TO RUN. HER legs barely worked, making her feet drag and trip her. Catching herself with her hands as she fell, she pushed up to keep moving. She glanced over her shoulder, sprawling again as Bell appeared, staggering toward the fire. With her only thoughts on getting away, she pushed up and fell yet again after only a few feet of progress.

Huddled against the ground, she held her head, hearing and not understanding. Bell didn't have to rape her. He knew he could have had her without force. He didn't have to rape her. Then he went out to fight them to keep them away from her?

She held her hands over her ears, not wanting to hear as she forced herself up again. She wouldn't go to the spring. He couldn't find her. He couldn't hurt or rape her again.

She fell head-first into a depression. Her hands flew away from her ears and the air rushed out of her lungs. Al exclaimed, "He's dead," and terror gripped her.

If Bell was dead, who would protect her? How could he be dead? He had fought them so many times before, and they had never so much as hurt him. How could they kill him?

Terrified, she had to get away and crawled, elbows and knees, down the slight trench run off had created. He couldn't be dead. She had to see, with only her head raised.

Bell lay still and quiet on the ground. Joey lay beside him, just as still, and Al leaned over Joey, awe in his voice when he spoke again. "He broke his neck. Man, I've never saw anything like it. Just like that, he broke his neck."

They all stood, staring down at Joey. Dago jerked out of the shock first, turned and kicked Bell in the side. Al jumped to stop him from kicking again.

Still trying to kick, Dago screamed, "He killed Joey."

"Over a bitch. You kick him again and we'll lose the deal."

Dago jerked his arm free. "Fuck the deal."

Al jumped at him, shoving him back. He said something that didn't carry to Annalisa, but she could see eagerness in Dago. He rubbed his hands together as they rushed to the tent.

She had the insane desire to laugh over the way they behaved when they found she wasn't there. Al crawled all the way through the tent, out the back slit, cussing and screaming. He walked over to Bell and kicked him.

"You let her get away, you stupid bastard."

"Maybe he let her go," Dago accused.

"He ain't that stupid. Get the bikes. We'll find her."

Oh, God, they'd find her, and Bell couldn't protect her. Annalisa squirmed down the shallow crease in the earth, her only safety in the dark. Bell couldn't protect himself from the kicks they gave him. He couldn't protect her. They would rape her, all of them, the way Bell had.

Worse! Oh, God, it would be worse. Annalisa pressed herself

down, willing her body to become part of the ground beneath her. She whispered a prayer when the bikes came her direction. Grinding her teeth together to keep from screaming, she let her breath out and went limp when they passed by only to tense again when Ready exclaimed.

"He's wet!" She knelt beside Bell with her hand down his pants.

Jolene stood beside her. "Maybe he pissed himself."

Ready shot to her feet and shoved her hand in Jolene's face. "Does that smell like piss?"

She sniffed, shook her head, and then knelt to put her hand in his pants. "He's shot it all though. He's soft."

"He'll come back up." She shoved Jolene aside to jerk at Bell's pants. "I told you he was lying."

"He's out cold, Ready. Al hit him really hard."

Ready straddled him to pull his pants down. "He'll wake up."

She backed off, saying, "Yeah, and he'll kill you."

Ready sat on his legs, contemplating that. "Not if he can't." She rose up to jerk at the pants again. "Get some rope."

"You're crazy! He'll really kill you for that."

"I'm having him!" she screamed. "He killed my old man. I got a right."

She scampered back when Ready jumped to her feet. Ready grabbed her by the arm and shook, urged in a voice that didn't carry, but her words convinced Jolene. Jolene left at a trot.

Ready pounced back on Bell. She rushed to get his pants down, panting from the effort, pushing him to his side. Joey was in the way. She stopped long enough to roll his body over a few feet.

From the light of the rising full moon, Annalisa watched, but felt no reaction. She saw it, but she felt no reaction to cold, callous disregard.

Ready jerked the pants over Bell's buttocks and rolled him to his back. Bell stirred. His hand searched for what disturbed him and found Ready's arm. She batted it away, still feverishly working to get his pants down.

Waistband down to his thighs, Bell jerked up only to fall to the side as Ready danced back out of reach. He caught himself with one hand and the other held his head. Twisting and pushing himself to his knees, he shook his head. Laughing when he tried to get his feet under him, Ready stood out of reach and laughed even harder when the pants around his thighs foiled his efforts, making him fall back to his buttocks.

Jolene ran up with some rope, and they both watched.

"He's groggy as hell," Ready commented.

"Yeah, but enough?"

Bell tried again for his feet, pulling at his pants and still holding his head. He shook it repeatedly, even after he gained his feet, feet wide apart to hold his wavering body from tipping over.

"We'll see," Ready cried, darting in to jerk his pants from the back.

Bell's knees buckled, and he sat down hard. Drawing his knees up, he held his head a moment before struggling back to his feet. The women backed off as he took two unsteady steps. Ready darted in again. She grabbed for his crotch. He recoiled, twisting away, his body moving but not his feet fast enough to stay up. He landed hard with his head bouncing on the ground and went limp.

"Think he's out?" Jolene asked.

"I'll find out." She jumped over his legs and swung her hand at his crotch.

Jerking violently, doubling up in pain, he moaned, making a noise for the first time as he rolled to his side. Holding himself with one hand and pushing up with the other, he went up, managed two steps, and fell again. Then he crawled.

Annalisa's panic built, pushing reason away. Though he couldn't know where she was, he moved in her direction. Even as groggy as he was, her mind screamed against logic that he was coming after her.

Ready stopped him. She ran up, shoved him off balance and skipped off. He sprawled, and she jumped on him, knocking him flat. Rolling to his back, his arms flailed in search of what attacked him, and she skipped out of danger.

Jolene, encouraged by Ready's success, joined in the torment. More helpless against them than Annalisa had been against him, he couldn't catch them to hurt them, and he couldn't keep their hands away to make them stop. He rolled back to his stomach, struggling to get back on his hands and knees. They both jumped on him.

They giggled and laughed at his uncoordinated efforts to twist his arms out of their holds while they tied his wrists behind his back.

"Tie his feet, too. I don't want him kicking me," Ready ordered.

That took less time than it had to tie his wrists. She rolled him to his back and sat on his chest.

"Now, get his pants down."

Jolene stood back. "I don't know."

"Do it!" she screamed.

"If you're wrong, he'll kill us both."

"I'm not." Her hands went between his legs. Bell jerked and stiffened when she touched him. "Hurt, baby?" she asked maliciously.

"Don't," he said, speaking for the first time.

Even as terrified as she was, Annalisa thought Ready had to be crazy. Bell was regaining his senses, and she was certain his strength was sure to follow, but neither did. Ready obviously knew more about that type of thing. She wasn't afraid, leaning down to put her face inches from his.

"It hurts good. You like a good squeeze."

The last was through clenched teeth, and Bell jerked his knees up, knocking her away. He rolled to his side, still doubled up. Jolene laughed, and Ready jumped to her feet to kick him in the back.

A heavy thud brought a jerk with a grunt of pain from Bell, but Ready was far from satisfied. "I'll fix you," she promised before running off.

Left alone, Jolene knelt behind him to fondle the bare hip showing pale and white in the moonlight. She ran her hand under the pants down to his thigh, then back. Bell lay passive and quiet until her caresses carried her hand across his buttocks to between his legs.

He arched his back, dragging his knees down and his hips forward to get away from her. "Don't," he told her in a slurred mumble. "Hurts."

"I'm gentle, baby."

Not gentle enough. He threw himself to his chest. She followed. He squirmed, pushing himself forward with his bound feet. She held. He threw himself to the opposite side, telling her again that it hurt and drew his knees back up to his chest, his back to Annalisa.

The desert moon gave her more than enough light to see his hands, clenched into fists. She could also see the puzzled look on Jolene's face, jumping back to keep from getting kicked when he threw his legs out straight.

"You squeezed him too hard," she told Ready when she ran back. "He won't come up in pain like that."

Ready shoved her aside impatiently. "Yes, he will."

Jolene saw what she had in her hands. "Hey, you can't do that." Ready knelt behind him. Jolene backed away. "You said some fun. You can't do that without him knowing."

"Are you going to help me?"

"Ready, he'll kill you for that."

"Who says he's going to live to kill anyone?"

"Al won't let you kill him. He'd lose the deal."

"The deal is already blown. He won't take what they did to him. Al will figure that out for himself when he gets back. Now cover his face."

Jolene didn't move.

"All right, but remember what I said," Ready said hatefully. "No fun for you." She shook out a coil of rope, tied one end to Bell's wrists and shoved the bulk between the rope around his ankles. When she leaned over Bell, reaching for his face, Jolene moved.

"Okay, but you better make sure he's dead when this is over."

She stepped over him, sat down, and pulled his head onto her lap. "I don't even know if I can hold him."

As soon as her hand covered Bell's mouth and nose, he fought. She wouldn't have been able to hold him down alone even leaning her body weight over her hand until Ready sat on his chest. He threw Ready off twice before unconsciousness overtook him.

Ready quickly pulled his ankles toward his wrists and tied the rope off at about a foot distance. Jolene sat at Bell's head. Whenever he showed signs of coming to, she held his face until he stilled again.

With no resistance to what she did, Ready worked his pants to his ankles, untangled the rope and looped it loosely around his knees. The branch she carried back with the rope, about two inches thick and a foot and a half long, went between his knees, holding his legs apart with sharp, ragged edges to unprotected flesh. Bell moaned when she drew the rope tight, pushing those edges into his skin. The rope, tied off to ensure the branch stayed in place, left still enough length to wrap around his neck from behind and be tied again at his hands.

Ready stood up, breathing deeply in satisfaction.

"That's hard work without the men to help," Jolene said.

"It'll be worth it," Ready said with relish. "I'll be right back."

———

Ready returned with two bottles of beer. She handed one to Jolene and knelt beside Bell. Vicious, she caressed his knee first and then hit the side with her fist, driving the stick deeper into his flesh. He groaned, and she hit it again, and then rose up, leaning her weight on his leg. "Wake up, Bell, baby."

She pressed harder as he twisted and groaned. He couldn't move away from it, and he mumbled, "Grant."

"I don't know who he is, but you're going to know me." She ran her hand down the inside of his thigh to his genitals.

"Grant," he shouted when her hand closed tight. "Michael— damn you, you whore."

"Who's Grant and Michael?" Jolene asked over his groans.

Ready retorted and stood. "Who knows?"

Bell quieted immediately, both in the insults he hurled and his twisting struggles. Quiet while they pushed him from his side to his back, he made no sounds, even when the rope drew tight around his neck.

Jolene stepped into the confined space between his spread legs, between the stick and his ankles and sat back on his feet. She used the stick like a handlebar and wiggled her toes under his buttocks. Ready sat on his stomach, facing his head.

"Wake up, Bell," she said, slapping him on the face.

"Maybe he had too much to drink," Jolene said with a giggle.

"Is that what it is, baby?" Ready asked. "Or not enough?" She tipped the bottle she held, filling his mouth. While he choked and coughed, she patted his cheek. "There, there, baby, just drink this down, and you'll feel good."

Jolene rubbed her hands up and down the inside of Bell's legs. "He is a stud. I always did like a man with strong legs."

Ready continued pouring beer in Bell's mouth while they talked, ignoring his choking. "What are you doing with a shrimp like Dago then?"

"You take what will have you. You know that. Dago ain't bad though."

"Be like doing it with a twelve-year-old."

"He's hairier," she said with a giggle. Her hands slid down. "This will be like doing it with a horse."

As soon as she touched him between the legs, Bell struggled. He choked and gagged on the beer poured in his mouth all the while twisting and squirming to be free of Jolene's hands and Ready's weight.

Ready finished pouring beer into him and changed position, facing his crotch. Jolene threw her beer away. Both women worked on him, Jolene with her hands, and Ready, disgustingly, with her mouth.

The ropes held Bell where they wanted him, in a helpless position with no vent for his anger other than shouting obscenities at them between gasps, moans, and groans.

"Is he hard, yet?" Jolene asked. Ready shook her head. "His balls are like goose eggs, Ready. They feel like they're going to bust. Are you lying to me?"

Ready jumped to her feet. "He's coming up fast." Her hands trembled, and she cussed when the buttons on her shorts didn't open fast enough.

"God," Jolene exclaimed, "he's huge."

"Anyone would be after Dago." She kicked her shorts off and straddled him, facing his head again.

"Hey, I ain't shitting you, you better go on easy."

"I've seen bigger." Ready said, wiggling down from his chest to his groin. "Guide him in."

They had tied him to prevent or restrict any movement but one. Bell threw his hips up, ramming himself in her. The force of it knocked her to his chest, making her cry out in pain and surprise.

She recovered quickly. "Oh, baby, you do like it." She wiggled down again. "Be easy, baby or…"

Bell wasn't easy. He thrust up again. She gasped, being nearly thrown off. "You filthy bitch," he told her. In a strained voice, his words came through clenched jaw while his hips rammed upward once more, then he went still, rigid, and moaned.

Ready straightened and stared in disbelief.

Jolene sat back and crossed her arms. "That," she said in disgust, "was a hell of a lot of work for nothing."

"You son-of-a-bitch," Ready screamed, slapping him with all her strength.

"Go back—" Bell growled, not finishing when Ready slapped him again.

Not satisfied, Ready jumped to her feet, kicked, and then

stomped, burying her foot in his stomach. That didn't satisfy her, even as his contortions pulled the rope around his neck tight and strangled him. She raised her foot again, changing its direction, still not contented with the way he writhed and gasped in pain. Her foot froze in mid-air.

Jolene scrambled to her feet.

The laughter came out of the trees, growing louder as the man walked to them. "A man's different, girls." The speaker, short and grossly obese, chuckled. "They can only take so much before they're no good."

"Fingers, we were just having some fun," Ready began.

"Unless you don't need their cock." He pushed them aside. Wheezing with the effort of moving his own weight, he stared down at Bell. "I don't need his cock."

A second man came up beside him. Smaller even than Dago, he stood with is head hanging.

"Fingers, he's…" Ready began.

The man cut her off. "You had your fun," he said, his tone ugly. He dropped to one knee and flipped Bell to his side.

Bell fell limply. He mumbled softly when the man leaned his weight on his hip. He stirred, trying to twist away when the man fondled him, but with a sickening difference than the women had.

The man wheezed, and a strange rattling sounded as he leaned his weight on Bell to keep him from moving away from his pumping arm.

He stood, wiping his hand on his pants, and Annalisa, from her hidden place, stared in shocked horror.

"Give me a hand, Blake," Fingers ordered.

"What do you need him for?" the small man whined.

"I want him," he said nastily. "I'm damn near to coming in my pants. Now get over here."

Fingers threw Bell to his face by the ropes. Wrapping his arms around Bell's waist, he raised him, while Blake used the stick to pull

Bell's knees under him. They didn't care that the ropes drew tight around Bell's neck and arched his back, strangling him.

The fat, repulsive man opened his pants, dropped to his knees and edged up behind Bell.

Annalisa hid her face, fighting sickness. Bell was vicious and cruel, but not depraved. Annalisa didn't think. She really didn't know. He deserved punishment, but no man deserved that, she didn't think. No man should have to suffer that kind of perverted treatment, no more than any woman.

She hated Bell. She wanted him dead. Yes, but no man deserved that. She held her hands over her ears, not wanting to hear what she had forced her eyes to keep from seeing.

Loud angry voices made her look and hear again.

Fingers faced Ready and shouted. "God damn it, why didn't you tell me who he is before I fucked him?"

"I tried. You were too hot to listen."

"Who wouldn't be after watching you? What the hell were you doing, anyway?"

"Just having some fun. He'd been mad, but it wouldn't have blown the deal. You'll have to kill him now."

"Where is Al?"

"Out looking for Bell's old lady. She split when she saw he was going to lose. When they get back, we'll have a real nice time with her."

"A new one?"

"Uh-huh."

Blake interrupted. "Are you going to burn him?"

"Huh?" Fingers asked.

Blake pointed at Bell. "Are you going to burn him?"

"Hell, I don't know. We'll see what Al thinks."

"You can Bell's bitch. It's been a long time since we've had a double blow out," Ready told him. "She's got a nice tight little ass, Fingers. You'll get two virgins in one night."

Annalisa cringed deeper in her hole, sickness burning the back of her throat. What they did was bad enough, but what they spoke of made the urge to vomit more than she thought she could hold back. Staying there, cowering in her hole until they moved away, Annalisa knew the time had come for her to get away, but when she sat up, she saw Bell. Her hand went to her mouth again to fight away the sickness.

Face down, the ropes held his legs and arms above his back. Hurt and unconscious, he was as helpless as she would have been against them, but she couldn't help him. She couldn't, not after what he did to her.

She hated him. She wanted him dead but not tortured to death. No one, not even Bell should have to suffer the things they talked of, but they only talked of them. They didn't say they would do them. The fault was his, anyway. This was the way he chose to live. No one made him live with those people, by their rules, and he always knew he might lose a fight. He told her that when he told her to go to the spring if it happened, the spring where she would be safe.

Oh, God, he did help her. He kept them from doing those things to her, but what could she do for him? She had no way to cut the ropes. It would take hours to untie them, hours in full view of them in the bright moonlight. In the shadows where she hid, she was safe. She could crawl away. She didn't owe Bell anything after what he did, or did she? What would they have done to her? But he was unconscious. She couldn't drag him away. She could barely support her own weight, and that was his fault.

"Oh, God, help me," she whispered and dropped flat again when Bell moved.

Even bound hand and foot, she was that terrified of him. He'd go after her, rape, and hurt her again. No, he couldn't. He was tied. He couldn't hurt her, but he could be hurt. If he wasn't tied, if he had his gun—*gun*? Her head snapped up to look at the tent.

The gun was there. If she had that gun, she wouldn't have to be afraid of him or them. She wanted that gun. She crawled on her hands and knees to get it, staying in the dark of the shadows. She listened for them to come back and watched him, reached the tent, and slipped inside, only to be trapped there.

———

Annalisa heard the bikes and dropped to the tent floor long before the lights struck the back. They came up over the depression where she had been hiding only minutes before and slid to a stop to keep from running over Bell.

Dago's bike stopped at an angle, casting the head lamp on Bell. Al's bike went down and skidded past him. Both men stared.

Al found his voice first as he got to his feet. "Fingers must be here."

"Yeah, but why'd he do that?"

Walking by the tent, Fingers answered, wheezing between his words. "You know me, boys. I see an ass, I just got to fuck it." He knelt beside Bell. "He's good, real fine."

Al and Dago grimaced in disgust when he knelt beside Bell, one hand fondling him.

"What was his ass doing out where you could see it?" Al asked.

"Girls had him down. We slipped in quiet like to make sure there wasn't any unwanted company. They had him down good. I got so horny I took over."

"God damn that Ready."

"We're all fucked now," Dago commented with a grimace, staring at Fingers and added, "You put any more fingers in, you'll rip him wide open."

"Knock it off," Al snapped.

"Gone too far now," Fingers panted. "I'm going to lay on him this time."

"I said knock it off. He's a runner, you damn fag. You don't blow up a runner."

"I'm not going to blow him up, just play."

"If you play with *him*, you better blow him up," Dago told him.

"Leave him alone," Al ordered again.

"Hell, what difference does it make now?" Dago asked.

"I hope he wakes up this time," Fingers wheezed. "He only gave me one good jump before."

"Wait a minute!" Al shouted. "He was out?"

"Whole time. I like a little more action."

"Then he doesn't know who did it?"

"So?" Dago asked.

"Or what. It could have been anything."

"Ready?"

"That bitch has it coming. When he comes to, if she's with him, what's he gonna think?"

"She did it."

"Right. Give me—Damn you, Fingers, get off of him."

"I got to, man, I'm busting."

"Give it to Blake then."

The scuffling stopped, and Fingers wheezed back by the tent, grumbling, "I hope he don't buy your frame. He's too good to waste."

"Give me a hand," Al said.

"What are you going to do?"

"Put him in the tent. Get his other arm." His voice strained as he lifted. "We'll put him in there and let Ready babysit."

Bell hung between them, and both men panted from the weight.

"He won't buy it, Al. He stinks of Fingers."

"She can wash him."

As they dragged Bell by the tent, Annalisa inched closer to the back. When they reached the front, she slipped through the slit, holding her mouth again.

"I never went the fag route, but this is one bastard I wouldn't mind balling myself, as long as he knew it," Dago claimed, puffing from effort.

"I'd rather ram a stick from his ass to his eyeballs," Al retorted. "Grab his feet."

Bent double, Al dragged Bell halfway in the tent and let him fall, crawling over him to get out.

Dago shoved Bell's legs in. "We could stake him out and make Prissy do it to him."

"That would be easy. She's like Bunny, screams every time you look at her."

"He damn sure had her screaming tonight. It makes you wonder if he was lying, and Ready is right."

"We could damned sure find out."

Al thought about it briefly before saying, "The deal is more important. We'll try to save it. If he doesn't buy Ready, we'll console ourselves to the loss with him."

"There's no reason he shouldn't once he's cleaned up. Fingers is so damned small an ass is the only thing that will fit him."

"Or a kid."

"Yeah," Al answered absently. He shouted at Ready. "Get over here." He whispered to Dago, "Have Jolene give her a dildo. That will cover anything Fingers did."

Annalisa was ignorant of what a dildo was. Without knowing, she knew it was something sick. She was ignorant of so many things she should have known for protection and warning, instead of being naïve and stupid. Would knowing what some people would do to others have helped her protect herself? Would warning have made the shocks any easier to bear? Hearing of atrocities was so much different than seeing or experiencing them. Hearing of a rape was so much easier than living through one. Hearing of terror so strong it numbed the mind and weakened the limbs meant nothing in comparison to actually feeling it.

Ready only had one question when told her chore. "Can I have a joint to keep me company?"

"Take what you want, but don't leave him."

"Sure, Al." The eagerness in her voice and bounce in her step indicated more than a forced acceptance.

Al chuckled softly. "She won't be able to keep her hands off him. Let's move the bikes and bury Joey."

They turned and started back to the rear of the tent. Annalisa quickly ducked back inside, shrinking away from contact with Bell's head. Her stomach twisted from the overpowering odor of human excrement and semen mixed with the rank smell of his body. All she could do was cover her nose and breathe heavily through her mouth to fight down the nausea.

For a few moments, listening only to the sound of his deep even breathing, forcing herself not to run was the hardest thing she had to do. She moved, afraid the sound would wake him. She knew her fear was unreasonable. He was still tied, but reason had nothing to do with it. He was there, even if at the moment, he was not the thing to fear. She had to remember that. Those outside were the danger. Al and Dago pushed their bikes up, and Ready came to the front. Annalisa couldn't slip out without the men seeing her, and Ready would soon be in.

If only she could find the gun, she would have a weapon. She looked around, patted the ground around her, frantically.

The knife! She fell toward Bell's feet, reaching for his pants. The knife was there in his left pocket. She'd seen him put it there when she handed it back to him.

"Where's the water, Ready?" Al asked.

"What do I need water for?"

"To wash him. You better do it, bitch, before you do anything else. We're gonna bury Joey, then check on you, and it better be done."

Annalisa dropped her head on her outstretched arm and relaxed in relief. How tired she was, and how easy it would be to sleep, but she walked up on her knees. She couldn't sleep now.

Finding the knife, she opened it quickly. Bell stirred, nothing more than a slight roll of his head and a change in the rhythm of his breathing, enough to make Annalisa start and cower. She froze, holding the knife to her breast with both hands until she was sure he wasn't going to wake. Easing down to her hands and knees, she kept as far from him as possible without brushing the side of the tent. That was when she found the gun, pushed up against the narrow space where the tent side sloped to the floor.

Now if Ready came back before the men finished their grizzly job, she would not be taken without having some way to defend herself. She had two, and Bell stirred again to remind her he had none.

"Do we have to do this now?" Dago complained. "I'm so horny, I'm about to bust. Fingers is driving me crazy."

Al thought it over, for a very short second. "Nah, it can wait."

Annalisa sighed in relief. Now she could get out. She leaned down on her hands, with the knife in one and the gun in the other. With the first step of her crawl to the back, she bumped Bell's arm.

Bell groaned. Damn him! Annalisa shoved him up, furious with herself for not being able to just crawl away. He groaned again when she let him down after slashing the rope around his wrists. With his hands free, when he woke up, he at least wouldn't be totally helpless, more than he had done for her.

She crawled out and dropped into a huddle again. Ready ran back, water sloshing out of the pan she was in such a hurry. "Now, I'll wash your ass, then you're all mine," she promised as she crawled in.

Water splashed, and Bell immediately groaned.

"Tender, baby," Ready cooed.

"Don't," he mumbled weakly.

"You're too tender, you prick. I'm not squeezing now."

Annalisa looked for a way out. Bright, silver moonlight surrounded the little pool of shadow where she hid. She peeked out, around the edge of the tent on both sides. They weren't all at the fire. She couldn't go either way without the danger of one of them seeing her as she passed through that light. Still trapped and forced to listen. Jolene squealed happily, and Bunny cried. Poor Bunny suffered while the others were enthralled. It angered Al.

"Hold still, damn you."

"It hurts," she sobbed.

"It's because you aren't hot. Get hot, bitch. I'm ready for a full night."

"You are?" Fingers bellowed. "I was all set for the blow out Ready promised me. I think I'll go see how she's doing."

"No, you don't." Al backed away from Bunny. "I'll give you something almost as good."

"No, Al, please," Bunny cried. "Please, I won't cry anymore. I promise."

The others hooted and hollered in excitement. Bunny's crying became hysterical. She hung on Al's arm, pleading with him. "I'll do what you want. I won't cry. Please, Al, please."

Al stopped in front of Bell's tent.

She grabbed his arm. "Please, Al." She ended in a scream when Al backhanded her, knocking her to the ground. She laid there in a heap, sobbing her heart out.

Al ducked down and stuck his head in the tent. "You got him cleaned up?"

"Want to feel him up, to see?" Ready asked sweetly.

He ignored her suggestion. "Make him comfortable." He backed out. Bunny sobbed wildly as he half-dragged and half-walked her to his tent. Jolene passed them, hurrying to Bell's tent.

"Brought you something. Figured you might as well have fun, too." She tossed it to Ready and hurried off.

Ready laughed throatily. "Thanks," she called, tossed the pan out, and zipped the flap. "Now you son-of-a-bitch."

Violent action inside the tent, shook the canvas sides, and with more strength than the last time, Bell said, "Don't."

"Now, don't you be loud, baby."

"Leave me alone," he slurred out.

Ready chuckled. "Sure, after I teach you a lesson. You know how big you are. You know it hurts when you ram in the way you did me. Now you're going to get rammed and good by a fake dick bigger than you are. There, that will keep you quiet."

No longer ignorant as to what a dildo was, it wasn't hard to figure out what Ready was going to do with it. Al had no worry over Ready convincing Bell she alone was responsible for what happened to him while he was unconscious. Ready would see to that.

In moments, Bell spoke again, muffled and distorted. The tent shook, and he groaned.

"Does it hurt?" Ready asked, making him groan again.

His voice, still muffled and distorted, definitely gained in strength and from the sound of it, his mind was clearing. He knew who she was, and he spoke clearly enough to understand even through what had to be a gag.

"Damn you, Ready." His breath caught. "Get away from me."

"I'm not through."

"Get the fuck away from me."

The rest was muffled too much to understand, but Ready's was clear, saying, "You're making too much noise."

From the fire, Al yelled, "Come on over here."

Annalisa silently thanked God. She didn't think she could stand much more. She peeked over the edge of the tent. Jolene stood at the front of Al's tent. Bunny was out of sight inside. The rest were at the fire. That made the way to the left clear. She dropped to her hands and knees. Now she could get away from the depraved sickness. Escape couldn't be too soon, but she couldn't hurry.

As much as she wanted away from Ready's hoarse whispering, she couldn't hurry. She had to place each hand carefully, so the gun or knife didn't click on the rocks, had to be sure her toes didn't drag and rattle the rocks, either.

Laying the gun down carefully, Annalisa sat up. She didn't need the knife and could move faster if she didn't have it in her hand. She folded it and pushed it down in her pocket. After a second of indecision, she put the gun inside her blouse.

Hands free did make moving faster and without holding

anything her hands didn't hurt as much. All she had to concentrate on was not dragging her toes. She couldn't think of someone seeing her. She couldn't let fear take over her senses.

Bunny screamed. Annalisa looked over her shoulder to see why, and something snapped inside of her. She didn't want to see, but she could not look away, didn't want to hear those screams of agony, but she could not close her ears. How the gun came to be in her hands, she didn't know, anymore than she remembered standing. What shooting would mean to her didn't matter. All that mattered was stopping them. The gun was in her hands, but as she brought it down to aim and fire, it didn't explode. She stared at it, unable to understand why. Nor could she understand why a hand was over hers. She twisted to free it, away from the thumb that blocked hammer from hitting the firing pin.

Bell stepped behind her. He locked a hand over her mouth, and he twisted the gun from her hand. "Don't or you'll trade places with her."

Her hands went to her face. Not enough. She turned and pressed her face to his chest. "God," she sobbed, choking again with the smell of him.

"Shh," he whispered. "Wait until we get out of here." He turned, keeping his arm around her and walked her away.

Annalisa cried, holding her hands in front of her face. She stumbled with her blindness. He caught her. She wept not realizing how many times he stumbled and caught himself with his hold of her or how many times he stopped, drawing great breaths of air. That he leaned heavier on her as they walked went unnoticed, until he fell. Only then did his condition penetrate.

He used her for support to pull himself up again.

"You're hurting," she stated tonelessly.

He pulled her close, wrapping his arm around her. "Don't let me go down and don't let me go to sleep."

"Are you tired?"

He held her close for another moment, pressing his face against her hair. "No, honey," he told her softly, "that's why I don't want to sleep."

He started her walking again.

'Honey?' Why would he call her honey? You called someone you loved honey. He didn't love her. You called a child honey. She wasn't a child. She was thirty years old. Not a child, but was she acting like one?

Tired? No, he wasn't tired, not in the ridiculous sense she had asked it. "Bell."

"What?"

"I hate your guts."

"I know. That's what keeps me from making a complete fool of myself."

The words and their possible meaning didn't register. "If it wasn't for them, I'd kill you."

"Just wait until I get you out of this."

"Then I will kill you if you ever come near me again."

"I'll remember that."

8

Doctor Thristen was not happy to have a call from Pratters. "Any change?" Pratters asked.

"Nothing significant."

"What's that mean?"

Thristen sighed in resignation. "I don't know why you won't settle for the vague little answers we doctors are famous for."

"I don't like them. Same, better, or worse?"

"A little better, but nothing to indicate he's going to make it."

"Thanks." He disconnected and dialed again. Her voice had the same apathetic sound to it. "Thought you'd like to know, there's been some improvement."

"Thank you."

"You really don't give a damn, do you?"

"Yes," she said and hung up.

Much to Pratters' irritation, he never seemed to have the upper hand with Mrs. Summers. He disconnected again and dialed the secret number.

"You don't give me much time," the man complained.

"I'm in a hurry. Got anything yet?"

"Very little. Our guy got into the financial records at the VA hospital. They show a lot of time in there, in and out." The sound of paper rattling came through the phone. "In-patient for six months, five-no-six operations in that time, physical therapy, and psychiatric sessions, before he was released to out-patient. More surgeries through the years, more psychiatric sessions then two years ago everything stopped until six months ago. He spent two days in for tests. Nothing since."

"I don't suppose you can tell me why?"

"Not from this. He's cost the taxpayers a lot of money. I can tell you the surgeons were neurologists, meaning there was nerve damage somewhere, oral, which explains why a partial denture was made, staff surgeons, and one specialist was called in, who happens to be a plastic surgeon.

"That's about it from this. I've got an appointment made with the chief of staff over there. I'll be able to tell you more about what it all was for after that. I've got a request into the credit check, a tap into income tax records, and a man on his way to the last known address."

"How long is it going to take?"

"For a complete background, a couple of days. If you'd tell me what you want, it'd help cut the time down."

"If I knew what I wanted, I wouldn't have called you."

He hung up, satisfaction making him grin. He had the son-of-a-bitch. After eighteen months, he found Bell's past. For the first time, he had a chance of finding a lever to use against him.

If he could wash it, Bell might dance to his tune, but he needed Prissy to be sure he could cover the whole thing up, Prissy and the answers to his questions about Mrs. Summers. How much easier it would be, if they were one and the same.

9

Submission

ANNALISA COULDN'T REMEMBER THE REST OF THE NIGHT CLEARLY, A jumble of falling, stumbling, and pulling Bell back to his feet. She woke to see dusk and Palo Verde trees leaning over her. Then stark terror seized her. She saw Bell and relaxed until more memory came through her sleep-slowed mind. She began to shake as she edged carefully away from him.

Rapist! Raped, defiled, soiled by a filthy animal. Dirt and filth from him. Hurt and pain from where he hit her, bruised her, scratched her, tore at her forcing himself in. In! Oh, God, filth. Wash it away. Water is here. Wash it away.

Frantic to be clean, she tore off nails clawing at the knots in her boot laces. She clawed at the buttons and tie in her blouse. When she took the pants off, his remains were there, encrusted on the inside of her legs to sicken her more.

Wash it away. Wash and rub, get rid of it. Be clean. It hurts but wash it away. Beat it out of your clothes on the rocks. Rub hard. Faster, rub it away. Oh, God, tired and washing won't make it go away, not ever.

Tears welled in her eyes, and she didn't want to cry anymore. Crying didn't help. Tears wouldn't make anything go away, and weeping hadn't made him stop.

Him!

He'd do it again. He'd rape her again if she stayed. Hurry, hurry back in the clothes but be quiet, don't wake him.

She jerked up straight and stared at Bell. Why hadn't he heard? He always heard everything when he slept.

"Bell." He didn't answer. He didn't move. She did, closer to him. "Bell." Still closer. "Bell, are you dead?"

As still as he lay, he looked as if he might be. Movement in his hairy chest to show he was breathing wasn't visible. His jacket was gone, and so was his headband, but his forehead felt warm.

She jumped back and cried out when his hand shot up to grab her wrist. She fell back as he rose up, and his other hand found her arm. Just as suddenly, he relaxed and laid back down, drawing her to him. He pulled her down until her head was on his shoulder and his arms around her.

"I thought you were dead," she told him, thinking how strange it was that he didn't smell so badly to her. Silly to think of that and talk of death.

"Just tired. Are you okay?" She nodded, slipping her cheek across his skin. "Why are you wet?" he asked.

"I took a bath."

He nodded, touching the top of her head with his chin. He was going back to sleep. She could feel it in the way his arms slipped on her back, and the way he jerked when she told him, "I'm afraid."

His arms tightened again. "They won't find us here."

"Of you," she whispered faintly.

"I won't hurt you."

She shivered, and her voice quivered with threatening tears. "You did. I could stand it if you didn't hurt me."

His arms tightened more. "I won't have to hurt you anymore."

No, he didn't. He had already terrorized her with pain, showing her what it would be like without submission. He didn't need pain any longer. She forced herself to lie against him, biting her lip when his mouth moved to her ear.

His voice was a thick whisper. "What happened last night won't happen again."

He rolled, putting her on her back to lean over her. She shuddered when he nuzzled her neck. She couldn't help it. He jerked his head back to stare at her in the fading light. Then, as abruptly as he had done the first time he'd kissed her, he pushed away, going to his feet.

She stared at him, afraid of what it meant. When he turned to walk off, she jumped to her feet and ran after him. "Don't leave me," she cried, grabbing him by the arm.

He stared at her for a moment before pulling her with him. Shaking loose from her hold, he moved some rocks. Beneath them was a bundle he shook out, dropped the contents on the ground and handed her the blanket. When he turned, reaching for his jacket on the rocks, she clung to him.

She knew what he was, what he would do, what he had done, but it was nothing to what she had seen them doing to Bunny, the same things they had talked of doing to her. What Bell did was nothing in comparison. She threw herself at him, pressing against him.

"Don't leave, Bell, please."

He held to her arms and pushed her away. "Get out of those wet clothes," he growled.

She obeyed. The only consolation to her modesty was that in the failing light, it was too dark for him to see more than her form. She threw herself at him again.

He held to the arms she wrapped around his neck, telling her, "I want you to want this."

"Yes, yes, I do."

"I want more than sex from you."

"Anything," she cried, frantically holding to him.

"I want you to leave with me when this is over."

"Yes, yes, anything."

His hands slid to her shoulders, ready to push her away. "I think you're lying."

Twisting out of his hands, she stepped closer, pressed against his body to prove it to him, and his arms closed around her. He held her in an embrace that threatened to smother her. His deep, irregular breaths blew on her neck as he nuzzled her, and one hand dropped to her waist to pull her close there. His hands were hot, burning on her cold flesh.

Rigid, she feared the change that might come. If she didn't fight, if she allowed him what he wanted without struggle, she might save herself that. He told her what she had to do. He wanted more than simple submission.

Bell led her to a narrow strip of sand and spread the blanket for them. Sitting her down, he sat facing her. One hand brushed her hair from her neck, uncovering it for his kisses. When his mouth reached hers, she parted her lips. She had to respond. While he kissed her, he lowered her to her back. While he fondled, her mind said no, I hate him. Her body said yes. His hands and lips, the way they sought and caressed sensitive areas caused the reaction. His body pressed against hers, his pelvis rubbed, and his maleness was between them, hard and waiting beneath his clothes.

Hands on his shoulders, her mind ordered them to hold him away. They obeyed commands from a different level. When she encircled him, pulling him to her, he reached between them to open his pants.

Submission with pain had been the first lesson. He then taught her response with gentleness. When he turned away to undress, she waited, aching to have him. She told herself she couldn't, but when he lowered himself to her, her arms and legs opened to take him.

No, he no longer needed pain. His only roughness came from

haste to enter her, yet he pulled back after the first bare penetration. Probing her depth for a slow entry only teased her. She thrust her hips up, wanting more.

Her actions gave him pleasure. Bell thrust full depth with a sigh. He kissed her while he drove deep, stroking slowly. He matched his pace to hers, increasing as she went into a frenzy of want. The release of her body in climax came for the first time in her life, waves and waves that brought a soft cry from her lips while she clung to him, quivering and moaning.

Joining her, working his arms under her shoulders to surround her with himself, he held her with his full weight and length over her. His body alternated from stiffness to thrusts with each pump of his body. Soft groans until his body was spent, slowed to limpness

Rolling to his side, still holding her, he turned her to him. Kissing and fondling her, he pulled the blanket up around them. The warmth turned her lazy feeling of contentment to drowsiness. She fell asleep in his arms.

———

When Annalisa woke, the sun was high, and she was alone. She had degraded herself for nothing. Satisfied that he had properly trained her, he'd left, knowing she had only submitted in fear, one that would hold her until he wanted her again.

She didn't doubt that he would be back, when it suited him, when he had the desire for satisfaction again in animal pleasure. Leave with him? Endure this kind of life forever? Suffer the shame? Never!

Dressed, she ate food from the bundle he'd taken from the rocks, filled the canteen, and began her journey. He would not find her waiting to pander to him.

He found her, instead, coming up the hill to the point. "What the hell are you doing?" he demanded.

She had learned deceit well. "Looking for you."

"I told you not to leave there."

He took her arm to walk her back, his hand cold and clammy.

"I was only going to the point. I wouldn't let them see me."

"Stay at the spring."

"I was just worried about you. Where were you?"

How easy the lies and false concern passed through her lips. If he could do it, there was no reason she couldn't. She watched him out of the corner of her eye for the effect her words had and took satisfaction in the fact that not only did he not look well, he limped.

His skin and clothes were saturated with perspiration. His face was pale, and his breathing shallow. She knew what was wrong with him, knew what to do for it, too, but she didn't tell him. If he got sick enough, she could take the gun. Then she wouldn't be afraid of any of them.

"After another stash," he answered, raising the bundle in his other hand.

"What do you do, stash supplies everywhere you go?"

"It pays to be safe."

"Why didn't you just go back to the camp for what you wanted?" she asked, believing that was what he had done.

"There's only one of them I'm interested in. He's not there now."

He had been back. "We have to wait?" she asked.

"We wait."

His breathing became more labored with the walk in the rough terrain. When they reached the drop to the small canyon, he fell the last few feet. Slow getting back to his feet, his arms trembled when he helped her down. He stumbled going to the spring and leaned against the rock wall to support himself. Leaning forward to cup water to his mouth, his hair swung down, shielding his face.

With spite, Annalisa said, "You ought to take a bath while you're there. It'd be a new experience for you." Hooking the long strands of hair behind his ears, he looked at her. "You really need one. This heat is too much for you in your weakened condition."

The deliberate sneer sent him to his feet, much too fast. He fell back to the rock wall, slid down it to sit in the small pool of water, and passed out.

Annalisa laughed until she realized he was unconscious again. "Bell." She moved closer. "Bell." She pushed at his shoulder. When he didn't move, she took the gun from his waistband. "Now I don't need you."

She left him sitting in the water, knowing when night fell, that he would go into chills. He deserved every sick minute heat exhaustion would give him. By the time the police got there, he would be sick enough to be glad to see them.

Feeling smug, she topped the crest and dropped flat, her heart pounding in fear again. *Them! They were down there!* She pushed back, her first impulse to run to Bell. He was useless, but she would be safe with him. He told her the spring was safe, that they wouldn't find her there. Her thoughts whiplashed again. She was safe where she was. She didn't have to go back to Bell, and if they did see her, she had the gun.

As she watched them, fear and panic subsided, and anger grew. Al and Dago rode bikes and Ready and Jolene drove her cruiser, searching the valley floor for her, using her own vehicle to hunt her down like an animal to do awful, heinous things to her.

They kept her from getting to her RV, to radio the police, forcing her to lay motionless in the hot sun. Without salt tablets— her pack was empty—she was in danger of developing the same problem Bell had. It wasn't fair, and the more she thought of it, the more her anger grew.

When they went back to their camp at sunset, she followed. She knew what they would do, eat, drink, smoke, and be merry, if merry was what you could call the perverted things they did. They would intoxicate themselves into a stupor of sleep, and while they slept, she would take back her cruiser. With it, she would go to her RV, reaching it quicker than she would have on foot. The police could be back before dawn.

If they heard her, they would follow her on their bikes. No, she would not let that happen. She would do something to their bikes. How hard could it be? A plan that seemed so simple and easy fell apart when she reached the bikes.

Light was no problem. With the hours they kept, the moon was high, and it was full, lighting the area like a distant flood lamp. She could see four bikes clearly, grateful the disgusting Fingers must have left, but she didn't know what to do to disable them.

A jerk at a cable on the handlebar tipped the bike over. She caught it, sinking under the weight. She let it down, not wanting to wrestle it back up and saw a pool of darkness spread on the ground, gas leaking from the tank.

She smiled to herself at the simplicity of what she could do. All four bikes went on their sides with the tank open. Now let them come after her.

Running to the cruiser, she reached to her pocket for the key. There was none. She slumped, fighting back tears. Bell had her keys, and not just the key to the cruiser. He had her keys to the RV on the same ring. She couldn't even get into it to the radio, let alone drive it away.

She'd been so stupid. The cruiser wouldn't even work with a key anymore. The wires they jerked out dangled by her knee. She reached for them, fully intending to pull them out in angry frustration and had them in her hands when she stopped herself, let go, and backed out. She stood for a second, looking at the outline of the point and back at the cruiser.

Pulling out those wires might disable it beyond repair. Disabling it to keep them from using it while being able to repair it, she did know how to do, and Bell knew how to make those tangling wires work. She had to go back anyway for her keys, and it would serve him right if she made him walk back to do it, no matter how sick he was.

Under the seat where she kept a small supply of tools, she pushed three flares aside to find a screwdriver and stuffed a miniature emergency kit into her pocket. Removing the rotor from beneath the distributor cap was easy work. She felt a flush of satisfaction when it was in her pocket, and she dropped the screwdriver back in its place.

Lowering the seat, she surveyed her work. The cruiser was disabled. She had the only means of fixing it. The bikes were disabled, and they had no gas to replace it. Gas! She twisted around to find the auxiliary tank switch under the dash. It hadn't been turned, more than enough for what she needed. Then she looked back at the bikes. All they had to do was take the gas out of the cruiser to fill their bikes. She had to do something more.

Tipping the seat back, she felt for the screwdriver again. Not knowing anything about the engines on motorcycles, she did know they ran on gas. They had to be similar, only smaller. Something had to be there that she could take off or break to keep them from running.

Her hand found a flare. She pushed it aside impatiently. They were good for nothing. They were out dated and dangerous, a terrible fire hazard.

Fire? Gas? She looked again at the bikes and held the flare. Why not? Fire purified and anything connected with them need purifying. A fire would certainly cause more damage than they could repair.

Three flares came out. Putting the cruiser in neutral, she pushed it away from the bikes, toward Bell's tent. She looked at that tent, thinking she'd like to burn it, too, but went to it instead.

They were too dead to the world to even know she was there, giving her the time to take anything she wanted or needed. Rummaging through his things, up-ending the canvas bag he used for a pillow, brought another surprise. Another gun fell out.

She damned her own stupidity again, shoving the gun back in to take with her along with a box of shells and his change of clothes. It was time he had a bath and put something clean on, even if she was getting used to his smell.

To save room in the bag she put on the black leather jacket she found. The canteen he'd thrown in to keep her alive when she was being punished went in as well. Tired of sleeping on the hard ground, she rolled up and included his sleeping bag. Under the canopy, she searched until she found salt and sugar, essential if she was to get him to his feet at all.

Did she have everything she needed? Food? Not needed, the two stashes he had were more than enough for no longer than she would let him rest. Water was certainly no problem. Getting it into him might be at first as sick as he was. She put several paper cups in. Then some of the plastic spoons, a can opener, and since there was room, a pan.

That she had to make do with what she could carry while they had all they needed chafed at her. Going without for a while would serve them right. A smile came to her lips. Yes, for them to do without would serve them right.

To lose all their supplies would prevent them from sitting around. A long walk to the highway would do them good, and it would clear the way for her when she made Bell come back to start the cruiser.

Bell was strong. With homemade electrolyte water of salt and sugar and morning's rest, he could make the walk. They could be there by late afternoon and still be to the RV with the cruiser, in time to have the police there to meet the others at the highway.

Even if they did make it to the highway first, it would satisfy her just making Bell drive himself to the police. She found another box of salt to pour in their water can but pulled the ice chest away from the canopy. They could have breakfast before their walk and let them figure how to carry the water in the chest to sustain them. If they were too stupid to think of it, they deserved what would happen. They had no business being in the desert if they didn't know how to live with it.

The first flare went at the bikes, the second to the canopy. She stood by Bell's tent, ready to throw the third when the first bike exploded. The sound was enough to wake them out of their stupors. A yell sounded and figures stumbled out to scream and dance helplessly around the fires.

Though Bell's tent was her first choice just because of what happened there, the last flare landed in middle of the three in a row. Depriving them of comfort gave her greater pleasure than burning down Bell's tent.

They were in too much of a stupor to comprehend what was going on. She ran off without any offer of a chase.

———

Exhausted, Annalisa arrived at the narrow canyon. Both guns were hidden away before she approached and sat on the canyon edge with her legs dangling over to look for him and rest. The bright moon cut a strip in the floor. He wasn't in it. On the edges, it was black as pitch.

"Bell." She heard movement directly below her. "Bell?"

His voice was weak and strained. "Where have you been?"

"For a walk. Move over so I can come down."

"I told you not…" His voice choked off, and she strained her eyes to see him on his knees, doubled over with his arms wrapped tight around his middle.

She knew what caused it. "Farther," she ordered. He had to crawl the few feet he made before he doubled up again, holding his stomach and retching in dry heaves. "Farther."

He shook his head and laid down. "Sick."

"Heat exhaustion. You're out of salt. That's what's causing the cramps and vomiting." She dropped the canvas bag down. "How many times have you passed out?" she asked, crawling down behind him.

No answer to her taunt. Not surprising. Though he wasn't quite in the strip of light, he was close enough for her to see he was drawn up in a ball on his side, shaking with chills.

"Get those wet clothes off. I'll fix you some salt water."

She dug a cup out of the bag. He didn't move. "You might at least have been smart enough to keep warm." He still didn't move. "Bell."

She started toward him, but stepped back, not trusting him in the slightest.

When he still didn't move after a push with her foot, she knelt beside him and rolled him to his back. The first thing she did was take her keys from his jacket pocket, but she couldn't find her rings. She dismissed them as unimportant, other than irritation at him for his carelessness with someone else's property. The keys were the most important. If she had to run from him for any reason, she'd have them. Only then did she make the salt and sugar water, guessing the correct amounts.

"Wake up." She shook him. He only rolled his head. She held his head and raised it. "Drink this."

He choked, trying to draw back into a ball. With careful tips of the cup, she coaxed the drink down him. What needed to be done next, disgusted her, but he wouldn't recover from the chills with those wet clothes on. Getting him well enough to walk to the camp was more important than her repugnance in touching him.

She removed his boots and turned her head away. Expecting a rank smell of unwashed feet, she was mildly surprised when there wasn't any odor. The next was the hardest, because of the area it covered. She jerked the pants waistband to open the buttons.

He grabbed at his pants, growling, "Leave me alone."

"You've got to be warm." She gripped the cuffs to pull them off. He kicked at her.

"Leave me alone," he shouted weakly, doubling up again.

"This is a stupid time to get modest," she shouted back.

"Prissy?"

"Who do you think it is? Get those wet pants off. I'll get the blanket."

"Not now, I'm too sick."

If the gun had been in her hand, she'd have killed him then. She vowed she would not do another thing, disgusting animal, thinking that was all she cared about. Not one more thing would she do for him if she had to walk all the way to Phoenix.

He rolled to watch her walk off. His voice shook with the chills. "Did you give me salt?"

"Yes," she snapped, picking up the canteen to fill it.

"Be all right soon."

She knelt at the spring. "Not if you don't get out of those wet clothes."

The cramps weren't just in his stomach. She could see it in the way his legs moved when he staggered to the blanket where she had lain the night before to serve his desires. He fell on it and worked out of the pants.

Shaking violently, huddled in a ball, he called to her. "Prissy?"

"Annalisa," she corrected hatefully.

"Can't call…you that…might ma…make a mistake."

"What mistake?"

"Would you…br-bring me the…other bl…blanket?"

"I'm not your slave," she snapped, but she did need him.

She screwed the cap back on the canteen and tossed the blanket to him, standing back out of reach. He tried to spread the blanket over him, but he shook too hard. Nor could he straighten for the cramps in his legs and abdomen.

"You need more salt."

"Did-didn't think…you'd hav…have…" He gave up finishing it.

She went for the cup. Still staying out of his reach, she set it on the ground by him. "Drink that."

He pushed himself over to reach it and drank too much too fast. It came right back up. He rose up on his hands and knees to vomit in the sand like a sick dog. When it passed, he fell back in the center of the blanket, shaking with the chills and contorted into a ball with the cramps.

Worse off than she thought, she had to do more, move closer, or he would not recover to help her. She covered him. She had to brush the shaggy, long hair back from his face to hold his head up to give him the drink in sips to prevent more vomiting.

Seeming to not know or care what she did, he didn't so much as roll his head to look at her. Within half an hour, the cramps eased, but he still shook with chills that had nothing to do with the temperature.

She touched him to give him more, and he jerked, grabbing for her. "Stop that," she yelled at him. Curling back into a ball, he mumbled something she didn't catch, but anything he had to say was unimportant anyway. "You need more. Do you think you can keep it down now?"

"Try," he told her through chattering teeth.

He couldn't even get it down. He rose up on one elbow, but he shook too hard to hold the cup to his own mouth.

She pushed his hand to steady it and held the back of his head. He shook hard enough to shake her hand as well. She took the cup away from him, and he slipped back to the ground. The chills started harder from the brief exposure to the cool night air.

She tried to lift his head to give him more. He pushed her hand away. "Wait...til...st-stop...shak...ing."

She took the jacket off and spread it over him. That didn't help. Neither did covering him with the sleeping bag. He still shook. Tired and chilled herself, she stretched out beside him, adding her body heat to warm him. When his shaking stopped enough to give him more water, she shivered.

As sick as he was, he still had the strength in his grip. He pulled her under the covers with him, wrapping his arms and legs around her. She might have been able to break away from him, but two things stopped her. Fear was foremost. She did not want to make him mad. Second was the fact she could find an excuse later to move away. Then she could get the gun, without alerting him first.

His shaking stopped, and something else began. She'd been stupid enough to get within touching distance of him and resigned herself to paying the price. She hated his caresses and kisses. She hated the feel of him, but her body betrayed her. In minutes, she turned to him, returning the kisses, welcoming the exploration of his hands, and her hands sought exploration of their own.

Never had sex been like this with her husband. Never! Bell was an animal, and he awoke the animal in her. When he pulled her hips to his, it was her hand that guided him in, the first time she had ever touched a man there.

The position of being on their sides was new and awkward to her, but Bell made it right. He moved her body, positioning her to fit, and the fit seemed perfect, as if the one had been created for the other. He sighed in the pleasure of submersion. She sighed in the pleasure of fullness and the touching of all sensitive areas even in a position foreign to her. The angle of penetration did not matter.

As before, her release seemed to trigger his. While her body quivered and shook, her hands, arms, and legs holding him as tight as humanly possible, his body pulsed, his arms wrapped around her. As each quieted, he snuggled her close to his chest.

"I've got to rest," he whispered.

Content to be held, she was happy he had not moved away, but passion subsided, and likewise the false state of utopia. Repulsion followed over what had happened, the position she was in, and that he had not withdrawn. He still lay within her, and their position held them coupled together by his leg hooked over her hip.

Moving in disgust to free herself, his arms tightened, forcing her to lay still with repugnance growing. For her to submit was one thing, necessary. To respond, to become as much an animal as he was, to her mind, was inexcusable.

She moved slowly, carefully, and he stirred. She waited. As sick as he had been, he had to be exhausted. He had to go into a deep enough sleep for her to get away from him, to remove him from her body. She lay perfectly still, listening to the sound of his breathing, feeling it on her neck. He had to be asleep, a really deep sleep, but when she tensed to move away, his arms tightened, and the thing within her twitched.

Even as she willed herself not to respond, something deep in her abdomen tightened in answer. His thing within her answered in turn, throbbing and growing, swelling to fill her. She would not want him, would not need him, but her body betrayed her. No conscious will prevented what he aroused in her.

His hand pressed her at the back, holding her tight against him. His lips sought hers. His other arm cradled her head, holding it while those lips traveled down to her throat. He began to move, slowly, gently, withdrawing, penetrating.

What he drew from her, she had never known existed, never experienced, and never expected. Her hips answered, just as her insides had. Hands and arms still obeyed commands that came not from her mind but her body until the demands of her body smothered out the wishes of her mind, answering his every move with passion, demanding from him. He obeyed. Her body quivered in spasms, triggering his release yet again.

He rolled to his back in exhaustion, and she rolled, following him, smuggling down close on his chest. Fondling gave her pleasure in the aftermath until his hand stilled, on her breast, and his breathing deepened in sleep. She returned to normalcy, repulsion at herself and hatred for him.

She wiggled a shoulder, moving his arm away. He stirred but did not wake. He stirred again when she slipped away from him, but did not rouse, and she was free.

Afraid to stay one second longer, Annalisa took the time only to find one gun. That and the one canteen was all she took in her haste to be away from him.

Once up the bank, she ran back up the hill to the point. She panted from exertion and fell to her knees to catch her breath. She meant to only lie there for a few minutes until her breathing eased. Instead she fell asleep.

———

Annalisa was in the same place when Bell found her, sleeping with her head on her arms. He ran, rattling rocks, and she woke before he reached her. She rolled to her back with the gun in both hands. He advanced two more steps before he skidded to a stop, realizing she knew who she pointed the gun at and had no intention of lowering it.

"What's that for?" he asked in puzzlement.

"I told you I'd kill you if you ever came near me again."

He squatted down on his haunches. "That was before…" He waved his hand vaguely toward the spring.

"That doesn't change what you did to me."

"What did I do that was so damned awful?"

He could rape her, and it wasn't anything to be upset about? It wasn't reason to hate him? She couldn't believe her ears, and his callousness infuriated her. She rose up slowly, holding the gun with both hands, pointing it at his head. He rose up with her, holding his hand in front of him.

"You bastard."

She wanted to kill him. She wanted to kill him so badly her hands shook as she pulled on the trigger. She ground her teeth together, using all her strength to force a gun that wouldn't fire.

He rushed forward to twist the gun out of her hands and backed off staring at her.

"All of that…" He pointed towards the spring with the gun. "…was an act? Why the hell didn't you just kill me last night?"

"I needed you, or I would have."

"You don't now?" He looked at the gun in his hand and threw it.

"I'd walk before I'd go through another night like that."

"You liked it, lady," he snarled.

Yes, she had, and she hated him even more for that. She hated him for saying it and leaped at him with her nails aimed for his face.

He batted her arms away with one hand and shoved her with the other. "Go back to the spring."

"To wait you at your leisure?" she asked hatefully from the ground.

"Or yours?" he countered in a snarl. "It wasn't all me, Pretty Prissy."

She threw rocks at him. He forgot the rape and only tormented her with the other. The first rock he dodged. The second he took on the arm to protect his head. Between them, she shouted, "I would never have submitted to you—"

He landed on top of her, forcing her arms back over her head. "Submitted?" he demanded. "You wanted it. All that sweet innocence was an act. You're as big a whore as Ready."

Unable to reach his mouth with her hands to shut him up, she delivered a head-butt to his mouth. His lip smashed against her skull, and she scampered to her feet when he recoiled. Before he recovered or realized what she was after, she dove for the gun, pointed it again at his head, unwavering with both thumbs pulling the hammer back.

Blood dribbled from his lips as he stared at her face, then the gun. When he turned his back on her and started down the hill, she screamed at him. "Come back here! You're getting my cruiser for me!"

Walking backwards, he yelled back at her. "If you're smart, you'll go back to the spring. If they find you, they can have you. I won't fight for you again." He jerked to a stop when dirt sprayed his feet.

"You're getting my cruiser for me."

He wiped blood from his mouth with the back of his hand, glaring at her. "You should have stuck to using your body."

"You bastard," she growled, firing again.

He flinched when the shot buzzed by his head. She could see his beard pulsate as he clenched and unclenched his jaw. In such a rage his body trembled, he swiped again at his mouth and deliberately turned his back to her.

"Damn you, come back here."

"Get yourself another stud," he called back over his shoulder.

"Damn you!" Dragging the hammer back, she fired again, screaming the same thing each time she fired. She still screamed when the hammer fell on an empty chamber, and he disappeared from sight.

"I hope they find you!" she screamed after him. "I hope they do everything they said they would! I hope you die, screaming in agony! Damn you! Damn you!"

He turned her into the whore he called her and condemned her for it. He raped her, beat her, humiliated, and terrorized her. Then he walked away, through with her. No, expecting her to wait for him to return when he wanted to use her again.

That wasn't going to happen. She would make him pay, kill him, if she had to chase him to the ends of the world. First, she needed more shells, and damned herself for not taking the time to get them and the other gun before she left.

Back at the spring, fatigue from her run wasn't her only problem. Fumbling with shaking fingers of enraged frustration, growling with fury, the spent shells refused to expel without perfect alignment and fresh shells slipped from her fingers.

Furiously resenting every second longer that it took her, she still took the time to check the other gun to be sure it was loaded. No more stupid mistakes, she swore, running with a gun in each hand. She slipped, tripped, stumbled, fell, and jumped back to her feet. This time he would pay for what he had done.

A breeze rose and the sky darkened as the desert she loved simulated her rage with fury of its own. Lightening flashed in the hills behind her. Thunder rolled in the distance, and the breeze built to wind.

The graceful movement the breeze gave the jojoba and desert bloom altered when the breeze picked up to a wild whipping wind, bending even the larger mesquite and Palo Verde trees while her rage left room only for instinct. Reason would have had her jump into the wash not fall headlong when the ground disappeared from beneath her feet. The fall knocked the breath from her lungs and sense into her head.

Killing herself with exertion, pumping the moisture out of her body, exhausting herself was senseless. She knew where he was going, back to the camp to friends he didn't know would no longer be there.

She sat there, drawing deep breaths to her aching lungs. As the pain in her chest eased, her heart lessened its pounding, and the roaring in her ears quieted. She was able to hear again, and she heard them.

Them! Him! All the same. All needed killing. All were not fit to live, to continue to torture and murder. She had the guns. They didn't have any.

Her breathing was even and smooth as she walked toward the sound of their voices, calm when she climbed the bank of the wash. She couldn't see them, but the words carried clearly in the wind to tell her what they did.

"Ever done it to a burnt hole?" Fingers asked, and the wind carried the smell of smoke.

Al answered. "Yeah."

"I ain't," Dago cried, excitement high in his voice.

"It's nice," Fingers told him. "You burn it, blister it good, then when you go in, those blisters break, wetting it up nice while you rub them raw. They scream their guts out."

The screen of desert brush whipped in the wind. She saw Blake's head dance and had sight as well for direction.

"They really scream when you cum."

"Cum's full of salt. Did you know that, Bell?" Fingers asked.

He was already with them. He would be the one she would shoot first, no longer afraid of them, no longer needing his protection. She had the guns.

The wash she fell into and crawled out of bent back on itself. They were in it, lower than she was. She moved more carefully, the brush between them thinning. She could see Al and Dago's heads.

Blake danced around Fingers. "Gonna play hide and seek? Find it through the pants."

"Gonna burn them right off." Fingers blew on the end of a burning stick he held. "Get the honey hole up."

Much the same thing happened to Annalisa then as when she saw what they did to Bunny. Fingers moved toward Al and Dago, and she saw that those two held someone between them.

Fingers held the stick in front of him, as if it were an extension of his penis. He moved forward while the victim struggled helplessly.

"I'm going to find me a nice sweet—"

Annalisa blew his head off. She fired again, and Blake screamed. Three more evenly spaced shots with the gun bucking with recoil in her hands while she moved to find new targets, tracking those who ran. With only a slight pause, she dropped the empty gun. One arm rose, swiping at tears from windblown dirt in her eyes. The other pulled the second gun from her waistband.

Two more shots and she no longer had targets from where she stood. She dropped down to the wash bottom, running by the three left behind. Bikes roared to life out of her sight and range.

With calm acceptance, she gave up the chase. They were beyond reach. She turned to those still in the wash. The gun still held ready her hands.

Blake sobbed hysterically. He crawled backwards as well as he could, holding an arm that spurted blood. He was not a danger. She ignored him.

Fingers laid on his back with his arms out-flung. The sand was dark around his mutilated head. He was no danger, but she hadn't succeeded completely. She had not killed all those she meant to kill, but she had stopped them.

10

PRATTERS RECEIVED A CALL LATE THAT AFTERNOON. THE BOYS IN the L.A. office had done a quick job on running down Caroline/Bunny's name. The only catch was they called it in to the supervisor of the Phoenix office, who wanted to give it to him personally. Pratters stood across the desk where the man glanced through the file.

"Thanks," Pratters said, knowing that wasn't why he'd been called in.

"Have you seen the papers?"

"No."

He unfolded the paper on his desk and handed it to him. "The press is raising hell. Someone gave them the details on Bell's file and the information that the FBI is going to, 'allow him freedom to continue his sexual attacks—frustrated and perverted by his impotency—on innocent young women that end in brutal, sadistic deaths in exchange for information on others who do the same thing.' It goes on about—"

"Does it bother to say we could never prove he actually did kill anyone?"

"It tells of the seven girls he claimed that were never seen again, after he took them off and returned covered in blood."

"All hearsay."

"You know damned well what he's been doing," the man retorted.

Pratters answered in kind. "Knowing and proving are, and always have been, two different things. He's one of the smart ones. Why do you think he takes them away from the camp to do it? No witnesses. Any who saw him take them aren't going to tell even that much in court. They're too damned afraid of him. The only body we ever found was so decomposed we couldn't identify it enough to even begin to prove it was one of the ones he took. The only thing we could prove was at one time he was within thirty miles of where she was buried. Take that to court and see how far it gets you."

"Pratters, you've got one of the best systems of informants around. You've got to be able to have gotten more on him than that."

"If I had, he wouldn't have been here."

"He has to go to trial. The public won't be satisfied with anything less," he half-shouted.

"That's the only satisfaction they'll get. They'll never convict him of murder."

"It was his gun that killed them all."

"A gun of the same caliber, and Al and Dago were self-defense, even if it was the same gun. There's a witness to that. After the beating he took, he can claim the same for Fingers and Blake, if he admits to shooting them."

"It wasn't self-defense if he provoked the fight," the man argued.

"Can you prove he did?" He went back to skimming the paper in his hands. "With Bell's condition, any lawyer would have a field day in court. The only bullet for ballistics was the one in Bell's chest. Assuming he only carried five shells in his gun, which he can easily claim, all of his shots were accounted for, and there's no evidence he had extras. There could be a gun that wasn't found or there could have been more of them out there that didn't get kil——"

The man said, "I see you've gotten to the kicker."

"Why didn't you tell me about this?" he demanded.

"I was going to," he said, surprised by Pratters' reaction. "It's only a possibility. They could just be making a big deal out of a coincidence. Girls that age take off all the time. There's really nothing to say there's any connection."

"She was seen in Cave Creek the same night bikers were."

The man looked from Pratters to the paper. "That's something I was going to ask you about. According to Bell's MO, he only took girls that hadn't been initiated. The doctor's report shows that this Caroline King had been subjected to that kind of treatment repeatedly. Is it possible there was another girl out there?"

Pratters stared hard at one line. Helene Fields was last seen filling the tank of her seventy Jeep. "It's possible."

A heavy sigh sounded from across the desk. "I hoped there wasn't. The county boys are going back out to extend their search." He sighed again. "They're concentrating on shallow graves."

"I'm going to the hospital."

———

The trip netted him nothing. Bell's condition was reported to him in the same vague terms, somewhat improved, but no indication of survival. Jane Doe had a previous visit from the county boys shortly before Pratters got there. The result was hysteria and heavy sedatives to calm her down. She was sleeping and would be well into the night.

With nothing for him to do there, he returned to his motel and called the secret number.

The report he received began with an interesting fact. "He got fragged by one of his own men."

"Revenge of some kind?"

"No, nothing like that. The guy got shot and dropped the grenade. The whole unit was pinned down, then overran. Your boy was one of those listed missing in action. He turned up six weeks later, more dead than alive. He'd been taken and tortured."

He paused to clear his throat before going on. "They sent a woman into him. He was cut to hell down there, abdomen, groin, and thighs. She stimulated him. Once she got him up, she laughed and walked out." He cleared his throat again. "He raped her."

"What!"

The man half-laughed. "That's what I said. The doctor said that was his reaction too. He still isn't sure it actually happened. It could have been your guy just wanted to badly enough he hallucinated it. The doctor said it was a physical improbability, but after getting to know him, he isn't too sure if he made up his mind to do it, he wouldn't have."

"Ruthless."

"Determined was the word the doctor used. He makes up his mind to do something and does. Getting away from them or walking out was a physical improbability, but he did."

"How did he get away?"

"Played opossum. After the thing with the woman stopped working, they went to the old-fashioned stuff, boots and fists. They had him in pretty bad shape, figured he was out, and turned their backs on him. He thinks he killed both, but one slipped enough it may have saved his neck."

"He broke their necks?"

"Damn sure tried, but he said the second one was sloppy. His words, he had to hurry, and he was weak."

"What a shame."

"They were killing him," the other man retorted. "It was nothing but pure guts that got him back to our lines the shape he was in."

"What are you getting defensive for?"

"I don't know. The way you said it, I guess. This guy went

through hell for years with all that surgery, and he never got over what they did to him."

"In what way?"

"Impotency. They've had him coming in for that for years. He called a halt to it two years ago. He just stopped going. That thing six months ago was for pain in the genitals. He stayed long enough to find out it wasn't physical, and then checked out again."

"Not physical? You mean he's a nut?"

"Not the way you mean. I told you the business with the woman stopped working. It wasn't physical then, either. He turned it off. He got a lot of infection in the wounds before he got back to our lines. They did a lot of surgeries on him. The damage was repaired. There was no reason he would not have been sensitive again, but he wasn't. He either couldn't or wouldn't turn it back on."

"What's the pain?"

"The doctor thinks it's trying to turn itself on, and he's fighting it."

"Why the hell would he do that?"

"The doctor says there are a couple of possibilities including guilt over raping or thinking he raped that woman, the sub-conscious association of pain with arousal, that he doesn't want it, or a combination of any or all of them."

Pratters considered it for a moment. "What's the background?"

"Not much on it yet. He was a career man, which explains how much older he is than the average Nam vet. The only other family is a sister. For all the doctor knew of what happened in Nam, he knew very little about anything else."

"Where's the sister now?"

"I don't know."

"Locate her and get all you can on him."

Pratters hung up, gazing thoughtfully. He knew now what made Bell tick. He was a man who had gone to war and found he liked it. The sex thing was just a new twist to an old story resulting from every war that had ever been fought. Bell thrived on the adrenalin high of combat. He enjoyed pitting his strength and cunning against an enemy. He sought it out and found it in the gangs, but he didn't want to spend time in prison. The answer to that was cutting a deal with Pratters, and that in itself was a contest and challenge of cunning.

Like all men, he had a weak spot. Bell didn't want anyone to know who he really was, either because he didn't want the sister to know what he was doing or because he kept that identity as a backup for escape if things got too hot for him.

Pratters was going to use that weak spot to gain control. Bell would dance to his tune when this was over—if he could wash the mess Bell had left behind. If not, Bell would be terminated.

There were definite advantages to having connections in more than two organizations.

———

The night passed without word of Bell. The morning came, bright and already hot. Pratters went straight to the hospital. The guard at the door nodded to him with animosity thick enough to cut. Pratters nodded back, unaffected. He glanced in at Bell, who looked no different. The nurse informed him Bell's vital signs had stabilized and were somewhat stronger. She would tell him no more, and Doctor Thristen was not available.

He went to Jane Doe's room, only to find he couldn't get in there. The county boys beat him in again, and if Jane ran true to form, she wouldn't be in any condition to talk to him when they got through.

His temper was very close to exploding when a nurse tapped him on the shoulder. He spun around at her, making her flinch. "What is it?"

"Doctor Thristen called. He'd like you in the ICU as soon as…" Her voice faded as Pratters walked off.

Thristen met him at the door. "I don't believe this," he said, and the look on his face proved it.

Pratters peered around him at Bell's cubical. The machines were still working, so Bell wasn't dead. Thristen waved a piece of paper in front of him. Pratters wanted an explanation, not notes. He glanced at it, only to snatch it from Tristen's fingers.

There were three letters, barely readable for the clumsiness of them. The first was a 'P', the second an 'R' with a third, no more than a single waving line. He looked at the doctor.

"He woke up." He sounded as if he still didn't believe it. "As soon as he realized he couldn't talk for the trach, he tried scratching on the sheet. I told him to rest, but he persisted so I stuck a pencil in his hand. He got that much done, enough so I understood and took it away from him." He finished the last, following Pratters.

Pratters stopped at the foot of the bed. Thristen moved around him. "He won't be very clear," he warned. He moved to the side. "Mr. Bell," he said without much volume.

Bell's eyelids fluttered. Thristen said the name again, and the eyes opened. Pratters shoved Thristen aside.

"You're ready to deal now, aren't you, you son-of-a-bitch?"

Bell's gaze had the unfocused look of drugs and weakness. His index finger scratched at the sheet.

"No writing," Thristen ordered. "You," he pointed a finger at Pratters, "remember he can't talk. Keep any questions to yes or no." He pointed at Bell. "You conserve your strength. Move your index finger for yes, middle for no."

Pratters dropped his hand over Bell's. "Did you kill them all? Joey? Fingers? Blake? Al? Dago? Did you burn the camp?"

Pratters half-shook his head at the answers and settled back on his heels. "You don't give a damn about anything as long as you save your own neck." He didn't expect an answer. He got it. The index finger under his hand moved. "What? Money?" he asked in scorn.

He jerked his hand up to stare at Bell's. Bell began tracing letters again, but Thristen shoved Pratters aside and stopped Bell.

"That's enough for now. You're too weak to continue."

Bell's eyes closed. Pratters pulled at the doctor to move him out of the way. "Bell, what the hell did you mean?"

Thristen shoved back. He turned on Pratters. "Get out now or I'll see to it you never come back."

Pratters backed off. Though it galled him, retreat was the only wise thing to do. He had only himself to blame for not asking the most important question first. He stared at Bell, rubbing the palm of his hand with his fingertips. He shrugged, turned, and walked out.

That last answer hadn't meant anything. Bell was just too weak to make sense. He was probably only trying to move Pratters hand away to write what he wanted. That last flicker couldn't have meant anything. Bell was the worst kind of bastard. Nothing held any value to him beyond his own safety, and he would use anything to assure that. The movement had only been to push Pratters' hand away to write out letters. What had he tried to draw out before Thristen stopped him? W-o?

Nagging at it accomplished nothing. He'd find out when he talked to Bell again. No good brooding over the problem of Helene Fields, either. That was the first question he should have asked, shielding the answer away from the doctor. The second should have been about Mrs. Summers.

The last was one thing he could do something about. He drove to her house only to find she wasn't home. Neither neighbor, on either side, knew where she was or when she'd left. One didn't even know who she was by her name. The other did say she was often gone for long periods of time.

Had she skipped? Had his badgering frightened her into running? If so, why?

He walked back to the front door, sheltered from view in a patio. The lock was easy to jimmy. He had the house to himself and searched through it carefully.

The rest of the house gave the same impression as the living room, neat, clean, well furnished with expensive furniture and good taste. Her clothing was all modest, the majority of the blouses and dresses, long sleeved. The bathroom held the usual womanly things and nothing masculine left from her husband.

As neat as she was, it was easy to move, look, and replace without disturbing. A quick search showed nothing out of tune. Even the second bathroom, converted into a darkroom, was neat and tidy. A file held indexed pictures of desert scenes, some with and some without animals. She didn't seem to have any works in progress. The counters and vats were clean and dry.

Had she already finished with the film she took while out the last time? Or had she been too busy to take any in the three days she would have had to have been out there because of flooding?

Wandering back to the family room and desk, he hoped to find something he needed in the neat, tidy records she kept. He pulled a drawer open, slammed it shut, and hurried back to the living room.

The car he heard sat in the drive, waiting for the garage door to open. Gleaming with a fresh wash job, water still dripped from the fender wells. It wasn't a Jeep, but a Toyota Land Cruiser was close enough for him.

She looked out of place in the casual setting of that kind of machine. She didn't look the outdoor, rough and ready type with her well coiffure hair hidden under a scarf and the pantsuit crisp and pressed. The only thing that did fit was the cleanliness. Dirt would look out of place in her garage. She pulled in next to the gleaming clean town car, and the door closed.

Annalisa came in the back door, straight into the kitchen. She never paused, dropping the things she carried on the table as she passed to reach the phone.

Something thudded heavily on the hard, smooth surface, and Pratters knew it wasn't the oversized briefcase. It had to be something in the canvas bag, something metallic.

She startled when he appeared and recoiled slightly when he took the phone from her hand. She recovered quickly, and instead of grabbing for the phone, she calmly suppressed the bar to disconnect the call.

"You didn't give them time to answer."

"What are you doing in here?"

"The door was open," he lied, handing her the phone. She hung it up, walking around the bar to the refrigerator, apparently not caring when he moved closer to the table.

"I didn't see your car," she told him.

Pratters smiled and didn't explain. He'd parked in front of a house farther down rather than wait for the mailman to leave the area in front of hers empty. Who would have thought his impatience would have been so rewarding?

He did care about what was on that table. The case looked like her, neat and clean. He had no doubt it contained her camera. The bag was what fascinated him. Worn and dirty, it was not something you would picture her so much as touching.

Fighting down anger at himself, he had no compassion for the signs of fatigue he saw in her face. He should have thought of her going back. An amateur nearly always did, fearing they had overlooked something.

"What did you forget?" he asked, his voice taunting.

She gazed at him over the glass she had filled with green liquid. "I wasn't aware I had."

He tried bluntness and surprise again. "I know you're Prissy."

He did surprise her, enough at least that she blinked those dark blue eyes of hers. She stared at him for a moment, blinked again, and lowered the glass. "I can't help what you think."

"Prissy had a Jeep."

"Four-wheel drives are very handy to have in the desert. That's why I got the cruiser."

He spun around and snatched up the canvas bag. She made no move to stop him, stated flatly, instead, "Be careful. That's a three-hundred-dollar lens."

"That's worth going back for."

She looked straight at him, holding the glass in front of her. "I took it out with me this morning."

He could feel the round cylinder through the stiff, dirty material. He started to put it down, feeling defeat. Another thought occurred to him. He opened the bag instead. If she had gone back to get it, it would have been out in the rain. The black metal surface of the telephoto lens gleamed shiny and clean to mock him.

In frustration, he shook the bag at her. "This isn't yours. It's not like you at all."

"It is a ratty old thing. I keep it for sentimental reasons, and it is handy."

He dropped it on the table. "I know you're hiding something, and I will prove it."

11

The Victim

Fingers tied a victim differently than Ready. She'd tied Bell's feet with the ankles crossed. When she forced his legs apart, the ropes tightened, but movement was allowed. Fingers had tied ankle bone to ankle bone. When they forced the legs apart, each blocked the other, forcing the ankles to bend at an unnatural angle. The stick was shorter, by necessity, not consideration, and Ready had not sharpened the stick on both ends. The right pant leg was soaked with blood. Only the seam on the left held the stick back from as deep a penetration. Blood only darkened the edges there.

All of Finger's ropes were tighter, cutting into the flesh around the wrists. Blood trickled in rivulets down the hands. The hands were held against the feet, instead of a short distance away. The neck rope was in the front, tied from knee, around the neck, and back to the opposite knee.

They had practice in how to tie their victims, holding them in a helpless kneeling, bowed position to be manipulated and mutilated. Already, and the real torture had not begun, there was agony. A screen of long hair masked the face, but blood dripped to the ground between the thighs.

Straightening was impossible for the neck rope and just as impossible to lie down. Falling to the side wasn't even possible for the distance between the knees. Yes, they'd had practice.

Blake screamed and sobbed when Annalisa moved toward them. She glanced at him, feeling no compassion for his fear or pain. She looked at Fingers the same way, feeling no remorse for his death or guilt with the knowledge she had caused it. He had once been a living thing, not fit to call human, merely living. He was no more. His feet lay a foot from the bound knees of his victim, his body no more than a lump of filth. She leaned over him, only long enough to take the knife from his belt. She needed it to cut the ropes.

Screaming, Blake staggered to his feet. Gripping his spurting, dangling arm, he ran, as much as he could. Annalisa didn't bother to look up or shoot at him again. Nothing mattered to her then but stopping the agonizing pain the ropes were causing. She dropped the gun and severed both ropes on the right knee. Knowing it caused more pain but had to be done, she pushed the leg to free the stick and threw the stick away from them.

She severed the ropes on the left knee and unwound what was left from the neck. The only sound was labored breathing, broken in gasps and stifled moans. When the ropes in the back separated, the arms fell from their own weight, not response from numb muscles.

1 2

PRATTERS FOUND THE DOCTOR IN HIS OFFICE. PERMISSION TO SHOW him in was given reluctantly. "I wish you'd let me attend some of my other patients," Thristen said as the door closed.

"How is he?"

Thristen looked up from the papers on his desk. "I..." The phone rang. "Excuse me. Yes, Mary, what is it? No, that's all right, put her on...Doctor Thristen...No, it's no bother. He's showing some improvement...I wouldn't feel safe in saying that. He did regain consciousness briefly this morning, but I still will not say he's out of danger."

He glanced up as Pratters edged closer. Before he could stop him, Pratters switched on the speaker.

"What are you doing?" Thristen asked.

"What?" the caller said.

"Nothing, I was talking to someone else."

The line went dead, but Pratters heard enough. She was worried and couldn't stand getting only vague information from the news.

Thristen was furious. "What do you think you're doing?"

"How often does she call?"

"That's none of your business."

"It is my business. You were ordered not to give out information on him."

"She has a right to know."

"She could be anyone."

"She happens to be the woman who found him and saved his life. She's afraid she failed to do everything she could have. She blames herself for not doing enough, and she's naturally concerned about him."

"Did she?"

"What?" Thristen asked, momentarily lost.

"Did she do all she could?"

That angered the doctor. "All anyone could have done under those circumstances."

"Because she flipped out?"

"She may have gone into shock, but she did all that could have been done by a layman in the field. If she had not closed off that wound, he would have died in minutes."

"He could have done as much by jabbing in his thumb."

"He wasn't conscious."

"That you know of."

"What are you getting at?" Thristen asked, the tone of his voice changing rapidly.

"Nothing." Pratters walked out, straight to the ICU ward. He stepped up to Bell's bedside.

Thristen stepped in behind him. "Standing there like a vulture won't accomplish anything."

"Why is it every time I come in here, you show up?"

"I don't trust you."

"I told you I want him alive."

"I've seen the way you look at him, so naturally, I don't believe you." He motioned the nurse out and took her place on the left side of the bed, across from Pratters.

Just as he touched Bell's wrist to take a pulse, the hiss-thump rhythm of the respirator broke. Pratters looked behind him at the machine. "What's wrong?" He turned back and saw that Bell's eyes were open.

"Didn't mean to startle you," Thristen told Bell. "I didn't think you'd be awake again this soon." Bell's finger scratched the sheet. "No writing."

Pratters quickly covered Bell's hand. Bell's eyes swung around to gaze at him. "Who shot you? Al? Dago? What did you mean this morning?"

With a jerk, he rolled his hand aside to stare at Bell's. He did the same thing he had that morning, jabbed him with a fingernail.

Free of Pratters' hand, he started scratching at the sheet. Pratters watched, waiting for more than had been traced out that morning. Thristen stopped him, coming swiftly around the bed.

"That's enough."

"Not by a long shot." He looked at Bell. "I've finally got a clue to where you came from and—"

"That's enough," Thristen cried, alarm creeping into his voice.

Bell's eyes closed, but Pratters knew he wasn't asleep and said so.

Thristen leaned over the bed with a stethoscope to Bell's chest. "Relax," he said, "just relax. Don't excite yourself."

"Don't you read the papers?" Pratters demanded. "Don't you know what you're wasting your compassion on?"

"If you don't get out of here, I'll have you thrown out."

"I'll be back."

———

Pratters didn't get to Jane Doe's room before the county boys intercepted him, pushing him into a conference room when he was already furious. He'd let his curiosity get the better of his common sense and blown another chance of asking Bell about Mrs. Summers and/or Prissy. The result of his mood was cruel bluntness.

They showed him a picture of Helene Fields, telling him they believed she might be a victim. They asked what, from his experience, they might expect to find if they were correct.

"A mutilated body."

"Is it possible they initiated her?"

"She's a cow. They wouldn't have taken her for anything but fun. That means a blow out." They were all insulted over the description he used of the heavyset girl. He didn't care. "She's aggressive, and she would have fought them."

"What makes you say she's aggressive?" one interrupted to ask.

"It wasn't her Jeep she took off in."

They withdrew behind sullen faces. Helene had at first been reported for car theft, not as a missing person. After a fight with her boyfriend, she drove off in his Jeep.

"Unless you've got more to tie her to them than being in the same town the same night, I wouldn't—"

"We found the Jeep, deliberately ran off the road."

"Near there?"

"Within ten miles of where we found Bell."

———

When Pratters did get in to see Jane Doe, she was too drowsy to make much coherent conversation, even for her.

"Caroline, you told me Prissy tried to kill Bell. How?"

"Hit him with the Jeep."

"Did she?"

She shrugged and snuggled down to get more comfortable. "He was hurt. It was hard for him to walk. It sounded terrible." She yawned wide and loud, shaking her head against sleep. "She screamed and screamed. Ready said he always could. She said he lied, and we all knew she was right when he…" She broke for another yawn. "…Prissy."

"Are you saying Bell raped her?" he asked incredulously.

"She screamed and cried." Losing the battle to keep her eyes open, her voice dropped to a murmur.

"Caroline." He shook her slightly. "Did you see him rape her?"

"Tent," she said with a shake of her head. "Gone when Al…" She yawned. "Looked…for…"

He shook her, then again, harder, to no avail. Giving up, Pratters walked back to the hall, rubbing the back of his neck. No damned wonder she wanted to kill him, but was it possible?

He went back to a phone, choosing a booth close to the hospital.

————

Pratters gave a name and title just as false as the man who first spoke to the doctor listed as Bell's at the V.A. hospital.

"How impotent is he?"

"I would like to know what this is all about before I release any more information."

"To save doubling over, what were you told before?"

"Nothing. He showed me his credentials and asked questions."

That gave Pratters room to concoct any story that suited his purpose. "He's been accused of rape and murder."

There was a moment's pause while the shock passed. When the doctor answered, it was definite. "He would not have done anything like that."

Pratters did not challenge or argue with him. "If you can swear under oath that there is no possibility he could under any circumstances, medically impossible, the case would fold." With no immediate answer, Pratters knew it would have been negative. "From what I got from my report, it isn't," he said, pressing his advantage.

"No, but not rape," the doctor answered.

"I also understand that he suffered from impotence as the result of guilt complexes deriving from—"

"Your man did not get that from me, and the cause of his impotency is not guilt."

"What is it then?"

"I believe it's a desire to avoid something that would make him vulnerable."

"Can you explain that a little more clearly?" Pratters asked.

"Two-fold, virile men need relief for a buildup of physical needs, the physical response made him vulnerable to pain."

"There are plenty of women who'll take care of that without asking for more than pay."

"Not for him. He's actually rather Victorian in his views about sex. He does not believe in it without love."

Pratters forced himself not to laugh. "After what he did in Nam?"

"If it happened, it was not for sexual gratification."

"What then?"

"Punishment."

"Intercourse with a whore?"

He answered slowly. "I think I shouldn't say anything more to anyone but his lawyer."

"I'm about as close as you can get without taking this to court. I think he's been through enough. I'd hate to see him go through a trial unnecessarily."

"Are you a friend of his?"

"I've known him for years. Look, we both know what he's been through. I've been out of touch with him for a few years, and I nearly fell over when I saw his name."

"You're a friend, but he's never discussed any of this with you?"

"Hell no, you know how closed mouth he is. I don't believe in a million years he did this, and this isn't all they want to charge him with. They've got several unsolved rape cases they're going to try to pin on him. I need all the help you can give me."

"I don't know that anything I can tell you isn't going to make it sound worse."

"It depends. Did he beat her when he raped her?"

"No, he only hit her once to stun her. He was too weak to even fight her."

"How did he punish her then?"

"Just by doing it," he said, sounding flustered. "She was a small woman."

"So?"

"If you want it in blunt layman's terms, he's hung in proportion the way he's built. He knew if he didn't hold back, he'd hurt her."

"From experience?" he asked, not hiding the sarcasm in his tone.

"Not like you mean," he retorted.

"How then, and, Doc, don't get mad with me. I'm trying to think of all the questions the D.A. is going to ask. That will be one of them, believe me.

There was a silence of reluctance. "He isn't going to like his personal affairs being talked about like this."

"Either that or trial."

"Yes, I know. As for your last question, he found out with his wife." Pratters perked up only to be disappointed as the doctor continued. "She divorced him, unable to cope with his injuries."

Pratters made no comment on how carefully the doctor said she dumped him. "Did he resent her for it?"

"No, he was actually relieved. Their relationship had become strained even before he went overseas."

"He couldn't satisfy her?"

"More the reverse. She couldn't accommodate him. They were only hurting each other emotionally."

The doctor was right. He was building a good case against Bell. "Let's go back to the woman in Nam. If, as you say, he didn't hold back, couldn't he have caused a rupture, possible death."

"The most would have been temporary pain, possibly some ripping of the vulva. His purpose was more insult and teaching her a lesson than actually pain. He had consulted a physician when it became apparent there was a problem with his wife."

The next question was more curiosity than anything. "Was his wife too small or him too big?"

"A little of both. Percentage wise, he should not have that problem. It was just unfortunate that those two fell together."

"He wouldn't have the same effect on every woman?"

"Percentages would be more toward wouldn't."

"Why didn't he want sex?"

"I'll answer that the way he did me. 'Should I try them out until I find one that fits, and maybe not be able to stand her or fall in love first and end up with the same problem?' For him, it was easier not to have the need."

"It seems he did. Wasn't that what the pain was?"

"I believe so. The sex drive is very strong. He's striving to suppress a normal function. His body is fighting to get it back. To control it, the mind is producing pain."

"Which is winning?"

"The mind or there wouldn't be pain."

"I see." Caroline, if he understood her correctly, said Bell had raped Prissy. "What could tilt the scales to the body winning?"

"The most important factor would be him wanting to."

"Just like that?"

"No, probably not," he said with a sigh. "He's suppressed it for so long."

"What would speed it up, drugs? Alcohol?"

"Or hypnosis. Anything that would weaken his subconscious control. If he met someone he cared enough about to take a chance, we could use drugs or hypnosis to help him get past the physiological blocks. He's refused both."

Bell refused drugs and avoided excessive alcohol. "How did he look when he was in six months ago?"

"Tired, a little run down."

"I meant in appearance."

"The way he usually looks."

"Was his hair long, short? Was he wearing a beard or mustache?"

"His hair was a little longer than usual, more like they're wearing it now and no mustache. He's always clean shaven."

"Did he seem bitter or resentful about anything?"

"No, he was as even tempered and pleasant as always. He has the most amazing ability to accept life, its bad points, then anyone I've ever met."

"Yeah," Pratters commented dryly. "Do you know why he dropped out like he did two years ago?"

"I should imagine it was because he had nothing to hold him in one place any longer with his sister in college. He was restless, which is understandable after all those years in and out of the hospital."

"How did he get along with her?" he asked, wishing he hadn't bound himself up with his lie about knowing the man for years.

"You must know how she idolized him. He just realized they were too dependent on each other. She wasn't making a life of her own. I believe it was the first fight they ever had when he forced her to go to college."

"It's been so long since I've seen her, how old is she now?"

"Oh, she must be about twenty-one or two."

"Which college was it?"

"I don't remember the name, but it was in Frisco, I believe. She ought to be just about to graduate." Pratters could visualize him straighten by the tone of his voice with the next question. "Why can't you ask him that?"

"He won't tell me," he said cheerfully before hanging up. He had the handle he needed now.

Bell hid his past for the sister's sake. Now he'd do what Pratters told him to keep it that way.

He couldn't see Bell again so soon no matter how hard he wanted to hit him with it. He did call Dr. Thristen. He asked one question, "Could those fractured ribs have been caused from impact, say with a car?"

"Possibly. Why?"

Pratters hung up instead of answering. If Annalisa Summers was Prissy, she did not have to shoot Bell, as he first suspected. She had a much bigger weapon with a heavy angle-iron tow bar bracket in the front to mangle and cripple.

———

Pratters began to doubt Mrs. Summers was home before she finally answered. She opened the door wearing the standard long sleeves and high-necked blouse over loose fitting pants.

"I'm working. If you want to talk to me, it'll have to be in the darkroom."

She turned as she said it. He hurried to keep pace. She waited at the door for him to catch up. "The space is limited, as you know. You'll have to stand against the door."

"How would I know?" he asked innocently.

She ignored the question, going to the far end to turn off a buzzer. The room hadn't seemed so small until the door was shut. Turning sideways left barely enough room for her to walk straight down the narrow aisle between the tub and a counter to reach another counter running along the back wall.

The area above the tub had wires strung across it. From those, prints and strips of film hung to dry.

He watched her remove a strip of film from a container of chemicals. In a short time, it hung to drip dry. She moved to an enlarger, halfway down the room from him. In the confining space, she was no more than two feet away with no bright lights behind her to throw her face in shadow. She went one better.

"Get the light, please."

After Pratters switched off the overhead light, the dim white light coming from the enlarger did more to distort and hide her facial expression than the shadows had while she adjusted metal bands on the base to the size print she wanted.

"How's your hands?" he asked in his friendliest voice.

"Fine," she answered tonelessly.

"I'm glad to hear that. I guess they were cut up pretty bad."

An envelope of paper came from below the counter. "You were misinformed. They're minor."

The white light on the enlarger went out and a red light went on.

"Good. Looks like you've been busy."

She continued with her work as if he wasn't there talking to her. A sheet of paper from the envelope went under the bands.

"Lose too much time keeping Bell company?"

She didn't answer. The enlarger white light went back on.

"Would you like to hear what I think happened?"

"Not particularly." The lights flashed from white to red. She moved to the trays of chemicals at the end counter with the exposed sheet.

He told her, anyway, watching her closely for reaction. "The bunch of them found Prissy's Jeep. Bell went back to look for the owner. He found her. I think that was you."

"You've mentioned that before."

"Yes, I have." She moved back to the enlarger. He leaned closer. "He took her back to camp. She was with them a couple of days before he lost a claim fight. She—you—got away, at least from the camp."

The red light flashed, and she fit another sheet of paper under the bands. The only one showing tension was Pratters. The lights flashing back and forth from red to white wore on his nerves.

"While he was unconscious the women sexually assaulted him. When the men got back from hunting Prissy, they went to other things, namely gang raping Bunny, and Bell got away. How's it sound so far?"

"Disgusting."

If it was to her, she wasn't showing it. She still worked steadily, perhaps a little too calmly.

"Bell waited a few days to start his vendetta. He was weak, I suppose, from what the women put him through. He started by burning their bikes and the camp. He missed two of them though. Fingers and his lover had gone for guns. The guns didn't do them any good. Bell ambushed and killed them both. Fingers was a homosexual. Did you know that?"

"The papers mentioned it."

"Blake was his lover."

She was back at the end counter, swishing the paper in a tray. Even if she wasn't Prissy, the things he told her should have been disturbing. They weren't, not that he could see.

"Bell had it made. The others were afoot, without weapons, but something happened he didn't count on. He assumed the desert killed you, and he was wrong. You knew how to live out there, and when you got the chance, you had some revenge of your own. You ran him down with your Jeep."

She still swished the paper in the bath. He realized it had been much longer than necessary. He moved up behind her, twisting his head to see over her shoulder to her face, near enough to touch her with his chin before she sensed him. She startled, whirling to face him.

"You don't have anything to feel guilty about. The bastard had it coming."

She looked at him for a long moment before backing away and turning back to the enlarger.

"You weren't listening to me," he said, moving up close to her again.

"No," she admitted.

"I know the kind of hell he would have put you through. It isn't necessary that anyone else need know."

She turned to face him. "I don't know why you persist in this. I've told you all I possibly can and no amount of badgering from you can change that."

His voice went flat. "Can and will are two different things."

"I really wish you would leave. I have work to do."

He exploded. "Work? Seven people are dead, one's lost her mind, another is nearly dead, another missing, probably dead, and all you think about is work?"

"It's all I care to think about. I don't want to know what happened out there. I don't want to know the kinds of things Mr. Bell is guilty of."

"Just want to hide your head in the sand, not know all the bad things that happen in the world. Just ignore them and they'll go away?"

"Someone else can deal with them."

"Your attitude is what's wrong with the world today. No one gives a damn, as long as it's happening to someone else."

He pushed past her to jerk the door open, not caring if she had paper out to be exposed. As he stomped down the hall, the door closed softly behind him.

13

The Storm

Annalisa caught the strands of hair to pull back from the face. The head turned away. "What can I do?" she asked.

"Go to hell," Bell told her, his voice sounding choked he was in so much pain.

He rose to his right knee, dragging the left leg to get it under him. The pain was too severe. He folded back down, holding the right knee with a swollen right hand. Blood oozed through his fingers. His left arm pressed to his left side, and he gasped to breathe.

She did not comprehend what he had said to her. She reached out to hold him, comfort, or help. He pushed her away with an elbow as she leaned close. "Get away from me," he growled out, hunching against the pain and holding his side.

"I want to help."

"You bitch," he hissed through teeth clamped together.

He didn't talk anymore. Barely able to breathe, he held his side. He straightened, tried it that way. Nothing helped.

She reached out to him again. He fell forward to his right hand to get away from her. His left arm still pressed to his side, and his body twisted that way with his breathing the most frightening. For each breath he attempted to draw in, the damaged muscles contracted, forcing it out in a grunt. She wanted to help, but through her dazed mind, one fact penetrated. He did not want her touching him.

The gun she'd laid down to cut him loose was a few inches from his knee. With his fingertips, he inched it to under his hand. She watched while he went again to his right knee and forced the left foot to the ground. He pushed his weight up and staggered to get the right leg up as well. He stood, torso hunched to the left side and face into the wind.

The brisk coolness seemed to revive him. He took a step, dragging the left foot into place quickly when the right leg threatened to buckle. He staggered a few feet forward to stand, staring down at Fingers' body. She rose to her feet and looked too, watching as Bell dropped to one knee and pulled at the necklace around Fingers' neck. When he sat back on his foot, unable to pull it free, Annalisa took it for him, untying the string from Fingers' neck. She also took the gun from Fingers' waistband, tucking it into hers as she held the necklace out to Bell. He fumbled the necklace into a pocket and struggled to his feet again. Following, she retrieved her gun on the wash bank, ejected spent shells, and fed in new ones from her pocket. Bell's pace made it easy for her to do while she walked. Finished, she stepped up beside him. He side-stepped away, nearly losing his balance. She walked behind him with a new thought penetrating. He did not want to see her.

As they walked, her mind worked itself from the stupor it had been in. "You can't stay up there now," she told him.

He didn't answer or alter his course.

"Bell, it's raining in the mountains. You can't stay at the spring now. That canyon will fill with water soon."

"Not raining." His words were slurred from the resulting swelling of his smashed mouth.

"It is up there." She pointed to the mountains ahead of them. He didn't look, but she knew he had to hear the thunder, see the lightning flashes, and feel the wind. "You can't stay at the spring."

He continued to walk. Jumping forward, she grabbed his arm. "You can't—"

He jerked free, staggered, and nearly went down. Biting at her lip, she dropped behind him and began a macabre game. His will kept him on his feet. Her persistence guided him. When she wanted him to turn, she stepped up on the opposite side.

When they reached a low spot on the wash bank, she turned him to climb it. When he drifted off course, she ran up to set him straight again. Gradually it took more than stepping beside him.

She had to touch him to let him know she was there. In too short a time, she had to pull him gently. Sometimes he looked up to see who she was and pulled away. Most of the time, he staggered blindly.

He should have been down, resting so he could breathe without gasping and resting the wounds to let the bleeding stop, but not out in the open. They couldn't stay where Al and Dago could find them. Those two would get over their fear and come back. Nor could they go back to the spring.

Shelter was important with rain only a matter of time before the storm reached them. Bell wouldn't be able to tolerate being wet and cold. He needed a place where he would be dry and warm, and she needed the blankets they had left at the spring to provide it.

Time was important, but she couldn't leave him by going ahead. Each time he came to an obstacle, a bush, cactus, or tree in his path, to avoid it he wandered away from where she wanted him to go. Soon, she had to guide him around those things he no longer saw.

When they reached the slope, it was too much of an added

strain. He went to his knees and started back up only to fall. His right arm kept him from falling completely flat. Throwing it out to stop the fall, the gun he carried clattered on the rocks as it slid away from him.

He either didn't know or no longer cared that he no longer held it. On his hand and knees, he didn't lift his head until Annalisa touched him. He sat back then, on his feet, using both arms to hold his side. With his head hanging low to his chest, the wind flipped his hair, hiding his face.

"Let me help you." She touched him on the shoulder. He didn't recoil. Kneeling in front of him, she gathered his hair in her hands to push away from his face. She wanted to lift his face, but her hands trembled, remembering the way it looked. She didn't want to touch for fear of hurting him more.

"Let me help you," she repeated, raising her voice for him to hear her above the wind.

She leaned forward with her hands at his neck holding the hair away, hearing the last words. "…can't make it."

She didn't understand how he'd gone as far as he had, but he couldn't stay there without shelter. Looked for something that would serve, she told him, "Stay right here."

He gave no indication he heard her at all. She had to leave him alone. She had to be sure of the place she'd thought of while following him. She had to be sure it would shelter them before she moved him, if she could.

Annalisa knelt in front of Bell, still hesitant to touch him if he did not know she was there. He was too weak to hurt her, but any sudden, violent move would hurt him.

The wind had increased, snatching her words from her mouth. She had to call his name three times before he raised his head and opened his eyes.

She didn't know if he actually saw her or if he would understand what she said. She shouted to be heard over the wind. "We have to move."

He nodded and reached for her with the right hand. She guided his arm over her shoulder only to have it hang limply down her back as he slumped forward, his forehead on her shoulder.

"Don't let me go down," he murmured.

If it were not for the windbreak her body made or the closeness of his mouth to her ear, she would not have heard him.

"I won't." She held him by the waistband and pulled. "Lean on me. Come on, move."

She tugged on limp weight, and his head moved in a shake.

"You can do it. Lean and move. This leg." She tapped his left thigh. "Move it and lean on me."

His arm tightened, nearly breaking her neck, not with viciousness but the reaction of his body to doing as she told him. The pressure increased, and so did the weight as he fumbled the left foot under him and flat to the ground. His weight was nearly unbearable when he forced himself up, leaning heavily on her. No more than four inches taller, he outweighed her by seventy or eighty pounds. She feared they would both fall before he reached his feet.

"Shift your weight so I can get beside you."

His movements were sluggish and uncoordinated, but he did as she said. While she edged to his side, he said, "I thought it was you."

"Don't try to talk," she told him again.

Labored breathing seemed to hold while he spoke, and he then panted and gasped to catch it again. He wouldn't stop talking. "I came to with Ready—"

"Bell, please!"

"I thought it was you screaming." He twisted, pressing his side even harder. He panted, caught his breath again. "I couldn't wake up…'fraid too late."

"Please don't talk. It's just a little further. You can sleep then."

"Too strong—hurts."

She didn't know how he could do it. Talking was difficult for her, and she wasn't hurt. She was panting from the exertion, but when she didn't answer, he stopped speaking.

Getting under the overhang was simple, but it hurt him. She knelt, and without support, he fell. His weight hit the right knee, and he passed out, falling the remainder of the way. Had she not caught his head, his face would have hit. She wanted to hold him then and tears blurred her vision, but there wasn't time.

Rolling him to his back, Annalisa used the sleeveless armholes of his jacket to drag him completely under. Even then she couldn't stop, no matter how exhausted she was. The overhang wouldn't protect him from the wind or the rain it would blow in, unless she blocked off the windward side. She had to have the blankets.

She ran up the slope and half slid down the back side. Going down the embankment to the spring, she fell worse than Bell had the day before, and she was slower getting up.

The sleeping bag seemed ten times as heavy as it had the night before, but with it zipped it served to carry the blankets and his clothes. A canteen hung from her shoulder.

Food, too heavy for her to carry, went to the bank, safe from the run off soon to fill the tiny canyon. Eating seemed of little importance with all else to consider at the time.

She fell back twice crawling up the embankment and thought she never would make it up the slope. Going down the far side, she was on her rump more than her feet. She nearly gave up when she saw Bell. He crawled, was crawling, out from under the overhang, pushing and dragging himself with one foot and one hand.

She dropped to her knees, feeling she couldn't possibly move him again. A large drop of rain fell on her face, urging her to try. She threw the blankets to safety and knelt beside him.

She held his head carefully to keep the damaged part from the dirt and rolled him to his back.

Eased his head down, she blinked back tears and grabbed his

jacket by the armholes. Moving him was easier. He helped, pushing back with his left leg.

Lightning flashed, and when the thunder clapped overhead, he jerked, yelling, "Get those damned assholes!" He nearly twisted out of her hands when he jerked down to press at his side, and he almost knocked her down when he pushed hard with his foot.

She had to turn him, taking him further out, to get him back in head first. The rain began in a deluge. Doing what she had fought to prevent, he was soaked to the skin in seconds. Herself as well.

"Get down, you damned fool, get down!" he shouted.

He pushed back again, trapping her feet with his weight. She went down, and he fell back between her legs. "Bell, please," she cried, working from under him.

As soon as she had him under cover, she left him to close off the end.

He shoved backwards until he reached the rear wall, and then up to lean back against it with both arms wrapped tight around his middle. The words about things of another time and place didn't stop. He dropped to a mumble by the time she had the blanket hung by driving small rocks into crevices with a large one. He still rambled while she weighted the bottom with larger rocks.

———

More floor space than in the tent, and without the sloping sides, more head space made moving easier, though standing straight wasn't an option. She could sit without the danger of bumping her head. She sat, and she stared at Bell.

All she wanted to do was sleep, but she couldn't stop. If he was still in those wet clothes when coolness of night came, he'd chill. The temperature had already dropped. She had to undress him. With numb acceptance, she walked close enough on her knees, pushed aside the blood encrusted beard to unbutton the jacket and wondered why he had to have it buttoned then when he never had before. The buttons didn't want to slide free of the wet material, making her struggle for something so simple.

When she saw his side, her stomach knotted. No wonder he held it so tightly. Already the huge bruise was swollen. Already? How long had it been? A few hours? A lifetime?

She pulled him forward to lean on her while she worked the jacket off. Folding his left arm to work it free, he jerked away, mumbling at her. He fell back to the wall, and his arms wrapped again to his side. When he started to slump, she pulled him back to her.

The right arm had to go out first. Once it was free, she worked the jacket from behind him, and then carefully down the left arm, moving it as little as possible.

With it done, she sat back, holding him against her, too exhausted to think of what had to be done next. She knew he had to be stripped, but how without moving and hurting him? What would it do to his leg when she pulled on those boots and pants?

She rested ten minutes, working out a problem that would have taken her only one any other time. She couldn't decide if she should move him first, then undress him, or undress him before moving him. Only an ingrain stubbornness gained her success. When she finally had him stretched out on the sleeping bag, completely nude, she sat and stared again.

As intimate as they had been, she had never seen the scars. She remembered the threat he made to show them to her. She could see now why it had been so easy for him to convince the others he was impotent. Why he should want to still escaped her, and it didn't matter. Not anymore. The scars covering his groin and upper thighs were old, not causing the pain. It was the other things. He was bruised and battered from his face to his swollen and discolored ankles. His shins were bruised and skinned. His knees were raw, and blood oozed from the ugly, dark hole on the inside of the right.

Bruises, scrapes, cuts, blood, and dirt covered him. He had to be washed, but she was too tired. She tried. She unknotted her shirt to rip the tail for a rag. She didn't have the strength to tear it.

———

Annalisa woke, stiff, shivering, and curled in a ball. Night had fallen, and the storm had quieted. The sky still lit intermittently with flashes of lightning, but thunder was too distant to hear as more than a slight rumble.

Moving to the edge of the overhang, a gentle breeze touched her damp clothes, chilling her more. She emptied the pockets of her pants in a neat pile, and took them off along with her shirt, and spread them out on the rocks, out from under the overhang where the morning sun would dry them. Rubbing her arms vigorously, she rose to find his dry clothes. They would do for cover and warmth until hers dried, and he didn't need them.

She jerked to an awkward, startled stop when he spoke.

"You think you're safe because I can't get to you."

"What?"

"If you get close enough, I'll show you what I can do. You won't think it's so funny then."

The things he said, too much like he had said one other night and the way he said them, frightened her. He used a calm, conversational tone to say things that sent chills down her spine. Her legs ached from the crouched position she had to use to keep her head from banging into the ceiling. They trembled when she backed out.

"You're going to wish you never teased me."

She turned to run. She heard him move. Reason told her he couldn't move far enough or fast enough to catch her. Reason was wrong.

His weight fell on her, forcing her to the ground. His hand clawed into her shoulder, throwing her from her stomach to her back. His weight fell back on top of her, knocking the air from her lungs. Sick and weak, he was ready to do what he intended.

"You think it's funny." His knee came down between her thighs.

"Bell, you can't," she cried.

He jerked his head back to look at her. "Prissy?"

"You're crazy!" she screamed at him, shoving him away, making him roll to his back.

Bell went limp. "It's raining," he said in wonder.

She sat up, realizing he was right. The storm or a second wave came down on them. "You're an idiot," she told him, working her arms under his shoulders to help him sit up.

His breathing worsened. "You...waited just long...enough."

"For what?" she asked absently while wondering how she was going to get him up without clothes to use for handles.

"For me...to need you." She pulled her head back to look at him. "...and still be...strong...enough to do...what you want."

She let go and moved back fast enough he had to save himself from a fall after sudden withdrawal of support.

"I didn't," she told him hatefully, "wait for anything, other than to get close enough, and I don't want *anything* from you."

"You still...want Jeep."

"You can have the damn thing."

"I—" The shout broke off. He had to control the volume he used, no matter how angry he was. Only in a whisper could he talk without gasping between words. "I never did anything to you to deserve that."

"No, not even you deserve that." She stood up, looking down at the lighter spot that had to be him.

The breeze picked up, working into a strong wind again, pushing the main force of the storm at them with incredible speed.

"You couldn't follow—"

The rest of what he had to say was lost in a flash and almost simultaneous crash.

"You can't stay out here," she shouted at him.

The soft drizzle went to a cloudburst. Even knowing where he was, she couldn't see him without the flashes of lightning.

In one flash he was still sitting. In the next, he was on his left knee and right hand with his right leg stretched out behind him. In the next, he was still in the same position. In the next flash, he rose up on his left knee.

She leaned down, found his arm and pulled it over her shoulder. He resisted for a fraction of a second. As much as he resented his need for help and her as the one to give it, she knew he had to accept.

Touching him again, without the fear of what he was going to do, she noticed something she hadn't before, his body heat. Going out in the mist must have cooled him enough for him to make sense, but with the fever in his body and the cold rain, his body trembled with chills before they got back inside the crude shelter. He couldn't crouch because of his leg. When he went down to his left knee, she dragged the sleeping bag to him.

"I hope you're satisfied. We're both drenched again."

"Cold," he said through chattering teeth.

"Lie down."

"Easier up."

"What is?"

"Breathe."

She sighed. Of course, it would be. That was one of the basic things she had learned in first aid, elevate chest or head wounds. She should have thought of it.

"You can't sleep sitting up," she said, looking around her.

In the flashing light, she saw what might serve. One section of the wall had crumbled, forming a drift of pebbled rock. It wouldn't be comfortable, but then neither was the rock floor.

Time and effort were necessary to move him, the sleeping bag, open the bag, and get him into it. She folded the blanket last for his head. Putting it in place was nearly too much for her exhaustion. Her hands stilled, holding the makeshift pillow when her head dropped to her arm. She fell asleep, vaguely aware of his arm sliding around her waist.

———

Warm and comfortable, Annalisa didn't want to wake. She wished groggily that Bell would be still and let her sleep. She raised her head to stare at him, memory overcoming sleep, though she was puzzled as to how she had come to be curled up next to him.

She rolled away, though what difference did it make? She was cold and tired and by him was warmth and the only bed. God knew she had shared one with him before.

A thought of revolting against passive acceptance crossed her mind. It didn't stay. Something overshadowed it. Bell hadn't been talking to disturb her nor to anyone else. He just talked, rambling in murmurs and mumbles. Some words were understandable. Most weren't. He was delirious, just as he'd been the last time he attacked her before the rain cooled his fever.

Of all the things she needed to do, she had to dress first. Her clothes were still wet. His were too big, but dry. She had to roll the sleeves of the plain, everyday shirt to uncover her hands, but all the buttons stayed closed.

The pants made her feel silly. She couldn't keep them up without holding them, and she had to roll the cuffs to keep her feet free even then. They were baggy and sloppy, but they covered, and dawn was breaking.

Once dressed, there was no reason to put off what had to be done. She knelt beside Bell and touched his forehead. It was hot, but his face didn't look as bad.

She looked closer. Yes, it did. It was still swollen under the beard. It had only looked better because the rain had washed the worst of the blood away. None of it looked quite as bad with the blood and most of the dirt gone. The bruises were more vivid, showing darkly on his skin, with even more visible than had been the night before. The scars on the lower part of his body were stark white lines.

She covered him, leaving just his right leg out. She could do nothing for the other injuries. Looking at it, she couldn't understand why he wasn't completely crippled. The puncture wound on the inside of his knee was an inch in diameter and deep. A swollen area as long as her hand kept the joint stiff and was already red with infection.

Her pocket size emergency kit held a tiny first aid kit, two sterile pads, one very small roll of tape, one tube of antiseptic soap, and an even smaller tube of antiseptic ointment. Enough for one wound and Bell had considerably more.

She began to doubt if anything she did would help. Yet while he was quiet, his breathing was regular, but he hadn't stirred, even with her touching him. Maybe he wasn't sleeping. Maybe he would never wake up.

Bell did wake as soon as the pad wet with soap touched his knee. He jerked and opened his eyes. They were glassy with the fever, but he knew who she was.

"Act II," he slurred out at her.

She couldn't make sense of what she thought he said, but she knew the tone. "I know it hurts, but it has to be cleaned."

"If you think it'll get you anything, forget it."

She flushed a bright red and dabbed too hard. He jerked, and she recoiled.

"Listen," she exclaimed, facing him, "I don't want anything —*nothing*—from you."

"Then why the Florence Nightingale trip? Guilt?"

"For what?"

"Setting me up."

"I never set you up!"

"You didn't burn their camp? You didn't wear my jacket to make them think it was me?"

She stared at him while he spoke, unable to believe he would really believe what he said. *Why not?* It was the kind of thing he would do. "You're despicable."

"Then why'd you go there?"

"To get my cruiser."

"You didn't take it."

"I couldn't start it," she told him, glaring at him.

"Back to despicable me to play nurse and lover?"

"Damn you, shut up!"

"You don't hate me for getting you dirty or roughing you up a little. You hate me for knowing what a whore you are."

"Whore!" Shooting up, her head struck the ceiling. Hunched down, holding her head, she shouted at him. "You made me like it, want it, but you won't enslave me. I won't live like an animal just because I behaved like one."

He rose up on his right elbow, the controlled, even tone gone. He shouted in a hoarse whisper. "Human, not animal. You're human, lady. I didn't make you do anything. I just found what was already there."

"You didn't have to bring me here."

He eased back down to hold his side with both hands. He closed his eyes not looking at her. "I wish I never had."

"Because you lost your precious deal. You don't care what happened to me."

"I didn't think you'd get hurt."

"Hurt!" she shouted, thinking of what he had done and shying away from any mention of how he'd raped her. "Oh, yes, you did keep me from them. I owe you something for that! They didn't get me after you shoved me under their noses! That's all! You used them to make me go blindly with you. I never would have been dragged into this snake pit if not for you!"

His right arm went up to lay over his eyes while she continued to shout at him.

"If you thought there was someone there, you could have just left. Your precious meet could have been rearranged."

"It was important."

"Not that damned important. It could have waited for a new

time or place. You didn't have to kidnap me, or you could have killed me like you did the others."

"I never killed——"

"You'd do the same to me, in time!" she screamed. "When you got tired of me or I got to be too much trouble. I won't let you! Long before then, you'll be in jail where you belong!"

He didn't answer, and she was out of breath. She was wasting air, anyway. Nothing she could say would change anything. She knelt back down to go back to cleaning the knee. He jerked once before tensing to hold himself.

Even with using all the contents of the tiny kit, she didn't feel it was enough. Nothing was left for his face or wrists, the worst of the open wounds, and those weren't causing him the most pain.

"Would it help if I wrapped your side some way?"

"You don't have anything," he said from under his arm.

"I could strip the blanket."

"You can try it."

She leaned close to reach the blanket behind his head. He raised his arm and opened his eyes. She could see the pain, fever, and something else.

Jerking the blanket out, she told him, "Don't look at me like that. I'm not falling for anymore of your green-eyed lies." She shook the blanket out, deliberately not looking at him, then or while she ripped the blanket in strips. "Sit up."

He tried raising straight up. He couldn't. He rolled to the right, up on his arm to push himself up. She didn't think he would manage any better. She slid her arm under his, pulling him up, and then slipped behind him to hold him there.

"When did you stop believing me?" he asked while she wrapped the first strip.

What was the sense in even discussing it? To his way of thinking, the worst he did to upset her was being too rough.

"Tell me when it's tight enough," she told him.

"You didn't…" He grunted hard. "Enough."

She loosened it to draw it tight again slowly. She stopped when he nodded. Nodding was much easier for him than talking. Wrapping the blanket awkwardly with him between her arms and making sure the knots were all to the front took her a long time.

When she eased him back down, he was exhausted. "Better?" she asked, worried that the help caused more problems than comfort.

He nodded for answer.

"I don't know what to do for your face."

He spoke in a whisper. "Nothing."

He was probably right. There was nothing more she could do. "I'm going after some food and water."

He nodded again.

"Think you can take a tablet?" His head rolled for a no. "Can you try? You need salt."

She had almost forgotten that. She had to make her brain start functioning again. There was a small tin of salt tablets in the emergency kit. She took out half of the eight, two for him and two for her.

"That's not the same stuff you had before," he said when she knelt beside him again.

Shaking her head absently, she watched his mouth while he talked. How could she possibly give him water without hurting that cut and swollen mess? She stepped over him, going to his left side.

That side of his mouth was not cut, and she tipped the canteen to the corner of his lips. He watched her, swallowing when the careful trickle finally hit the back of his throat. He didn't want the tablets.

"You need salt."

"If it is."

She was puzzled, then angry. She put two of the tablets on her tongue, sticking it out for him to see. After swallowing hers, she put his on his chest.

"If you don't take them and get heat sick on top of it, it'll be your own fault."

Dropping the canteen at his right side, she stepped over him to snatch up her boots. The rocks hurt her feet, but she didn't stop to put on her boots until she was out of sight. She didn't want him to see the gun she'd shoved inside one.

———

Annalisa was surprised to find the spring canyon with no more than a trickle of water running through it. The wash above it started higher in the hills and traveled out to the valley. It should have been full of muddy run off. Since it wasn't, she took full advantage, crawling down the bank to see what she had missed in her hurry the day before. There wasn't much, a can of chicken spread. She tossed it up on the bank before going to the stash hole to see if he'd left anything there.

What she found told her clearly why he had been so determined to go back. Ten, neatly banded stacks of cash, the spoils of his hideous little world, were all wrapped neatly together. She saw no reason for him to have it, and the police would probably find it interesting.

She used his bag to create a stash of her own. He said it paid to be safe. She was going to be. Two more guns were somewhere on the path from where he went down to the overhang, but she'd find them.

The gun she had, the extra shells that were left, a small supply of food, and his money went in the place she chose, safely buried away beneath a stack of rocks, carefully replaced in a slide.

Now, if something did happen, she would have the stash to rely on. If not, it would be an easy spot to find when she led the police back.

With the food in the front of the oversized shirt, she went down, not over to the overhang first. Without any trouble, she found the gun he'd dropped. She had to look harder for the one that fell out of her waistband.

She didn't need two guns to control him, and two guns would be twice as hard to keep away from him. She hid one at the base of the slope.

Her efforts all seemed ridiculously unnecessary when she got back.

Bell was much worse. He'd thrown off the cover and tossed restlessly, stirring slightly when she dropped the cans, but he didn't wake. Nor did he, in any coherent manner, fight to keep her from replacing the cover.

"Hot."

"It's the fever."

"Hot," he insisted incoherently. "Hot—wet, all the time wet—fungus grows on you—leaches worse—hate leaches."

Maybe the bag was too heavy, but he needed cover to retain his body moisture. He was losing it too fast with perspiration. She tried the blanket. He threw it off.

She covered him, reached for the salt tablets, covered him again. Picking out two tablets, she picked up the canteen, covered him while she opened it, covered him while she moved over to his left side, and covered him again while she tried to pour water in his mouth.

The battle to keep him covered exhausted her. They were in the shade. At least the sun wouldn't hit him directly to burn and evaporate the moisture away too fast. With the humidity up, it wouldn't as fast, but with the humidity, the natural system of cooling wouldn't work as well, either.

She lifted his head, rousing him. He responded to what she wanted him to do, but not enough to know who she was any more than he knew what it was she had him swallow.

She fanned him to evaporate the moisture on his skin and cool him. When his skin was dry, she sponged him with the tail ripped off his shirt.

He asked her questions she couldn't answer, and he didn't wait for one before asking another or just talking. He often repeated the names she had heard before and numbers.

She left him only long enough to make the tedious trek back up to the spring, to refill the canteens with fresh water. The dry canyon still puzzled her, but she was grateful for the fresh water. Filling the canteens, she listened closely for the roar of a possible, approaching flash flood. Something had to be blocking the runoff that should have been in the wash, and she didn't want to be caught down there when it let go.

She hurried back, and Bell was even worse. He wouldn't rouse enough to understand he was to drink. She put salt, a pinch at a time from a crushed tablet, in his left cheek to be absorbed into his body. The only moisture she could safely give him was with sponging.

The worse he became, the more frightened she got with a different kind of fear than she'd felt for herself, but still selfish. Deliberately or not, she had caused what happened to him. Her fear didn't lessen until she began to feel she was winning. His temperature lowered, and his breathing began to level off. His forehead felt almost as cool as her own when she fell asleep beside him, listening to his regular, but shallow breaths.

———

A roaring woke her, coming through the ground to her ear. She raised her head to look at Bell. The sound wasn't coming from him. He was still and quiet beneath her hand, sleeping peacefully, but the sound was still there, growing louder. She jumped to her feet and ran to look back over the ridge, toward the sound coming from the mountains behind. She stared in awe.

"What is it?" Bell called out to her.

"Flash flood!" she cried in excitement. She'd been right. Something had been damming the wash higher up. "Look at it!"

Wild water cascaded down the mountain, more a waterfall than creek. When it reached the spot where the bed dropped beneath it at the spring, it shot out from the mountain side at least twenty feet before it fell.

"I wish I had my camera. I'll never see anything like this again."

The great wall of water disappeared behind the ridge, sucking a twenty-foot tree down with it. She twisted to look at him.

"Did you see that?"

Bell had pushed up to sit, watching her. He shook his head.

She wanted him to see. She wanted to share the spectacle. She forgot who he was or what had passed between them. Only that moment mattered. She spun back around, tracing the wash's path for a spot he could see from where he was.

"Look, down there, watch."

Where the wash bent to restrict the great wall of water, it jumped over it, gouging out a new path for the water behind to follow. If the wash was too shallow, it spilled over, out on the land, mowing down trees and brush ahead of it.

When it reached the spot she pointed out to him, she twisted, shouting her question. "Did you see it?" She didn't wait for an answer. She saw it in the way he watched. "Isn't it fantastic?"

Annalisa didn't wait for an answer, twisting back around to watch the finish.

The head water, that great rushing wall, was gone from sight. The water behind was lower. The overflow began to recede, pulling back to the banks of the wash. It was all dull after that first monstrous rush.

She sighed in regret. "I wish I'd had my camera." She turned to go back. "You shouldn't be sitting up," she exclaimed, realizing for the first time that he was.

She hurried back, drawing up short when she saw how intently he watched her. "Don't look at me like that," she snapped. That look annoyed her, reminding her how silly she must look in his clothes, and it was one of those gazes she couldn't decipher. He was also very nude.

His eyes dropped as he eased himself to his back. He didn't lose his breath from the movement or exertion.

"Looks like you feel better. Think you can eat something."

"No."

She did. She went to the small food supple. "It'd be better for you if you rinsed it out with salt water, if you could stand it. Do you want me to fix some?"

"No."

"Suit yourself," she told him with a shrug. She sat back with a can of chicken spread, a plastic spoon, and opener. Pausing between bites to scratch her head, she didn't look at him or speak to him while she ate.

Several minutes later, he broke the silence. "That wash runs between here and the highway. You'll have to have the cruiser to cross it, if they haven't already taken it."

She scratched and answered, "They can't."

"Why not?"

"I took the rotor out." Her full stomach made her sleepy. She crawled past him for the blanket.

"I should have known you'd think of something like that."

"You still think I deliberately—"

"Why'd you fire the camp?" he demanded.

"To make them go away," she retorted furiously.

He didn't answer. The sun was setting, making the area under the overhang dark in shadows. She couldn't see his face clearly enough to see his eyes, but she knew he was staring at her.

Determined not to let it bother her, she told him, "I'm going to sleep." Out from under the overhang, she spread the blanket, well away from him. She wanted to sleep, but after an hour of trying, she gave up. Every rock under her poked and bruised, and whatever bit her had in several places, making her whole head itch.

She went to the overhang for a canteen and nearly jumped out of her skin when he lit a match. "You don't smoke," she said, staring at the cigarette in his mouth.

"You've never seen me. There's a difference." He had the leather jacket in his lap and slid a cigarette pack into a pocket. "Nice of you to bring them for me."

"It wasn't on purpose," she told him, annoyed at the thought of doing him any favors. "Should you smoke now?"

"Why not?" He touched the nearly burnt out match to the cigarette and deliberately blew the smoke at her.

The match went out, putting them back in darkness.

"I suppose the right kind of cigarette would make you *feel* better, but I doubt if it's going to help your lung any."

"It's not marijuana, and there's nothing wrong with my lung— no thanks to you."

She countered just as hatefully. "What would have been wrong with you if I hadn't shot Fingers' head off?"

"What would have happened if you'd done what I told you and stayed at the spring?"

"You were sick!" The exclamation shocked her. She didn't know where it came from, and she didn't want to. She hadn't gone to the camp for his sake. She hadn't. "Damn you, take care of yourself."

She turned her back on him, patting the ground to find her things.

"Do I get my clothes back?"

"I wouldn't take anything of yours." She shoved things furiously into her own pants pockets.

"You'll take some of it."

"What's that mean?" she demanded, jerking buttons open.

"Lice, lady. You sleep with the dog, you get his fleas."

"Damn you." She jerked the shirt off and threw it at the glow of his cigarette. "Take your damned filth."

She sat down, jerking at the pants to get them past her boots.

"Do you like undressing in front of a man?"

"If you could see me." One foot insisted on hanging up. "It wouldn't be anything you haven't seen before."

"You know what happens to a tease?"

The foot popped free. "If I want to tease you, I'd light a match." She threw his pants at him blindly. She couldn't see the cigarette, but she knew where he was or should have been.

She gasped in shock when he grabbed her. That he knew where she was, when she couldn't see him wasn't fair. Neither was it fair that he still had the strength to wrap his arm around her neck and drag her bare body against his.

His mouth was at her ear. "Don't ever think a man can't because he's hurt."

His arm choked her. She held to it with both hands and pleaded, "Bell, please don't."

"Another woman teased me. I was worse off then, but I didn't let her go until I was through with her."

When he let go of her, she was too frightened to move. He shoved her, slamming his hand into her back. She ran on her knees to her clothes and crawled out, clutching them to her. Away from him, gasping to catch her breath. She stopped out of his reach. "I wasn't teasing! I was mad! You told me I had those filthy things on me!"

"That's not all you're liable to have, unless you've had yourself fixed. Or is that what those pills you carried in your pocket really were? Did you come prepared to have a good time without the worry?"

"Damn you! Damn you! You made me do it. You made me want you. I never wanted anyone else before. You made me a whore. You forget everything else and call me a whore! I hate you! I hate you!"

"Until you need me again."

"I don't need you. I never did."

"Then why did you come back?"

She didn't answer the question. She couldn't, but she had an answer for an earlier one. "If I had your spawn, I'd kill it before I'd bring anything from you into the world."

She heard him move and ran. Still naked except for boots, she fled from the fury she was sure she had roused in him with her hate filled words.

———

The flood was no longer fascinating. The wild creek running bank to bank frustrated and frightened her. She could find no place narrow enough to jump or shallow enough to wade.

Bell had been right again. Damn him. She would have to have the cruiser to cross the flood water, but she fought giving in. She walked the creek banks, praying for a way across. Stumbling often, she once walked too close, and the bank gave way beneath her. The water pulled at her feet and legs while she held tight to a flimsy bush to save herself.

Regained solid ground, she sprawled, numb with fatigue. Tears threatened and desperation, the feeling that none of the struggle was worth it. The temptation to let sleep overtake her with the hope she would never wake nagged at her.

A sound sent her back to her feet with her heart pounding and her mouth dry. Her first thought was it was Bell.

His reasons for wanting her now would be different. Now he hated her as much as she hated him. Unfairly, he thought she had done something she hadn't. She would never feel safe again until he was locked behind steel bars or dead.

She walked again. When the wash ran parallel to the road, she knew it was hopeless. She could follow the wash until it crossed the highway, but that could be dozens of miles, and she no longer had the strength to walk. Unsure any longer if she had the strength left to walk to the camp, she had to admit it was her only hope. She could put the rotor back and without anyone to disturb her, experiment with the wires until she made them work.

Only a few miles, but each step was harder. Her feet and legs grew heavier with each one she took. Gray dawn brought light, and she could see her cruiser. Beyond it a tiny thread of smoke rose into the air.

Annalisa knew the smoke wasn't from any fire she set. Those were long since dead, drowned in the rain. It had to be a campfire, and it had to have been built last night to still be smoldering.

They weren't gone.

How many were there, or which ones, didn't matter. Only one to fight her would keep her from the cruiser.

Then Bell was there.

A sound first, very slight. A shadow moved, and he walked from under a tree where the black jacket and dark Levis hid him in the shadows. He had a staff to walk with, leaning heavily on it to move his right leg. A darker spot at the knee of the pants she'd worn such a short time ago showed the wound bled. The binding she had put around his chest didn't show under the shirt and jacket or keep him from pressing his arm to his side. His breathing labored again from the strain.

She straightened from the slump of defeat, and her hand went to the butt of the gun in her waistband.

He stopped. "I don't want to fight with you anymore," he told her softly.

"What do you want?"

"I just…" He broke off, staring at her. "A truce and trade. I'll get the Jeep going, and you give me a ride to the highway."

She knew what he really wanted, a chance to get the gun and her again. She'd just see that he didn't. "Okay."

He half-shook his head, looking at the ground. "Give me the rotor."

"I'll lay it on the fender." She walked by him, making sure she stayed out of his reach. With the rotor on the fender, she was on the far side, keeping the cruiser between them before he reached there. He unlatched the hood from his side, leaning on the fender.

When he picked up the staff again to go around, she told him, "Just stay there."

She unlatched her side and helped him raise the hood. He needed the help. He used only his right arm, and she was the one who kept the hood from falling back on the windshield, where she left it leaning. That was much easier than pulling the prop up. Besides, the prop was on his side.

During that, her back was to the surviving tent. He faced it. He leaned over, reaching for the distributor. "They're coming."

She glanced over her shoulder, only to snap her head back when he spoke again.

"That gun's different than yours. It's a single action, not double." She looked down at it, then back up at him. "Didn't you even know you were using your own gun?"

She knew he could see she didn't and how shocked she was. If he had her gun, he had been to her RV. That meant he did and had always known where it was.

"Tracks," he said to answer her unasked question. His eyes shifted back to the tent. "You better watch them. If you can't shoot them, catch them with those boots coming in. You're good with them."

The bruises on his shins. She had never known she had succeeded in hurting him. "You deserved it," she retorted defensively.

"Not all of it, lady." He raised his voice. "You don't look too good."

Ready shouted out an order that was physically impossible. Annalisa blushed, not turning to look at her.

Bell ignored it, but asked Ready, "Al give you that for letting me get away?"

Annalisa looked then. Ready had a livid bruise on her jaw, and she wore Bell's headband. Jolene stood behind her.

"You gave it to me, you prick, with your head."

"You're lucky I didn't kill you."

"You liked it. I showed you, you really can."

She started forward, and Bell straightened. "Next time I will," he warned.

Ready stopped, looking him over. The cruiser hid his knee. The jacket and shirt hid the bindings, and his beard, hair, along with the way he held his head, hid most of his swollen face. Nothing hid the slurred speech from his damaged mouth.

"You don't look too good either, baby," Ready taunted. "Did that nasty angel blow dust in your eyes? Or did you get stung again by a nasty yellow jacket? Or both maybe?"

Jolene touched her arm in warning. Ready shrugged it off with a laugh. "You really tripped out, baby, flying higher than a kite."

"She's going to try," Bell warned in a voice only Annalisa could hear as he leaned back down to what he was doing.

"I bet you don't remember Fingers. You were so wiped out, you didn't know the difference between a dildo and a real hot prick." Ready shouted and laughed at Bell's reaction.

His eyes swung to Annalisa, and she looked at the ground.

Ready continued to taunt, moving closer. "Fingers said you really enjoyed it. I sure did, but Pretty Prissy screamed her head off."

Annalisa twisted her head to look at Ready, saying, "Shut up."

"Did he find you again before he lost it? He was sure in a hurry. Was it better when he was coming down? Did he let you juice up before he slammed that hunk—"

"Shut up!" she shouted.

"Or what?"

Annalisa turned to face her. Ready's mouth fell open when she saw the gun. She half-stepped back, then laughed. "Boy," she told Bell, "you must have really got better. You sure got her trained."

Annalisa backed to where she could watch both of them. "Get it fixed," she snapped at Bell.

Ready laughed even harder. "What's the matter, Prissy? Didn't he get better? Tired of two humpers?"

Bell stared at Annalisa, but his warning was for Ready. "You better shut up."

Ready looked at Annalisa, saw the way she trembled and still laughed. She moved a step closer and froze.

Annalisa's trembling was not with fear. As long as the gun stayed in her waistband, she didn't look threatening. When she pulled the gun out and stepping into shooter's stance, it was much different. She stood with her feet apart. Her arms were straight, with both hands holding the gun and the hammer back. She pointed it at Ready's head, and she no longer trembled, but was furious for forgetting Bell's warning. She hadn't cocked the gun. She'd put it on safety.

Ready stepped back again in indecision, looking at Bell.

"Better go back to that tent and keep your mouth shut," he told her.

Jolene took no more urging. She turned and ran. Ready looked at Annalisa, still undecided.

"Run," Annalisa said in a still calm and deadly voice.

Ready backed away, and the gun moved, staying in line with her head. She broke and ran.

Annalisa watched until Ready's foot disappeared inside the tent before she turned to face Bell. He stood with the rotor in his hand, staring at her.

"Fix it!" she yelled at him.

His head dropped. He stared at the rotor in his hand for a moment. Glancing once more at her briefly, he leaned over the fender. He fumbled with the rotor, gasping and holding his breath as if he were performing heavy physical labor.

She snapped at him in impatience. "Quit stalling, damn you. Get around here. I'll fix it. You can start it and don't try anything." She started around the back of the cruiser. "Don't look at me like that. I don't believe it."

He dropped his eyes. Humble? Contrite? Like hell! Everything he did when he seemed decent was a lie. He leaned on the staff as if he couldn't walk another step without the danger of falling on his face. He hunched, holding his side like it suddenly hurt beyond endurance. He gasped and held each breath. When he lowered himself to the narrow running board, he held tight to the steering wheel.

She didn't believe that was the only thing to keep him from going to the ground in a heap. Annalisa was not going to fall for his act. She'd seen how he stood and moved when Ready was there. All that gasping was all to put her off guard. She couldn't see him while she leaned over the fender, but she listened to every move he made. She straightened just as the cruiser jumped forward.

His pain was real that time. The door frame must have caught him in the back when the cruiser jumped. He hadn't taken it out of gear before he tried getting it away from her. He was on the ground, holding his side with both arms.

"That was a stupid thing to do," she told him dispassionately.

He pulled himself back to the running board. Then his hand went to the windshield frame, and he pulled himself to his feet. He fell against the side.

"What do you think you're doing?"

He answered her by leaning back from the waist far enough to shove the hood forward. It landed in place with a crash, and he fell back with his chest on the windshield.

"Damn you, get it started," she told him, snapping her side of the hood.

"Show you."

"I'm not getting that close to you."

The next was more sigh than language. She picked out, "In… gun…start," while he pointed to her, the gun, and dropped his hand to the wires.

He really did look bad, but she still didn't trust him.

"Back off while I take it out of gear."

He hung on the windshield, long enough for her to think he wasn't going to follow orders. The first word of a threat formed on her lips just as he did move. He didn't move away from the cruiser. He used it in place of his right leg, inching his way down the fender.

"That's far enough, but keep your back to me," she said, tired of waiting on him.

He turned his back to her, leaning his right hip against the fender for support. She still kept the gun pointed at him, half-shaking her head when he fumbled to latch the hood on that side. Staying as close as possible to the right side of the seat, Annalisa stretched her leg out to press the clutch and shove the gear shift to neutral.

His progress back was just as slow. She waited on the passenger side, leaning in on one knee, the gun in both hands pointed at him.

He fumbled with the wires. The starter whirred, but the motor didn't catch.

"Gas," he gasped out.

"Yes, there's gas."

"Give gas."

That was right. She always has to pump it to get it started when it was cold, but how without getting close to him? She stayed on her knee, leaning on the seat back and stretched the right leg out. She had to put it in front of the floor shift lever to reach it with the side of her foot and couldn't quite reach to have leverage. When she rose up on her knee, she lost her balance. Catching herself she had to hold the gun in one hand and hold herself steady with the other.

With the gun still pointed at Bell, she hooked her wrist over the windshield top for more balance and pumped the accelerator. He touched the wires. The motor sputtered and died. She pumped again, holding it down. He touched the wires. The motor coughed, sputtered, and she pumped furiously. The engine sputtered once more then roared to life. Relief flooded through her, but she got careless. She concentrated too much on getting it started, and Bell snatched the gun out of her hand, fumbled to keep his hold of it and get his weight off the cruiser. She jumped behind the wheel, threw it in gear, and backed away from him.

He'd done it again. He had the gun and the force to win, but she was not going to let him. He was not going to get away.

Twenty feet away from him, she slammed on the brakes. She could still win. She threw it in first and hit the accelerator, his chest in line with the point on the tow bar.

14

PRATTERS WENT BACK TO HIS MOTEL. HE WANTED TO SLEEP BUT couldn't. Something was there, something out of tune that he couldn't hone in on. Anything off bothered him, worried him, and he couldn't bring it to the front of his mind where he could examine and dissect it.

He paced for hours with no relief. He didn't have enough information and wasn't going to get it out of Mrs. Summers, whatever her part was in the mess, unless he could trip her up some way. So far, he had failed miserably at that.

Bunny/Caroline would be in a drugged sleep that time of night, useless to him.

Bell might not be. He'd surprised the doctor twice already with waking up unexpectedly. This might even be a chance to talk to him without a witness.

He went into the hospital through emergency entrance, using his credentials to impress anyone who thought to stop him. It also got him past the guard, but not out of sight.

Word must have come down that he was not to have a private interview with Bell again. The guard stepped inside to watch. The nurse stepped from behind the station desk to stop him. Pratters had one on both sides.

"He isn't awake," the nurse said. "He isn't to be disturbed."

"I won't. There's a scar I have to check. I won't even have to uncover him."

"Well," she glanced at the guard, taking assurance in his presence, "as long as you don't disturb him, I guess it's all right."

The cubical curtain was open, and no nurse sat at the bedside. Pratters left the curtain open, knowing if he shut it, he'd have the nurse and guard both on his back. He did move to the head of the bed, out of sight of the nurse's station. The guard wouldn't think anything of him leaning on the bed. The nurse would.

Not much of a jar, but enough for Pratters to know if Bell could be roused. He was grateful for the dimness of the lighting and hoped the machines wouldn't alert the nurse. Bell's eyelids ticked. Pratters slid down the rail, leaning over as if he were looking at the scars on Bell's face. Bell's eyes opened.

"The guard's watching me," Pratters warned, using a soft tone that carried no more than a few feet.

Pratters eased back and dropped his head, assuming an attitude of deep thought, for the guard's sake. "You really screwed up."

Bell's index finger moved, a tick no larger than the first indication he was awake.

"You son-of-a-bitch, you don't care how hard you make it for me."

Bell answered yes.

"If you're trying to tell me you do, I don't believe it."

Bell answered yes.

Pratters straightened quickly, but not soon enough not to be caught. The nurse came after him.

"You'll have to leave. I told you not to disturb him."

"I didn't," Pratters exclaimed innocently.

"You touched the bed. I'm going to have to report this."

"I didn't do anything."

"You jarred him. There was a definite jump in his pulse and breathing."

There was no beating the machines. Even with Bell's eyes closed, the nurse knew Pratters had done something.

"I really am sorry. I didn't know just touching the bed would hurt him. He really is doing better, isn't he?"

"He's stabilized. Goodbye."

———

Pratters went back to the motel and again called the secret number.

"I don't have much more yet," the man complained immediately.

"Just give me what you do have."

"Okay, but it's only the basic stuff. I tapped the credit bank. He hasn't applied for any in five years, so the information is that old. At that time his credit was A-one. He only had one payment, on a seventy-five, pick-up truck, since paid off. He had every credit card there is practically, a savings and checking account, and a steady yearly income."

"What did he do?"

"Laborer."

"How much in savings?"

"A hundred and seven thousand."

"What!"

"That's what it says."

"Where did he get that kind of money?"

"That it doesn't say. I have to tap his tax reports, and that takes more time than you've given me."

———

When Pratters finally slept, he overslept. He still made it to the hospital on time. He walked in while the county man finished identifying himself as Detective Davison and his partner, Detective Conners.

The man paused to give Pratters a hateful look then read his rights to Bell. "Do you understand these rights?" he asked of Bell when he finished.

A stenographer stood behind him, making the appropriate squiggles in her book to indicate Bell's positive finger twitch.

"Do you wish to remain silent?"

Bell answered yes, and the man turned on Pratters. "What have you been telling him?"

"Not a damned thing. You can ask the doctor."

"You—" He shifted his weight, hitting the bed with his hip.

"Get off the bed!" Thristen shouted. "Nurse!"

The respirator made crazy half-jumps, and Thristen leaned over the bed. Bell contorted with his efforts to breathe. The nurse rushed by Pratters and pushed her way through the crowd at the side of the bed to reach the IV tubes to inject a syringe full into the catheter.

"Get out—no, lie still." Thristen was furious, shouting at them and fighting to keep Bell's hands down.

Pratters jumped forward, knocking the county man aside to catch Bell's right hand. Thristen looked up to give him a hateful look before he talked to Bell. "Relax, let the machine do the work."

The machine pumped air, raising Bell's chest. The muscles of his chest contracted, forcing the air back out. Every muscle in Bell's body contracted. Tendons in his neck and arms protruded, looking as if they were about to burst through the skin. His grip of Pratters' hand was painful. Only one thing could give a man as weak as Bell the strength to grip that hard. There no faking. He was in agonizing pain.

"The drug will take hold in a minute. Try to relax, let the machine do the work. That's it. That's it, just let the machine breathe for you"

Thristen listened with the stethoscope. Gradually the tendons dissolved back into the flesh and the grip on Pratters' hand lessened.

"Good, good." Thristen looked across at the nurse in a signal. "That's fine, just fine, let the machine—no..." The respirator jumped again. "...let the machine do it."

Bell opened his eyes and stared at him.

Thristen smiled. "I know it isn't easy, but you've been doing fine until now. Don't think about it. That lung will settle down just fine by itself, and the machine will keep it going. You ought to be feeling that shot. It'll ease the pain. You'll feel drowsy. Go with it. Rest is the most important thing now."

Pratters let go of Bell's hand. It immediately rose, going toward his face. Thristen blocked it.

"Lie still." He looked at Pratters. "Keep it down until he goes to sleep." Back to Bell, he said, "I know it's uncomfortable, but it has to stay for now. I'm going to turn your head a little."

Pratters thought Bell was after the trac tube. Thristen obviously knew better. He rolled Bell's head to the right side, easing the pull of the tube through his swollen, lacerated nose.

The nurse stepped up, folding a towel into a small pad. It went under his right temple, giving his head support and to keep any weight off the swollen cheek.

All the gentle care and concern turned Pratters' stomach. Bell would never bother showing the slightest concern and certainly would not put himself out with care or help. He was the kind who would throw a drowning man an anchor and laugh when he went down.

"Holding his hand in more than one way?" Davison asked from just outside the cubical with his silent partner and stenographer behind him. He should have kept his mouth shut.

Anything Pratters had to say was cut short by Thristen, reminded of how angry he was. "Get out," he ordered.

The man pointed at Pratters "If he stays, I stay."

Thristen straightened, looking as if someone had just replaced his backbone with a steel rod. "We will see about that."

He nodded to the nurse. She stepped up to take Pratters' place.

He walked, and Pratters followed, curious as hell to see what was going to happen.

They walked by the threesome, and Thristen gave every appearance of not seeing them, which began to worry the overbearing Davison. He followed, and the still silent partner followed him. The stenographer fell in behind to complete the procession.

The good doctor raised hell that reached all the way to city hall. By the time he was through, Davidson wished he had not gotten out of bed that morning.

Thristen's favorite phrase was, "total disregard for the physical welfare of a critically ill man." He always followed it with, 'gross negligence'. For good measure there were several mentions of civil rights, constitutional, and human rights.

He ended with, "I better not see his face in this hospital again." He handed the phone to Davidson. "He wants to talk to you."

"Thanks," he said faintly.

He said, "Yes, sir," a few contrite times and hung up, looking slightly sick. "He said to go back to headquarters. He'll meet us there." He turned to Pratters. "He'd like for you to accompany us."

"Shit," Conners mumbled. "This is going to look great on my record."

The partner was wrong. The only one to be called on the carpet was Davison. Conners was excused after telling his version of the incident. The stenographer gave her version, reading it word for word from her pad, right up to the last line Thristen spoke before he left to start his action.

Pratters was asked one question. "Does that sound accurate to you?"

Pratters nodded for an answer. Satisfied, Sheriff Hudson, head man of the Maricopa County Sheriff's Department, headed for the door, telling Jefferson, Davidson's superior, "Take him off the case."

The door slammed behind him, and Davidson began to argue with his captain. "You can't take me off the case."

"You're off."

"I've got an interview with the Summers woman in ten minutes."

"I'll interview her."

"But you aren't——"

"Davidson, you..." Jefferson broke off, looking at Pratters. "Would you mind waiting outside for a few minutes?"

Davidson received his chewing out in tones loud enough to carry through the wall and door. He stomped out, jerking a thumb at Pratters to indicate he was to go back in.

Pratters shut the door softly. "He didn't mean to hurt Bell."

"I know that. It wouldn't have happened if you hadn't been there."

"He was wound up and ready to go off before I ever showed up."

"Why were you allowed in before us?" he asked sharply.

Pratters sighed mentally and reached into his pocket. "Thristen thought I'd been asked for." He handed the slip of paper over the desk. "I suspect Bell was trying to ask about Prissy."

The 'P' was clear. The 'R' was barely readable. The last could have been anything, and Pratters had used that to explain away why a criminal would be asking for him.

"That was a dirty trick," he said, handing it back.

Pratters shrugged. "The doctor said he asked for me. I didn't argue."

"Or read any rights. Anything he answered won't be worth a damn in court."

"He denied everything anyway."

"He's guilty. We've got more than you're aware of, and he's going to pay for it."

Pratters sat down. He wasn't really interested in a cozy, friendly chat. He was making sure he was still there when 'the Summers woman' came in. "There's no reason we can't work together on this. We do want the same thing."

"That isn't the way I understand it."

"I want him stopped. From what I've been informed, you don't have enough. A good lawyer—and they have plenty of them available—will make hash out of it."

"We have plenty. He got greedy. He tried to take the drugs without paying for them."

"Oh?"

"The coke came in with Thomas Holt AKA Fingers. Bell had it, and there wasn't any money."

"Maybe it got burnt up."

"None in the ashes."

Pratters thought about that. It just didn't seem like Bell. "If he tried anything like that, he'd be fair game in the gangs. I don't think he would."

"He—excuse me." Jefferson answered his phone. "Bring her in."

Pratters moved to a chair in the corner. He nodded in acknowledgement to an introduction, hoping Annalisa didn't do anything to cause more tension by showing he'd already talked to her, without their knowledge.

She didn't. She barely looked at him and sat in a chair in front of the desk. Dressed in a stylish pant suit of a light weight material, long sleeved as usual, her hair was neat and shiny, as always, pinned to the top of her head. Her face was pale, and the dark circles of fatigue makeup didn't hide were even more prominent than before.

The captain sat on the edge of the desk facing her.

"We appreciate you're taking the time to come in, Mrs. Summers."

"You said it wouldn't take long." She used the same listless voice. "I have another appointment at two."

"Then I won't take a moment longer than necessary. There are just a few things we aren't clear on."

Davidson walked in and shoved a picture in front of her.

"Which—"

One word was all the man got out. Annalisa gasped, paled considerably more, and quickly covered her mouth. The other hand when to her stomach. The small purse she carried fell to the floor as she lunged to her feet.

The stenographer behind Davison took over. She dropped her pad, took Annalisa's arm and quickly escorted her to the nearest facility.

Jefferson snatched the photo from Davidson. "You stupid son-of-a-bitch."

"What'd she do that for? She's seen it before," Davidson asked in amazement.

"Yeah, and how did she react? Get the hell out of here."

"I just—"

"Get out!" He shoved him. "And stay out of sight."

Davidson left in bewildered confusion. Pratters had little sympathy for him. Fools rush in where angels feared to tread. Davidson one of the fools, trying too hard and blowing it.

"May I?" he asked pointing to the picture, curious as to what had made her so violently ill. She was ill. No one could fake that sudden color loss.

Jefferson handed Pratters the photo, then paced, waiting for his witness to return. "If he screws up again, I'll put him on patrol so far out, he won't see a car for weeks."

Hume had stayed more professional than he mentioned when he'd walked into that mess out there. He had to have been the one who took the picture. Al and Dago were in the foreground, the heads mutilated, and their bodies in grotesque positions only found in death.

In the background was the RV. Bell and Annalisa, her holding Bell, were in the doorway.

Pratters wanted that picture.

"Was this the only one taken at the scene?" he asked.

"What? Ah, no, just a minute."

Jefferson handed Pratters a packet of prints from his desk top. One was what Pratters wanted, a clear close up shot of Mrs. Summers and Bell.

Pratters shifted through them, picking out five. They gave him a shot of each of the corpses, and the one he wanted. "Mind if I keep these for my records?"

"No," he answered absently, rushing to the door as she returned.

"I'm so very sorry," Annalisa said as he escorted her back to the chair.

The stenographer retrieved her pad and retreated to the back corner, opposite Pratters. She indicated, by raising her hand to her mouth and out, that Mrs. Summers had vomited.

"I'm the one to apologize." He handed her, her purse. "Do you feel well enough to go on?"

"Yes, but please don't show me anymore pictures."

"No, no, of course not. A diagram will be fine." He sat on the front of the desk. With a pad and pencil, he drew out a rough sketch and held it up in front of her.

"What we need to know is which bike Bell was on."

She stared at her hands in her lap while she stated, "He wasn't on a bike."

"I know he wasn't riding one when you found him," he said patronizing. "What we need to know is which of the bikes were there when you found him."

"There wasn't."

"Excuse me, Mrs. Summers, but there had to be."

"There wasn't."

Jefferson looked up at Pratters with an expression suggesting he saw their case falling apart. He began, without any patronizing in his voice, "You said you found him on the side of the road."

"Yes."

"Then there had to be a bike there."

"There wasn't."

"He had—look, if he'd been walking, he'd have been wet and muddy. It rained just before you called."

"I called several times. No one would answer me. I was afraid he'd die before someone did."

"How long did you call?"

"For hours."

"Before the rain?"

"Yes."

Jefferson looked at Pratters again. His case was going right out the door.

"Why didn't you just drive him in?" Pratters asked, giving the impression he was helping. He had no worry that she would have an answer.

"The roads were flooded."

Pratters looked at the sheriff and shrugged. "Did he say anything to you during that time?" he asked, knowing what she'd answer.

"No. I guess he tried. He made noise, but he had so much trouble breathing, and his mouth was so swollen, I couldn't understand him."

"You said in your statement he was quiet all the time," the sheriff said.

"I thought he was unconscious. I guess he was just resting. He heard the noise and got right up."

"Did he threaten you in any way?" Pratters asked.

"No."

"He must have frightened you."

"Yes, he did."

"Didn't you see the gun?"

"Yes, I saw it."

The sheriff interrupted. "Did you touch it at any time?"

"I moved it when it fell."

"When was that?"

"When he fell, going in."

"You didn't mention that in your statement."

"No, I didn't think of it. It didn't seem important."

"I was curious as to how your prints got on it."

"I moved it. He must have seen me. He didn't have any trouble finding it after he knocked me down."

Pratters and Jefferson looked at each other. Jefferson spoke. "He knocked you down to get the gun, not to protect you."

"I really don't know. I'd like to think it was to protect me. I'd like to think there is something good in him." She looked up for the first time at Jefferson "They're saying I should have let him die."

Pratters could see Jefferson getting lost in the depths of those deep blue eyes.

She dropped her head again. "I couldn't just leave him hurt like that."

"No, and you shouldn't have," Jefferson said kindly. "It isn't for you to judge. It's for the courts to decide."

Pratters interrupted the touching scene. "Did he know you were calling for help?"

"I didn't think so, but he heard the bikes, so he must have heard that, too."

"He made no effort to stop you?"

"No."

"Mrs. Summers," Jefferson asked, "can you remember who shot first?"

"Them, I guess. I suppose that was what made the glass shatter."

Jefferson's chin sank. "Do you have any idea how they knew he was there?"

"No, unless they saw him through the window when they passed."

"They passed, then circled back around?"

"I think so. I couldn't see, but it sounded like it." She raised her hand and pressed it to her forehead. "I'm really not sure. Things aren't—I don't remember too well after he knocked me down."

She straightened, drawing in a deep breath. "Please, if that's all, I don't feel well."

"There is just one other thing." He sounded as if he hated to bring it up. "I understand your husband left you a gun."

"He had one when he died."

"Did you have it out there with you?"

"No."

"Where is that gun now?"

"At home." She stood up, swaying slightly. "I hope that is all."

"I'd like to send a man out for it. In fact, I'd like to have someone drive you home."

"I'm not going home. I'll be back there by four." She turned for the door. "You can send someone then."

"I'm not busy," Pratters said quickly after nearly starting out of his chair at the mention of her having a gun. He damned sure hadn't seen one when he'd searched her house. "I'd be happy to drive you wherever you're going."

"I don't need anyone to drive me."

Pratters moved faster than she did. He reached the door first and held it closed. "I really don't think you should, and unless your appointment is vital, I think you should go home."

That was the first time he saw the glimmer of anything in her face. Pale and wan as she was, he saw anger.

"I'm going to the doctor." She straightened, turning to face Jefferson. "I don't know why you want my gun, but it's under the mattress on the bed, right side. The back door is unlocked."

"It's against regulations to go in without you being present."

She'd turned while he said it, to stare at Pratters' chest. "If you don't move, I'm afraid I may vomit on your feet."

Pratters stiffened slowly, not sure if she meant it or not. The stenographer was smarter than him. She dropped her pad. In moments she had Annalisa past Pratters on her way back to the restroom.

"I wish I hadn't had to put her through that," Jefferson said.

"You talk like you grilled her with hot lights," Pratters snapped back at him.

"I don't know what you're hot about."

Pratters didn't, either. Everything seemed to be going his way. The county boys were losing their case, thanks to Mrs. Summers, and were no longer going to be competition. Maybe.

"What did you get on that body you found?" How neat it would all wrap up if it was Prissy.

"It's Helene Fields. She died of exposure."

"Raped?"

"No, she was just foolish. She had a fight with her boyfriend. To spite him, she took his Jeep. She ran it off the road. There's no prints on it but hers. She told him when she left, she'd leave it someplace he'd never find it. She just picked a place too isolated. The walk home killed her."

"Nothing to connect her with them?"

"Absolutely nothing."

Prissy was a loose end again. "You gave it a good try."

"I'm not through. Bell is not getting away with those murders."

"I don't see how you can prove it."

"He burnt the camp."

"He wouldn't have burnt his own bike." The realization startled Pratters as much as it did the sheriff. It came from the back of his mind without him knowing it was there until it was out. He explained it, as much to himself, as he did the sheriff. "There were six men and six bikes. Two were at the shooting scene, four burnt. Bell would not have burnt his own."

"If Al and Dago were part of the camp, two of those burnt, would have been theirs." Pratters nodded. "So how did they get the two they had when they went after him?"

Not that he believed it, but it helped. "When they killed Fingers and Blake and took them."

He sank back in his chair. "Damn!"

———

Pratters went to Caroline's room first. He took the picture out and held it in front of her face. "Is this Prissy?"

She looked at it for the longest time. She touched it. Her fingertip traced Bell's face, then Annalisa's and followed the line of Annalisa's arm to Bell's chest.

"Is this Prissy?"

"He's asleep."

He moved the picture closer and pointed to Annalisa. "Is that Prissy?"

Pratters was never to know what went through her mind while she looked at the photo, but she didn't answer, saying, "Ready said Prissy hated Bell. She liked to hurt him. She made him fall."

Pratters put the picture away. "I want you to think real hard. What happened after Prissy hit Bell with the Jeep?"

"It was a terrible sound, and Ready said, she hit him. She made him fall, and it was hard for him to walk. He was nicer than Al. He didn't make her do bad things, and he didn't let them hurt her. Al made me do bad things. He let them hurt me. He hurt me."

Her eyes filled with tears suddenly. "I can't go home. I'm bad."

Pratters pressed the call button for the nurse.

"I was afraid to go with her. I was afraid to go with Bell. He said he wanted to take me home, but he came back covered with blood, and Al said he must use a knife for so much blood."

The longer she talked, the faster she talked, and the faster the tears fell. "Ready said he lied, and she wanted him, but he didn't want her, and she did bad things to him. She made him mad, and he came back."

The nurse took one look and reversed her course out the door.

"I got lost trying to find Al, and I got so scared. I wanted to go with Prissy when she said to, but it would've made Al mad. He hurt me when he was mad, and I didn't want to be hurt anymore. I wanted to go with Prissy, but Bell scared me. He came back covered with blood, and Al said he had to use a knife for so much blood. I don't like knives. They scare me more than guns, but Bell didn't shoot anyone. He told them he carried the money so he carried a gun, and they couldn't have fun with his old lady, and it made Al mad. He said Bell should share."

Bunny never faltered in her monologue while the nurse gave her an injection or when the nurse asked softly if Pratters would stay with her until she was asleep.

"Bell never shared, and Ready said he lied, that he always could, and Prissy screamed and cried, and he moaned something awful, and Ready said it made her mad 'cause he shot off too soon, and that was the reason he lied, 'cause he couldn't hump more than twice before he…"

She broke the constant stream for the first time in a sigh. The drug took affect fast after that. "It made Ready mad. She wanted to hurt him. She liked hurting him and Prissy…" She talked, dropping in volume and slowing until her eyes closed and the words ceased.

The nurse slipped in quietly and whispered, "Doctor Thristen would like to see you in ICU."

———

Pratters stopped outside the cubical to listen to the conversation behind the curtain. A nurse and Thristen were with Bell.

"Judging from these scars, I'd say you've gone through this kind of thing before," Thristen said in his cheeriest voice. "You'll feel a little discomfort. Try not to tense. It'll make it easier. Now, I'm going to distract you. I'm going to poke around on you. Let me know if I hit a sore spot…Oh, found one, did I? I can see why. There's still some distention here."

His voice dropped to a murmur while he talked to the nurse. Her answer was a murmur. Strange how the voice dropped with serious matters.

Thristen's voice rose again to talk to Bell. "Seems we're going to have to bother you more. I'm going to call x-ray up here to take a look at that spleen, and I'm going to have to disturb this tube. Now would you like the good news?" He chuckled softly. "Was that a look of disbelief?"

The nurse answered. "Maybe you should have given him the good news first."

"Possibly, but I've a feeling you know the best. You're awake to hear it. That's the biggest part of recovery. Your kidneys were not functioning. They are now, on their own. That means we can relieve you of some of these tubes. No, not that one, not yet. I want to rest that lung for another twenty-four hours. If there's no further bleeding, we'll inflate it. If there's no bleeding, then I'll remove the trach."

The curtain slid open. The nurse stepped back to warn the doctor as soon as she saw Pratters. The look of alarm on her face was enough for Thristen to know who was there even though Pratters was still out of sight.

"Be right back," he told Bell. He reclosed the curtain when he stepped out, and he walked Pratters away from it. "Now what do you want?"

"How is he?"

"Amazingly well for the condition he's in." He turned to talk with the nurse. "Yes."

"It'll be fifteen minutes."

"That'll be fine. Prepare a tray. We'll get it done first."

"What's wrong?" Pratters asked.

"Besides the obvious?" It didn't provoke the reaction Thristen expected. "Someone pull your fangs?"

Pratters shook his head. "I'd like to talk to him."

"I'd rather you didn't right now. We're going to exhaust him enough for one day."

"Doing what?"

"The drainage tube is obstructed. I'm going to have to clear it. If I can't, we'll have to take him back to surgery."

Pratters turned to stare at the cubical curtain. "I need to talk to him." He looked back at Thristen. "Just a few minutes and it's important."

"It always is," he said with a sigh. "You can have as long as it takes us to get ready, and for God's sake, don't upset him."

Pratters already moved. Bell watched him when he walked through the curtain, and there was a difference in the way he did it. The unfocused look was gone. Still pain, but Bell was not half-asleep with drugs.

"I have to know about Prissy. Did you kill her?"

Bell answered with his head. He regretted instantly when the tube pulled on the damaged tissues of his nose when he rolled his head no.

Pratters caught his hand as it went up. "Leave it alone," he told him.

He barely had it out before Thristen was there again. "Oh," he said, sounding relieved, "after the tube again. That's the only thing he gives us a bad time about."

"Why don't you put the damned thing over the rail instead of under it, so it doesn't pull so much?"

Thristen stared at him in astonishment.

"I wasn't through talking to him," he retorted defensively.

Thristen raised an eyebrow. "I think you are."

More frustrating than anything, if Thristen said he was, he was. He threw Thristen a look designed to wilt. Thristen was totally unaffected and walked out with Pratters to the hall.

"You two have the strangest relationship I've ever seen."

"We don't have any relationship."

"You certainly aren't friends, but..." He glanced over his shoulder at Bell. "...if he weren't the bad guy and you the good, I think you could be. You'd certainly balance each other's personalities. You're the volatile, and he's the passive."

"Passive? Him?"

"Passive, yes. He's one of the most phlegmatic people I've ever seen."

"He's too weak to be anything else."

"Have you ever been critically ill?"

"Yes."

"How long was it before the doctor wished he'd never seen you?"

"As I recall, it was the other way around, as soon as I could open my eyes."

"That's what I mean. You probably fought everything they had to do for you. He doesn't. He knows it has to be done, and he goes along with it, passively. Just like that tube. In his condition, any annoyance can be unbearable, yet he'd never done more than move it. You'd have jerked it out."

————

"What have you got?"

"Very little. I'm waiting on the tax reports, and I haven't been able to locate the sister. I did find out why."

"Well, don't keep me in suspense."

"She ran away, packed up everything, and skipped while he was at work one day."

"Why?"

"According to the landlady, he was a tyrant. The girl never went anywhere, never had any friends. She was his slave and got tired of it."

"When was that?"

"Two years ago. No one was too clear on dates, but it all seems to fit in. Not too long after that he got a call at work. The next thing anyone knew, the foreman had a broken jaw. That night he demolished the apartment. He just went berserk, busting everything he could get his hands on. As big as he is, it meant anything there. She said there were even holes in the walls."

"Did she swear out a warrant for him?"

"No. He calmed down later. She got a check for a thousand and a note to let him know if the damages came to more. The address was a post office box, and he still has it. That and his trip to the hospital six months ago are the only things I've found so far that show he's been alive for the last two years."

Pratters hung up. The sister was no hold on Bell. Prissy was still alive. Mrs. Summers was having second thoughts about helping Bell, and if it began to look like Bell would go free, she might decide to come up with what she knew.

Prissy might as well. She might be hanging back, keeping her mouth shut, waiting on his injuries or the law to finish the job she started.

As much as he wanted to turn the tables on Bell, he couldn't chance his own safety. He found the nearest phone and dialed the operator.

"This is Dealer. Go with the Three."

"There's no way to avoid it?"

"No, damn it or I wouldn't ask for it."

"Okay, okay, they'll move tonight, but it's going to be touchy. We don't have the connections there we do here."

"No one will be expecting it. There won't be any trouble."

———

Pratters stayed available in his motel room for the bad news. It came first from Thristen, so mad he could hardly talk.

"Would you slow down? I can't understand you," Pratters told him even though he knew what he was saying.

"It's too soon."

"Too soon for what?"

"Damn you, you could have waited. He's too weak. It can throw him back into shock."

"I still don't know what you're talking about."

"You ordered him moved!"

"No, I didn't. It must have been your county friends."

"It said federal."

"If it was federal, I didn't know anything about it. Hang up, I'll find out."

He called the local branch, asking questions though he already knew the answers. They had not ordered Bell's transfer.

The alarm sounded, and Pratters was there, pacing and cussing just like everyone else. He dropped into stunned silence, just like everyone else, when the news came in.

The ambulance had been found in the desert, in flames, still holding Bell's body.

Pratters walked to the parking lot with Thristen, listening to his shocked ramblings.

"I can't believe it. Who would do a thing like that? My God, he was helpless. He'd only just started breathing on his own. He couldn't hurt them. Why—why would anyone do a thing like that?"

"To make sure he didn't talk."

"I can't believe it. I just can't believe it."

"I tried telling you the kind of people they are. It was the article in the paper that did it. They didn't want him caught in a trap he couldn't get out of without making a deal."

"Those men had all the papers."

"They've got strings to every branch of law enforcement. A real judge gave them the official blanks to forge."

They reached his car, and Thristen leaned against it wearily. "This will shock people into listening."

"I doubt it. There won't be any sympathy for Bell. The papers saw to that, too."

"I know one person who will care. I need to call her, so she doesn't hear it on the news or read it in the papers."

Pratters agreed. "I'll do it if you like." It might be interesting to see Annalisa Summers' reaction.

Though it was after midnight when he arrived, she wasn't dressed for bed. To judge from the time it took her to answer the door, he guessed she came from the darkroom.

"I apologize for calling so late, but…ah…may I come in?"

"Does this fall under the heading of harassment?"

Her words suggested a threat, but he ignored it. He stepped inside, forcing her back and found the switch for the light before facing her. "It's Bell."

"I know he's doing better."

"He's dead."

She stared at him for a moment before shaking her head. "He's doing better."

"He was doing fine until they took him out of the hospital and set fire to the ambulance he was in."

She half-turned away from him, shaking her head. "I think you're lying."

"You've got a radio and television. Turn one on. It's big news, and they're broadcasting it already."

She turned full away, still shaking her head, and walked to the kitchen to stand facing the counter. She twisted the knob on a radio to find a news broadcast.

Pratters followed and found the light switch.

Notes of music, disjointed and spasmodic, came from the radio. "Police…" sounded and she backed the dial.

"…are investigating the abduction and fiery death of Simon…"

"No," she said softly.

"…Bell. He was spirited out of the…"

"No," she said louder.

"…Maricopa County…"

"No!" She screamed it, and her fists slammed down on the radio.

"…Hospital earlier…"

She screamed again, slamming her fists down. The case shattered, and the words she didn't want to hear stopped. She didn't. She raised her fists again, and Pratters jumped forward to stop her.

Shrieking at him, she twisted and drove her fists at his face. As soon as he backed off, she twisted back. Her arm swung, driving her fist at the radio. The debris flew across the counter to the wall and bright red blood spattered the clean counter top.

Pratters jerked his handkerchief out. He reached for her arm, and she turned, swinging at him.

"You did it," she screamed at him.

"You did it yourself," he exclaimed.

Her arms dropped limply to her sides. Blood dripped to the floor, and she murmured, "Yes."

When he reached again for her arm, she attacked viciously, hands at his face and a knee to his groin. Instinct turned him to take the blow on his hip, not where she intended, making his gasp more of surprise than pain. He recovered in time to make a grab for her when she ran by. He missed, dodging an elbow. He swung around the bar and skidded to a halt, holding his hand protectively in front of him.

In that split instant, Pratters knew he was a dead man, and there was nothing he could do to stop it.

She pulled the trigger, and he flinched, but nothing happened.

She wailed, dragging the hammer back again with both thumbs. Tears ran down her cheeks, but they didn't blind her.

Pratters lunged at her, striking her just as she pulled the trigger again, and his ears rang from the concussion as the pistol fired. They fell into the table and went down in a crash. When Pratters grabbed the gun, she gave it up without resistance.

Sobs ripped from deep in her throat. She didn't struggle while he wrapped the handkerchief around her wrist and knotted it clumsily. She didn't seem to know or care he was there until he moved to pick her up.

A wildcat again, she kicked and screamed, pumping the blood out of her wrist. Pratters backed off.

"You have to go to a doctor."

"No." She started up only to fall to her knees. She saw the canvas bag, knocked to the floor when they hit the table and dragged it to her by the strap. Hugging it in her arms, she swayed back and forth as if rocking a baby.

He went to the phone, and for once, he didn't growl when he spoke. "This is Dealer. I need a doctor."

"For yourself?" the voice asked in concern.

"I misjudged someone's mental stability. I pushed too hard. She slashed her wrist."

"Take her to emergency."

"I can't," he said, looking back at Annalisa. "She won't let me for starters, and it finishes with, I don't know how much she knows."

"About what?"

"Peddler."

"How did the three go down?"

"Without a hitch."

"Then what's the problem with what she may know?"

"She may know about at least two of the different parts I play."

"Jesus Christ, what's going on?"

"I don't know. That's why I need a doctor."

"Maybe you should have held off on the three until you did."

"Are you going to help me or not?"

"I can't. I told you we don't have the connections over there. I can't just snap my fingers and come up with a safe doctor."

With nothing more to say Pratters hung up. Arguing only wasting time. He called the only doctor he knew there.

"I need some help."

"Pratters?" Thristen asked sleepily.

"I blew it. She came apart and slashed her wrist. She won't go to a doctor, won't let me take her, and you're the…"

Thristen's voice cleared of sleep. "Give me the address." As soon as he had it, he asked, "Have you controlled the bleeding?"

"Not completely."

"Artery or vein?"

"Vein."

"Keep pressure on it until I get there."

———

Thristen took over when he arrived, pushing Pratters back and out of the way. She didn't fight Thristen, but then he didn't try to pick her up.

Once he was satisfied the bleeding was not an immediate danger, he gave her a shot. She didn't fight that, either. When the shot took effect, when she went from nearly catatonic to drowsy, he helped her to her feet and walked her to the bedroom. The door was firmly shut in Pratters' face after a curt suggestion from Thristen that he spend the waiting time, cleaning up the mess.

Thristen came from the bedroom an hour later, remote and distant in his attitude, and stayed that way. "What did she do it on?"

Pratters pointed to what was left of the radio. "I guess she thought if she shut it up, it wouldn't be true."

"It's fortunate you didn't have her turn the television on."

He picked up the phone and dialed a number. He waited, letting it ring for some time before he got an answer. "Mrs. Webster, this is Dan Thristen. I know you're retired, and I know it's the middle of the night. I wouldn't call you like this, but it is an emergency and personal…Twenty-four hour, at first anyway." He nodded to himself as the invisible party spoke. He gave the address, his thanks, and hung up.

Watching Pratters clean the last of the blood from the counter, he asked, "Did she try to shoot herself?"

"No."

"There's a funny smell in the room, a gun on the table, and a hole in the wall."

Pratters swept what was left of the radio into the sack of bloody paper towels. "She tried to kill me."

"Any particular reason?"

"I was the messenger that brought the bad news." He went around the counter to the table, picked the gun up, and set the sack in its place.

One by one, he ejected the shells left in the cylinder. The last, the one that should have been in his head, he put in his pocket. The gun dropped in the sack with the rest of the evidence to disappear.

"Do you have the right to take her personal property?"

Pratters rolled the top of the bag down, closing it tight. "It's a thirty-eight. She won't miss it."

"Are you saying that's the gun Bell was shot with?"

"I'm not saying anything," he said, facing him. "What happened out there doesn't matter worth a damn now. He's dead." He headed for the door but stopped just before it. With his back still to Thristen, he asked, "Will she be all right?"

"Physically, yes. Mentally, emotionally, I don't know."

"Tell her I'm sorry. If I'd known, I wouldn't have told her like that."

"You knew. I told you she blamed herself. She became emotionally involved with him when she held him in her arms, fighting to save his life with nothing to fight with."

"Tell her I'm sorry."

Pratters left, knowing he did not have to warn Thristen to keep the affair quiet. Thristen knew that when he called an old friend out of retirement and told her it was personal.

————

Pratters waited until morning, and he used the phone, keeping distance between them. He was wise in doing so. Thristen was still furious.

"Do you give a damn?" he asked in answer to Pratters' question.

"Yes, I do. How is she?"

"I really doubt it, but to answer your question, she's resting comfortably. Only time will tell how serious the trauma is or the lasting effect."

"Nervous breakdown?"

"That's as good a name as anything, severe shock. I'm sure it's difficult for you to understand. Being involved in violence as much as you are, it wouldn't affect you the same way. Nor would living with being responsible for a man's life in the aftermath. You would do what you could and walk away without a second thought."

"You don't have to explain it to me."

"I think I do. That accusation you made was irresponsible."

"I didn't make an accusation, nor will I. What happened is no one's concern, but it's going to be hard for her to live with. There are specialists who deal with rape."

"Rape! Is that why you think?"

"Damn it, listen to me. I know a hell of a lot more about what happened out there than you do. She's going to need help to sort out her conflicting emotions. She was grateful to him, yet she hated and feared him. She wanted him dead and was scared to death he'd die, leaving her without protection. She'd never been tried or tested before in her life. She got thrown into a hell pit of fire and came out tempered steel. She did what she had to do, when she had to do it. Now she has to learn to accept it, rationalize it, and fit it into society's concepts of good and bad."

He paused for breath and realized Thristen had grown quiet. He also realized he had said too much. He shut up.

Thristen said, very soberly, "Tempered steel bends very little without breaking."

"It takes a lot to break it. Has she broken?"

"I don't think so. Last night, I feared the worst. Today it seems she's found something in the back of that mind of hers to hold on to. The most important thing now is the physical. She's exhausted."

"Did you tell her I'm sorry?"

"I did. She made no comment."

"Just as well."

He hung up. Uneasy, he knew he'd made a big mistake, one that could be very serious to him if Thristen cared to ferret out more of his feelings than he cared to show. Perhaps he wouldn't. The chances were he wouldn't, no more than he had Pratters' explanation of her reaction.

Maybe she hadn't meant to shoot Bell. Perhaps panic that subsided to fear had driving her to switch guns with Dago when she realized what she had done. That would better explain why she cradled Bell in her arms, stroking his head.

She may even have imagined herself in love with Bell. As ridiculous as it seemed, it often happened in kidnapping cases with the victim developing that illusion. Bell would have kept the others from her, for his own hideous reasons.

Whatever happened, no longer mattered. The case on Simon Bell was closed. The only question in his mind was would Annalisa survive living through the aftermath of terror strong as tempered steel or brittle and broken? Only time would tell, but he wouldn't be there to see it.

THE END

———

Turn the page for a preview of book 2
AFTERMATH

———

Don't miss out on your next favorite book!

Join the Satin Romance mailing list
www.satinromance.com/mail.html

AFTERMATH

AWAKENED BY FIRE # 2

1

TWO WEEKS TO THE DAY AFTER HIS RETURN FROM PHOENIX, Pratters' superior, Daniels, sat on the corner of his desk. Pratters worked, trying hard to ignore him. The subject was one he wanted to avoid ever since he'd had a gun pointed at his chest and the hammer hit. Only a fluke of a dead shell saved his life that night when he told Annalisa, Simon Bell was dead.

"This will be the biggest round-up in history," Daniels said. "I can't understand what Bell had in his head."

"You can bet whatever it was, it was for his benefit."

Daniels stared at Pratters sadly. "He had one saving grace, those girls he saved. Sure, Bell scared the hell out of them. He had to, to keep them quiet, but he saved them from a lot worse. One of those girls prays every night for him."

"For his death or salvation?"

"Saving them is what got him killed."

"Being what he was got him killed," Pratters countered.

"There's no give in you at all."

"Not for scum like Bell."

Daniels gave up, standing slowly, and laid the heavy folder on the desk, patting it slightly. "I'd still like to know where he came from and what made him do it. Did you get anything on that list of vets?"

"None that weren't accounted for," he answered, still without bothering to look up.

"Too bad. Sure, you didn't miss one?"

"Give it to Lewis if you think I can't do my job."

"You do it, too damned well. I think you ought to take some time off."

"I'll think about it," Pratters answered indifferently, pushing the folder out of the way.

He didn't look up until the door shut, leaving him alone. Only then did he take the folder to leaf through it. He, however, already knew what it held, plus more that only he would ever know, Annalisa being one, and what Simon Bell had done to her safe, comfortable life.

He pulled a bullet from the change in his pocket, rolling it between his fingers. If it hadn't misfired, it would have torn through his heart, his punishment for misjudging what Annalisa Summers' reaction would be when he told her Bell was dead. Though he knew more than anyone else about what happened out there in that desert, there were still things only Annalisa knew and wouldn't tell. As the last girl Bell saved, she both hated him for kidnapping her, yet possibly loved him for keeping the others away from her, right up until the minute she shot him with the same thirty-eight pistol aimed at him.

Pratters had a quirk about ringing phones which accounted a lot for the way he answered them. One never rang that it didn't mean bad news, more work, or an interruption to sleep or work.

He jerked it up to stop the noise and growled his name.

"I love the way you answer a phone. It makes me want to hang up immediately."

Pratters ignored the criticism of his phone manners. He knew the voice. Greetings weren't necessary. "Is it Barrows?"

"I thought you'd like to know, he's regained consciousness."

"How bad is he?"

"We knew there was paralysis."

"Yeah, go on."

"We can't be sure at this point to what degree the damage will be permanent. I want to stress that. What we see now will not be the end result. At this point, we just don't know the full extent of the brain damage or how much improvement there will be."

"What is it now?"

"His mind is a blank."

Pratters groaned and leaned forward in his chair to rest his head in his hand. "He's a vegetable."

"No, no, he's awake, and he responds to light, sound, and touch. It isn't hopeless by any means. From the tests we've ran, we believe the damage to be localized in the memory centers, not learning or motor."

"Motor? You mean he can't move? At all?"

"Remember, I said the damage was in the memory centers."

"What's that mean?"

"It means he's going to have to learn to do it all over again, as well as regain use of the paralyzed areas."

"Learn what?"

"At this point, it looks like everything. It's very early yet."

"Wait a minute. You said everything. You mean like read and write?"

"I mean like walking, talking—"

"You mean he's an idiot?"

"No, I don't. There's nothing wrong with his intelligence, not that we know of. There's no reason we can't affect a near hundred-percent recovery with retraining and therapy. It depends on him and how hard he'll work for it."

A light on the phone blinked insistently at Pratters. "Look, I've got another call coming in. Will it do any good if I went to see him?"

"It wouldn't hurt. Come by tonight."

Pratters pushed a button to switch the call. He didn't growl his name. He didn't feel like it. "Pratters."

"You sound tired."

He straightened up with a jerk. "Who is this?"

"Annalisa Summers."

For one of the very few times in his life, Pratters was dumbstruck.

"Are you sick?" she asked.

"No. I just-ah-a friend-I-I just…" He recovered from the shock, found his tongue normal sized, and began to make sense. "I just talked to the doctor. A friend is pretty bad off."

"I'm sorry. I hope he gets better."

"They think he will, but there was brain damage."

"Oh."

The long-distance lines clicked while they each waited for the other to speak. Then they spoke at the same time.

"How…"

"I…"

"Go ahead," Pratters said quickly.

"I just wanted to tell you how sorry I am for the way I acted and what I did."

"That's okay."

"Not really. It wasn't your fault."

His dropped to his hand again. "I'm sorry. I'd never have told you like that if I'd known."

"You had no way of foreseeing the reaction I'd have. My problems aren't visible and go back for so long. It's like when I was a child, one time there had been a bad storm, and a branch broke in the tree in the backyard. It had a nest with baby birds in it. I wanted to save them. My father told me it would be useless, and the birds were only pests, not even worth trying to save. I tried anyway. I propped the limb up with a piece of wood. The parent birds came back to their babies, but the next day, the neighbor's cat got them. I hadn't propped the limb high enough. I hadn't done enough or done it right. I threw rocks at the cat." She paused before adding, "It seems a silly comparison."

"I understand what you mean."

"I let it form the way I looked at life. I gave up trying or caring, until Bell. I failed again. In a way, you were my father and they were the cat. No matter what he was, it made everything I'd done seem so futile and hopeless and not worth doing anyway."

Pratters skipped over the last part of her comments. "You didn't fail. He would have lived."

"Until the cat came."

"There wasn't anything else you could have done. You had no way of knowing what was going to happen."

"No, but I think you would have known they'd have gone after him to keep him quiet."

"I anticipated it. I ordered a guard put on him. I'm sure you heard the news reports about the false papers they used to take him." He didn't add, of course, that he ordered Bell taken from the hospital and his ambulance set on fire.

The silence lengthened uncomfortably again. "How are you?" he asked quickly.

"Fine. I have to take it easy for a while, but I'm fine."

She didn't sound much better. She still had the listless quality to her voice.

"I'm sorry."

"You don't need to be. It would have happened sooner or later. I was shutting myself behind a wall, not feeling or caring deeply enough for anything to touch me. It made me defenseless when something did. I look at things differently now. I was forced to.

When you break down, things always look different. You're looking up. I learned a lesson."

"Not to try?"

"No, that's the mistake, but you have to accept failure when you do."

"You didn't fail."

After a hesitation, she answered. "No, I really didn't. I'll let you go now. If you ever come this way again, stop in. I'll be a better hostess."

She was being polite, ending the conversation casually. He answered in kind. "I'll do that."

He had no intention even as he said it of ever seeing her again. Annalisa needed no reminders of that time of terror in her life. She needed time to recover from the aftermath. He picked up the folder Daniels left behind, the one barely covering the man Simon Bell was.

THANK YOU FOR READING

Did you enjoy this book?

We invite you to leave a review at the website of your choice, such as Goodreads, Amazon, Barnes & Noble, etc.

———

DID YOU KNOW THAT LEAVING A REVIEW...

- Helps other readers find books they may enjoy.
- Gives you a chance to let your voice be heard.
- Gives authors recognition for their hard work.
- Doesn't have to be long. A sentence or two about why you liked the book will do.

ABOUT THE AUTHOR

Oklahoma born, L.L. Brooks now makes her home in the high desert country of Arizona, her desert used as the setting in this story. They gave up the asphalt and concrete of Phoenix and the heat, choosing instead dirt roads and distant neighbours. When she finds time for other activities, she enjoys reading-no surprise-a good movie, crocheting, a night out with hubby, spending time with the family and friends, playing with her dog, and—yes, she admits it—shopping, thrift shops and garage sales her favourite kind, even if the nearest gas station is a good ten miles away. Always thrilled to hear from fans, you can email her any time at L.L.Brooks@hotmail.com and find a growing author page on Amazon.

www.llbrooksauthor.webs.com

www.ingramcontent.com/pod-product-compliance
Lightning Source LLC
Chambersburg PA
CBHW050513260626
47157CB00004B/1305

Totally Bound Publishing books by Jaqueline Snowe

Out of the Park
Evening the Score

Classic Curves
Whiskey Surprises

Finch Books by Jaqueline Snowe

Cleat Chasers
Challenge Accepted
The Game Changer